The Antarean Odyssey

The Antarean Odyssey is about the birth of a people and the fiery end of their home-world. This is a story about a people, their adventures, love, heartbreak, sorrow and of overcoming difficult and often dangerous situations.

The Antarean Odyssey

Assignment Earth

Book Six

Sabrina's assignment is to see if Earth is ready to join the Planetary Alliance. When she returns to Earth she feels like she is stepping into Jonathan Wright and her parent's footsteps. But freeing Earth of the Altruscan influence had become even more dangerous.

The Antarean Odyssey

The Labors of Jonathan

Book One

One evening Jonathan Wright overhears a conversation about
a world-wide Cartel, an interstellar trade agreement, and
aliens called Altruscans.

The Antarean Odyssey

The Original Four

Book Two

This story is about four girls coming from diverse cultures
and backgrounds, and they are the beginning of the Antarean
people.

The Antaean Odyssey

Loss of Eden

Book Three

The ending of childhood might feel like the loss of Eden. It is time for the Original Four to meet the world. They story is about an expedition going terribly wrong. Sabrina races home against time and death only to find a deserted ship. The Antares is only manned by androids.

The Antarean Odyssey

Starship Trefayne

Book Four

Sabrina didn't mind leaving Acheron. But she was not too crazy about having to drop her studies and the being a guinea pig integrating a Chiron Starship.
If Captain Thalon aka Sargon though to have Sabrina safely on the Trefayne, he will soon learn otherwise.

The Antarean Odyssey

Misalliance

Book Five

Now is the time for Commander Sarah Thalon, Chief
Medical Officer of the Worldship Antares to leave home
to become an intern on Madras to fulfill a requirement of
Starfleet of the Planetary Alliance.

The Antarean Odyssey

Inge Blanton

iUniverse, Inc.
Bloomington

The Antaren Odyssey
Assignment Earth

iUniverse books may be ordered through booksellers or by contacting:

iUniverse
1663 Liberty Drive
Bloomington, IN 47403
www.iuniverse.com
1-800-Authors (1-800-288-4677)

ISBN: 978-1-4620-3585-4 (sc)
ISBN: 978-1-4620-3586-1 (ebk)

Printed in the United States of America

iUniverse rev. date: 07/20/2011

The Antarean Odyssey

Book Six

Assignment Earth

Prologue

Sargon had gone, and for Sabrina assuming command not only meant running the ship, but she commenced a complete overhaul of the governmental structure of the Antares. Since she was also a lawyer, she revised the legal codes and incorporated interstellar laws. Very often she would bundle up her two boys, and using Spitfire, fly to Acheron or Khitan to confer with other lawgivers. In her spare time she edited the information saved from the time Sargon and companions first discovered the Antares and the construction of the Antares' environment. All the records were now available in the ship's extensive electronic library.

Ayhlean was in charge of the planning and handling of the ever expanding and more complex operation of Antares' societal structure since new people had been added.

Joran had set up a banking system approved by Sargon.

Sarah, as she had so often stated, was the Chief Medical Officer on the ship.

Kamila, busy with her horticultural science, was reshaping Antares' landscape. She introduced new varieties of grain, fruit-trees and shrubs, something she wanted to do for a long time.

Benjie was in charge of the educational system.

Chapter 1

It was fairly late and the house seemed quiet when Sabrina returned from Khitan. After putting her boys to bed, and before turning in herself, she checked the computer for messages. She found a communiqué from Aram Valdor ra Sandor, Acheron's ambassador to Madras. It was short. It only said: Sabrina, Ras al Khazim claims Sarah was kidnapped and he is pressing charges against Yoshi. I think you need to prepare a response. Aram.

In irritation, Sabrina bared her teeth and growled just as Medea, wrapped in her robe, walked in.

Surprised, she looked at Sabrina. "Bad news?"

"I don't know yet. You think Sarah's still up?"

"It's kind of late, Sabrina. She might have retired. Don't you think this could wait until tomorrow?"

Sabrina pursed her lips. "I don't know. By the way, what are you still doing up?"

"To see if you need anything."

"Thank you Medea. I'm fine. Go to bed. I'll see if Sarah is still in Sickbay. If not, I'll go to bed myself." To Medea's doubtful look she added, "Okay?" and raised both eyebrows.

"Seeing is believing," Medea muttered before she left.

After the door closed behind Medea, Sabrina put a call through to Sickbay.

She caught Sarah just going off duty. To her surprised, "What's up?" Sabrina replied, "I need to talk to you. Can we meet in your office?"

"I'm on my way to pick up Davida. I'll have to bring her along."

"That's okay."

When Sabrina walked into Sarah's office, Nesrim was there. "Night duty?" Sabrina asked, as she sat down in a chair.

"Regretfully, yes. What can I do for you?"

"Sarah should be here in a few minutes. She's bringing Davida. Would you mind babysitting?"

"Not a problem."

The door was barely open when Davida, dressed in pajamas and with her teddy-bear clamped under one arm, ran in ahead of Sarah, demanding for Sabrina to pick her up.

Sabrina complied, and hugging her asked, "Are you a night-owl?"

Davida giggled. "Only when Mommy works night-shift do I have to go to bed in daycare. But I can stay up with you, if you want me to."

"Thank you. That's very nice of you. But would you mind very much going with Nesrim so Mommy and I can have a talk?"

"Sure. Maybe Nesrim will read me a story?" She slid off Sabrina's lap and taking Nesrim by the hand, said. "Nesrim, did you know what Melissa said in class today . . . ?"

"Oh, Nesrim," Sabrina called after them. "Before you get too involved in what Melissa said, would you mind sending this to Sargon," and handed her Aram's message. "By the way, do any of you know where he is?"

"Last I heard, he is on Acheron," Nesrim replied.

"Okay, try Acheron first, and if he isn't there, the Explorer."

As they watched Davida leave with Nesrim, Sarah asked, "Now that you got my curiosity up, what's going on?"

Sabrina told her about Aram's communiqué.

Incredulity and confusion fought each other in Sarah's face. "Of all the conniving things he could have done," she finally exploded, "that's plain spite." Then she frowned, "Do you think he's contemplating getting me back?"

"You think that's what he is after?"

"No, I don't think so. If it's anything, it's probably getting back at me through Yoshi."

"Give me a rundown on this individual."

"Well," Sarah said, then stopped and scratched the top of her head. "I don't know where to begin. Ras can be a charmer, kind . . . but I think those are only social veneers. He's a liar. I know that for a fact. He's a schemer, and he likes to play games."

"What you are telling me is that he is an accomplished actor?"

"Yes, that's a good way of putting it. I mean, he fooled me all the way."

Before Sabrina could ask another question, Nesrim stuck her head back into the room. "There's a message in from Madras. I thought you'd like to see it."

"Have you been eavesdropping?"

"Sabrina, I didn't know we had eaves on the Antares," Nesrim said innocently, repeating an age-old joke.

"Nesrim!"

"Of course I've been listening in. Sarah's my sister. I hope you remember."

Sabrina chuckled. "Nesrim Love, get out of here."

3

Nesrim stuck out her tongue before closing the door behind her.

"Let's see what we have here," Sabrina said, putting the dispatch up on the screen. As she began to scan, "I think we better print that," she told Sarah.

As the missive came off, both began reading it. "Oh, this is information on Madras," Sarah said. Then suspiciously, "Sabrina, what are you up to?"

"Aram says that I'll need to answer this. It means going to Madras to clear Yoshi of this ridiculous charge. It could get to the Alliance's headquarters, and on his record."

"I never thought about that," Sarah said, dismayed. "I guess we better do something."

"Yes, and as soon as possible. Would you mind babysitting Logan? I can handle one baby, but not two."

"You think he'll stay with me?"

"If he's with Davida, or you could ask Soraja if she would help. He's pretty well bonded with his siblings."

"Yes, Soraja probably would be a big help since she scores high on telepathy. She could dispel Logan's fear of you being gone. When are you going to leave?"

"Early in the morning."

"You're not waiting for Sargon?"

"No. I think the sooner this is nipped in the bud, the better. I'll have Medea take Logan to the daycare in the morning, and you could pick him up from there if Sargon isn't back."

"You think this message will bring him home?"

"You can bet your boots it will. Also, I want you to give me any additional information you can about Ras al Khazim. You know, about Nala. About the woman who came to look at Davida. Give me any other impressions you can think of, and the reason why you needed to be picked up in such a hurry."

"I'll have it all written down before you leave."

Sarah went to get Davida, then, left Sickbay with Sabrina. After saying goodnight, Sabrina went back to her own home. Picking up the phone, she roused Benjie from his sleep and told him about Ras al Khazim's charge.

"That's a bunch of bunk," Benjie grumbled. "What does he mean by pressing kidnap charges? We didn't kidnap Sarah."

"I know that. I want you to write a statement to that effect, and I want you to contact Yoshi and have him do the same. I want a copy of everything you two have, then, I want one copy forwarded to the Fleet Admiral Hikaru Okada. We won't have a blemish on yours, or Yoshi's record because of that stupid individual."

Chapter 2

Sargon arrived on the Antares before Sabrina's message reached him. So, the only business on his agenda was an invitation to join Kamila for breakfast. Also, there was a memo that Ayhlean was right now in a meeting, but need to see him as soon as possible.

After a very pleasant morning with Kamila and Soraja, he went to see Ayhlean. She immediately briefed him about Ras al Khazim's charge against Yoshi, and that Sabrina had left this morning for Madras.

"I wished she'd waited," he told her.

"She thought it needed immediate attention. Will you follow her?"

"No, since she can be back anytime, I will wait for her here. Then, I was promised a tour of the Antares by Kamila."

"About all the new stuff she did?"

"Yes . . ." Sargon suddenly stopped in mid-sentence. "She didn't take Logan?" he asked, astonished.

"No, she left him with Sarah. Why?"

"He is fretting because his mother's gone. Where is he?"

"Probably in daycare since Sarah is on duty."

"Let's go."

When Sargon and Ayhlean arrived at the daycare center they walked into a slight altercation between Kamila and the care-giver on duty. Soraja and Davida were looking on. As soon as Davida saw her father, "Daddy!" she squealed, and ran to him with outstretched arms.

Sargon broke into a wide grin. "Hey, how is my big girl?" he asked, as he picked her up. He hugged her tightly, her small face pressed against his cheek.

Soraja impatiently tugged at his sleeve. "Dad, Miss Ada doesn't understand why I have to stay with Logan."

Sargon looked at Ada. She was a new-comer to the Antares and probably had not been briefed about his children.

"Sometimes, listen to what the children tell you. Soraja was probably instructed to stay with Logan."

"But Sir, she's supposed to be in her class . . ."

"I understand. But Logan's mother is gone. He is in distress because of it. I'm sure Soraja was asked to look after him." Turning to his daughter, "Its okay, Soraja," he calmed her. "I'll take care of Logan." And to Miss Ada, "Where is he?"

"He is with the other three-year-olds."

In the meantime, Logan sensing his father nearby, mind-called for Chen to come and get him. Charging around the corner, and way ahead of Chen, Logan's "Daddy, Daddy, my Mommy is gone," erupted from him as soon as he saw his father.

"I know, Son. She will be back soon. If you want, you can come with me and we'll both see what Kamila has done to the Antares."

Logan gave a sigh of relief. As soon as his father put Davida down, he held up his arms and demanded to be picked up.

"Hi, Dad, hi, Mom," Chen was finally able to interject before someone could rat on him. "I helped Logan because they had him stuck in a playpen. He tried to run away all morning."

"That's being a good brother, right?"

7

Chen pulled both shoulders up to his ears. "Well Dad, what was I supposed to do?"

"Its okay, Chen," Sargon told him, and gave him a reassuring pat on the back.

Before leaving, Sargon turned to his oldest daughter, "Soraja, thank you for taking such good care of Logan," and gave her a quick hug.

"Oh, it was nothing," Soraja assured him, very adult, and with a negligent wave of her hand.

Sargon chuckled as he watched his three offsprings walk off in Ada's wake to return to their respective classrooms.

"Will I see you before you leave?" Ayhlean asked Sargon.

"How about having supper with me?"

"You're on."

After Ayhlean left, Sargon turned to Kamila. "Now to you. In your last communication you reported that you did some landscaping and some village building. Now, what do you mean by village building?"

"I thought that would intrigue you enough to come home," Kamila teased him.

Kamila took Sargon's free arm while he carried Logan on the other, and they left the daycare area to walk through the adjacent park. They emerged at the Academy-complex and she led him to the shopping area behind the hotel and through an opening in the wall into a village.

"When did this spring up?" Sargon asked, astounded.

Kamila pulled Sargon around to face her. "Well, it happened this way. Karsten came up with this bright idea about a village, and Ayhlean and I bandied it around for a while. Do you recall the Luithians? Well, they wanted a place that reminded them of home. So, with their help we drew up a plan and built this village. I hope you like it?"

8

"I'm a little late to object."

Kamila laughed and putting her arm through his again, led the way. They strolled down the first street. On both sides were single family houses surrounded by gardens. When they came to an open plaza, he saw a beergarden with tables and benches and recently planted trees. The plaza also sported a church and town hall. There were sundry shops and a village green with a duck-pond.

"Well, who thought up the beergarden? Sargon wanted to know."

"Well, believe it or not, it was Karsten."

"And I see you haven't forgotten the butcher, baker and candlestick maker and the grocery store," Sargon said. "I think I like it."

"Come and see what else I have." They walked on in companionable silence until they passed by an arched gateway. With a sweeping motion of her arm, Kamila said, "These are the Luithians' fields. We will leave them for now. What I really have been waiting to show you is the wilderness we're going to have. Eventually, the water from the duck-pond will flow down this depression here," she said, showing him a deep ditch, "then continue along here," indicating a deeper channel.

They followed it until they passed through another arched gateway. After a while they came upon a massive depression in the ground. "This is a collecting hold for the water that later will become a lake," Kamila explained.

After they had gone halfway around its rim, Sargon gave a gasp of surprise. The floor suddenly dropped away into the level below.

Kamila chuckled at Sargon's delighted expression. "Yes. It's going to be a waterfall. I also had steps built at the edge to lead down. Using two of the cavernous cells, I thought to let it go

9

wild. Right now, I'm having robots spread another layer of soil. When this is done, I will let the seeds fall where they may and then see what springs up. I'm not going to plan it; I'm going to let it happen."

Putting his free arm around Kamila he said, "You've done a great job, girl. This is going to be marvelous."

"Also, the wilderness will aid with the air on the Antares. I had to release two canisters of artificial air last week. Our air is being used up more quickly with the new people. But then, soon the grain will grow and the trees put on leaves. This will help a lot."

Logan, nestling against his father neck had been dozing, now raised his head and stretched. Sargon, making a quick scan of his son, said, "Kamila, we have a little boy with a full bladder. You don't mind a little fertilizing, do you?"

Kamila laughed. "No. It might even help."

Logan giggled as he tried to see how big an arc he could make.

"Feeling better?" Sargon asked. "I bet you're hungry. Want to eat?"

"Yeah, go eat," Logan agreed.

They walked back the way they had come, then, sat down in the beergarden, on a bench, underneath what someday would be a sizable shade-tree.

Logan went to get himself a booster-chair. Looking at Kamila, he voiced his uppermost concern, "Kamila, my Mommy is coming home?"

Kamila ignored him as Joseph, the proprietor, came to the table.

"We have fresh sausage, potato salad and beer. Would that be to your liking?" he asked, curiously eyeing Sargon whom he had never seen before.

"That would be fine," Sargon told him.

When Joseph left, Logan again asked Kamila, "My Mommy come back soon?"

"Logan," she told him impatiently, "your Daddy said that she would be back soon. Now quit asking."

"Kamila, impatience does not become you," Sargon reproach her in Galactic. "Logan always becomes anxious when his mother is gone."

"Soraja does just fine when I'm not with her all the time," she replied somewhat tartly. But what Kamila didn't voice was that Soraja had attached herself to Karlana.

"Soraja is not bonded to you. When Sabrina was raped, she had to withdraw her consciousness completely from him. Since then, Logan worries when she's gone."

"She was what?"

"She was raped, Kamila. That's how Jason was conceived."

"How dreadful! How did that happened?" Kamila said with passion. "That must have been a nightmare. How could she have gone ahead with the pregnancy? How can she love that child?"

"Kamila, she loves Jason as much as she loves Logan. They are both her sons."

Logan became indignant at being left out of the conversation and not having his question answered. He banged his spoon so hard on the table it bounced off.

For a moment, Sargon looked at Logan with a raised eyebrow, then, retrieved the spoon. Cupping his face gently in his hand he assured him that his Mommy would soon be coming home.

Kamila looked at Logan somewhat appeased, understanding his anxiety, but she still resented his being here. She had made sure Soraja was well taken care of so she could spend this time alone with Sargon.

They were both silent as Joseph brought the food and continued their silence while they were eating.

Sargon looked at her with his unreadable cat-eyes. He knew her well. Kamila didn't really like children and was inclined to become irritated with them. She even took exception to the attention he gave their daughter. When she thought him too preoccupied with Soraja, she became nettled. She always liked to be the center of attention and catered to. Only pregnancy had given her that. The one who greatly surprised him was Sabrina with the joy she showed in her sons and the love and care she gave them. He remembered how often she stated that she did not want, nor had time for a child.

When they parted, Kamila smiled at him, but it was only a ghost of a smile.

*   *   *

Heartbreak and weariness swept over Kamila as she left Sargon and she wanted to cry. She knew it had been a big mistake to show how much she resented Logan's presence.

She sighed heavily.

After her return from Ganymede, she had thrown herself into reshaping Antares' landscape. She had reveled at surprising Sargon during his infrequent visits by showing off her creations. His praises had made her feel alive and appreciated, and he seemed to enjoy her company. As far as she could tell, he still loved Soraja, even after Sarah had brought Davida home. Everything had seemed secure and so happy.

Then one day, months ago, he retuned home, and his demeanor had been somewhat distant. Being used to it, she rarely gave it a thought. Until one day, at a small reception, he introduced everyone to his wife and daughter. He was married!

After that, all her old insecurities had raised their ugly heads again. He had a wife. Now, she was not important anymore. Soraja was now just another daughter. She hated it.

She had wooed Sargon ever since she knew him. Even as a twelve year old, she had been aware of his masculinity, of his strength and the power emanating from him. He had power. Aligning herself with him meant safety. She remembered her mother's submissiveness and her constant fear of falling out of favor.

For the rest of her life, Kamila allied herself with people she thought would give her safety, instead of finding the strength within herself. She understood early on that Sargon would never marry any of the Original Four. As long as the others couldn't have him, it was all alright with her.

This morning, when he returned alone to the Antares, it had awakened a small twinge of hope. He came home without Chantar. Their breakfast together stirred old memories and awakened old feelings. He had enjoyed being with her. For a moment, she had spun a day-dream that Chantar did not fancy living on a worldship. Maybe things were too difficult for her here. Maybe she went back home to stay. Then Kamila chided herself for being too imaginative. She had seen the radiant love between them.

Now, he had no need of her.

For some time she stood undecidedly in front of the Academy's headquarters then looked across at the apartment complex where she lived. Should she go home or up to her office?

She never cared for all that hoopla about founding a house and having one of the nursery-cells. She liked her big roomy apartment and being close to the shops and the entertainment center. There was often a concert or a dance at the hotel, also, the kids put on shows for visiting guests. This took care of her lonely evenings when she couldn't stand being cooped up in her apartment.

With a sigh, Kamila lifted both shoulders and desultorily trudged up to her office on the second floor. She sat down in her chair, staring dry-eyed at the wall, thinking about how she had envisioned a whole day alone with Sargon. Now all that had been ruined by Logan being there.

Kamila roused herself and called Abie, Ayhlean's secretary. "Abie, will you find out where Ayhlean is?"

"Sure, just a minute."

While Abie hunted Ayhlean, Kamila chewed on her bottom lip and contemplated how to approach her without sounding too unhappy. She knew Ayhlean would show little patience with her.

"Kamila, Ayhlean is in a meeting, but should be out in ten minutes."

"Thanks, Abie."

Ten minutes later, Ayhlean walked into Kamila's office. "Hi Kamila, what's up?"

"You sound cheerful."

"I just won a round with Ethan. We need new infrastructures and he hates to let his engineers go. He complained that I would need them far too long and often, and he had other projects." She gave Kamila a closer look, then, asked, "What's with you?"

"I just wanted to ask how long I can keep the robots."

14

"There's no problem; as long as you like. But now, the real reason that brought me here?"

"I didn't think I was that transparent," Kamila grumbled.

"Kamila, quit hedging."

Kamila thought for a moment, then, decided a straight approach would be better. "Ayhlean, I will soon be finished with my projects. What do you think Sargon would say if I told him that I wanted to go back to Ganymede?"

"Why would you want to go back there?"

"I have friends there."

"You have family here," was Ayhlean's curt reply.

"I know. But, you think he will let me go?"

"I don't see you fettered to the Antares. If you really want to go, I doubt he would stop you."

Kamila balled her fists in her lap and felt a surge of hot emotions. She swallowed hard, trying not to cry. This wasn't t what she wanted to hear. She had hoped Ayhlean would beg her to stay, then, she could graciously give in.

"I want to leave because I'm not important here. What I do is not important to anyone," Kamila said hotly. "Nobody has time to visit. Everyone is too darn busy with their own lives. You have your job, and I know you have little time for anything else. And Sarah, well, she's running Sickbay, besides teaching science classes and training nurses in her free time. Sabrina, oh well, most of the time she's gone. I'm always alone. No one seems to care, and no one loves me."

Ayhlean had heard all that before. It was one of Kamila's oldest ploys when she didn't get her way. "That's not a nice thing to say," Ayhlean exploded. "What put that bee in your bonnet?"

Kamila sighed deeply and raised her hands in a helpless gesture. "I feel like I don't belong. I never fitted in. I always felt like a fish out of water."

Ayhlean gave her a studied look. Kamila had always feigned a kind of helplessness which prompted her and Sarah to come to her aid. No, this time she was not going to give in. Sabrina was right, Kamila only wanted attention.

"Kamila, you will have to make up your own mind about what you want to do. I advise you to talk it over with Sargon before you jump into something too quick and then regret it."

After Ayhlean left, Kamila, still in a bad mood, went shopping. She purchased a lovely blouse, and with her hurt feelings a little assuaged, went home. When she opened the door, Soraja came toward her, but retreated when she saw her mother's face.

"Kassim!" Kamila called.

"Yes, Kamila," he answered, coming from the kitchen. When he saw her sad face he cajoled her with, "Come, I have fixed something special for you." He never understood how Soraja would know her mother's moods. She had warned him and he had taken the time to prepare some delicacies.

Handing him her package, she only frowned at him. Kamila considered Kassim an old man, posing no threat to her. Since he endeavored to please her, she tolerated him. He had attached himself to her during the time she had been pregnant with Soraja.

When she entered her living-room, he had already set out a small table with lighted candles and the pretty dishes she liked. As soon as she was seated, he served her with tidbits from Ganymede she especially craved during her pregnancy.

Kassim watched her surreptitiously. He knew he was in for a difficult evening. While she ate, he prepared her bath and all the oils and astringents he would need to massage her body. He also prepared a special drink she liked, hopeful that she would relax. Maybe she would be nice to him and, maybe even sleep with him. Before going back to the living room, he went to the kitchen and told Pietry to take Soraja and see if she could stay with Zaida, one of Kamila's little sisters. Pietry was a young man she had fancied some time ago and brought with her on her returned to the Antares.

Kassim sighed. Ever since their return from Ganymede, Kamila had become more moody than usual.

Chapter 3

When Sabrina orbited Madras it was noon, but her internal clock said it was morning. Contacting the control tower, she asked permission to land Spitfire on the planet instead of mooring it on the space station. After a slight delay, it was granted. The weather report said it was cool but sunny, with very little wind. After landing and shutting down Spitfire, she dressed herself and Jason according to the weather report. Usually, when she was away from the Antares, she wore Acheron's fashion, which consisted of loose baggy pants and a long over-dress. Also, she had packed the necessary supplies for Jason and a small bag for herself. Hoisting her son on her hip, she disembarked the ship.

"Well Jason," she mused, "let's see what we're going to do?" In answer, Jason babbled at her. "I'm glad you agree to renting a taxi and letting the driver find the ambassador's home. Also, I think it would be a good idea to first call ahead. Don't you?"

When she called, the butler answered with, "No, his lordship was not at home, and could she call back later?"

After ascertaining his name, Sabrina's peremptory reply was, "Well Mister Parma, you will have to receive us without his Lordship being present. And I would advise you to inform him of our arrival."

When she arrived at Aram's house, a dour-faced butler opened the door.

After being invited into the vestibule, she asked rather tartly, "Have you informed the ambassador of our arrival?"

"No, Mrs. Hennesee. He is in a meeting and can not be disturbed," he informed her frostily.

"Surely if you had tried he would not have minded being disturbed. Is he coming home for lunch?"

"Yes. He should be here in about twenty minutes."

"Good," Sabrina said, undaunted. "Put another plate on. But, before you do, show me to the bathroom."

She undressed Jason, and to the boy's delight, gave him a bath. "Can't have a stinker you know," she told him as he splashed happily in the water.

When she came out of the bathroom, she heard Aram's voice asking. "What's the second plate for?"

"A Mrs. Hennesee . . ."

"Has made herself at home in my house," Aram finished.

He was rewarded with Sabrina's laughter, and carrying Jason, she came into the dining room.

"Hello, Aram," she said cheerfully.

He gave her a flash of a smile." Well, hello yourself. When did you get here?"

Checking her time piece; "Just about thirty minutes ago. I'm afraid the bathroom is a little wet," she informed the butler. Turning her attention back to Aram, "Is Thalia here? I know she was on Acheron, but I was told she was coming here."

"That was on her agenda, but she was re-routed to Daugave."

"Aram, can you put us up for a time?"

"Of course," he replied. When he looked at the baby and saw his eyes, "This isn't Logan!" he exclaimed in surprise.

"No, this is Jason. I left Logan on the Antares. One baby is enough to handle; two would be a disaster."

19

Aram turned to the butler. "Parma, make sure Lady Sabrina has a nice room and everything she'll need."

An exclamation from the open door made Sabrina turn,

"Lady Sabrina! How nice to see you again. Are you staying with us?" It was Batton, Aram's valet whom she had met a long time ago in the House of Sandor.

"Hello, Batton, I'm happy to see you too. And yes to your question."

"Lord Aram, with your permission, I will look after Lady Sabrina's comfort."

"Agreeable?" Aram asked.

"Very," Sabrina told him, then, smiled at Batton. "I bet he knows all about me from Tomas' gossip."

"Lady Sabrina, Tomas does not gossip," Batton returned, imitating Tomas' stuffy demeanor.

Suddenly, a little girl rushed into the room. "Father, I'm so glad you came home," she burbled.

Aram turned red in the face as he saw Sabrina's surprised expression.

"Father?" Sabrina asked.

"Ahem. Sabrina, Thalia arranged for a . . ."

"Temporary consort," Sabrina finished, now familiar with Madras' custom. Amused, she noticed his face turning even redder. "My dear Aram," she informed him, "you're positively turning into a beet." Turning toward the door, she looked at the young woman standing hesitantly there. "Well Aram, introduce me to your consort." Then, with a widening grin, asked, "By the way, does Lahoma know about her?"

Ignoring the barb, he continued with his introduction. "Sabrina, this is Lucinda and my daughter Asara."

"Lucinda, I'm glad to meet you," Sabrina said amiably, but had trouble biting back a wicked grin at Aram's discomfiture.

"My lady," Lucinda curtsied. "I'm sorry Aram, but Asara heard your voice and before I knew it, she was out of the room."

"Can she have lunch with us?" Sabrina asked.

"What are you up to?" Aram asked, suspiciously.

"Me? Why does everybody think I have to be up to something," Sabrina protested, then gave Batton a quelling look as he tried to stifle a snicker. "Put two more plates on," she told the butler. "Come Lucinda, sit down beside me." Sabrina suppressed a giggle, then, with an expression Lahoma used, she told Aram, "Don't be so fidgety."

Now that Sabrina knew, and he saw that she didn't mind, his embarrassment subsided. "Lucinda, please join us," he invited her.

"I think Lucinda is a godsend," Sabrina told him. "She could help me. She has information which otherwise would be unobtainable to me."

Stroking his chin and looking at Lucinda, Aram said, "I see what you mean."

Lunch was conducted in a light, pleasant atmosphere. Aram and Sabrina exchanged gossip about Acheron and the Antares, and every once in a while they were interrupted by a demand for attention from Jason or Asara. When Aram pushed his chair away from the table, Sabrina said, "Now if you don't mind, I'd like to borrow Lucinda."

"Be my guest. I have to go back to this infernal meeting. I bet you two will get along well."

"Would you mind coming up to my apartment? I have quite a few toys your son might like to play with."

Lucinda's room was light and sunny. A couch and several chairs were covered in warm, rose colors; there were books, and children's books in a bookcase. Jason's eyes immediately zeroed

21

in on the toys. With a squeal he arched his body, demanding to be let down.

"Can I get you something to drink?" Lucinda asked.

"No. Let's get to work."

Sabrina told her Sarah's story.

"First on the agenda is to learn more about the family background of Ras al Khazim. And Lucinda, I want straight language, no euphemisms."

"I understand. Ras al Khazim comes from a very illustrious family. The family is old and rich. Ras al Khazim is the President of the Space Port Academy. The post was arranged by his family. Let's call him Ras. He has good manners, but is a manipulator. His wife, Renara, who handles his finances, is said to be put out with him. Ras is supposed to be oversexed," Lucinda blushed, but bravely continued. "His wife finally became overwrought by his constant demands. She was pregnant the first five years of their marriage. After that, she arranged for him to have a concubine. Later he had two. It is hinted that even the concubines became weary of him and moved to an estate he owns in the mountains. Then, I'm not too certain, but it is whispered that he procures very young girls for his aberrant behavior."

"He does," Sabrina informed her. "How would he go about procuring those children?"

"There is a black market. Very poor families who have too many girls, sometimes sell them to people who promise to find good homes through adoption; or if they are older, gainful employment. But, mostly these girls wind up being used for sexual gratifications. To marry off a girl, cost too much. Most dowries are high. And if you want your daughter to marry into a good family, you have to have a substantial dowry."

"I bet this often leads to female infanticide," Sabrina said.

"Yes, it does. It's forbidden by law, but it still happens."

Sabrina then told her about Sarah's observation when she was working at the children's hospital in Sikar. "Sarah said that the girls exhibit no illness when they were admitted. But within two or three days they developed a pathology that led to their death. I need to find a Silvan Algoron."

"Algoron? There was a death notice in the newspaper about a Marsala Algoron. I think I have an address. I will try to find it for you."

"Then, we come to . . . I don't mean to embarrass you, but what is a temporary consort?" Nevertheless, Lucinda was embarrassed. Sabrina felt sorry for her, but she needed to know.

"A temporary consort very often is someone like me, an orphan. No money. Some relatives are reluctant to sell a baby to a broker. They do care a little about the girl. There is a contract drawn up for the duration of the affiliation, so if a child is born, it will be legitimate, but it belongs to the father. If the association is amiable, there is a monetary compensation at the end of the contract. Lady Thalia has provided a very generous recompense; also, I can keep my daughter."

Sabrina opened an attaché case and brought out a document. "Would you read this?" she asked, giving it to Lucinda.

"A marriage contract?" Lucinda asked, astonished. But when she looked closer, she shook her head. "Sabrina, at first glance this document looks like a marriage contract. But I don't think that's what this is."

"What do you mean?"

"This paper looks like one a marriage contract is written on. But since the writing is in an archaic style and language, I can't be sure."

23

"Who can read this?"

"Aram's secretary."

"Do we go to him, or does he come to us?"

Lucinda smiled deprecatingly, "If we want him to be cooperative, we better go to him."

"I see. Then we'll do just that."

After Sabrina picked up Jason, while a maid took care of Azara, she followed Lucinda. Before entering the secretary's office, they could hear Aram dictating a letter. Lucinda hesitated, but Sabrina pushed the door open and entered.

"Aram, Lucinda thought your secretary might be able to read this," she said, and laid the document on the desk.

Picking it up, Aram scanned it. "Can you?" he asked, handing the document to the secretary.

"Yes Sir."

"Explain this document to me," Sabrina said.

He gave Sabrina an intent look, but at a nod from Aram began to interpret.

"This is a contract for a temporary consort. It states that this was drawn up to give legitimacy to any child born during the duration of this union. This contract is binding for a Sarah Thalon, and can only be terminated by Ras al Khazim. After the contract is terminated, there is no compensation in any form for Sarah Thalon."

"At a glance this document resembles a marriage contract, does it not?" Sabrina asked.

"Yes, very much so."

"Is this the language used when drawing up such a contract?"

"No Ma'am. The language now used is written in the vernacular."

"What would you conclude from this document?"

"If it was drawn up by both parties still able to read this archaic writing, I'd say it's admissible. But if only one party could read this, I would say there was a deception perpetrated."

"Would you give a deposition signed by a notary to this effect?" Sabrina could see that he was squirming, but after a glance at Aram, he agreed.

"Aram, can this deposition be done now?" When he gave Sabrina a surprised look, "I'm worried about Logan. He is almost unmanageable when I'm not with him." When Aram gave her another quizzical look, she said by way of an explanation, "I disappeared on him much too often."

Aram still didn't understand, but left it alone. "There's a formal tea tomorrow, and I expect Ras al Khazim will be there. You want to go?"

"I don't have anything to wear to go to a tea."

After Aram studied her, he said, "You're about Chantar's size. Last time she was here, she left clothes that couldn't be cleaned in time."

"Yes, Chantar's things would fit me. I guess I'm going to a tea . . . oh god, what to do with Jason? Kid, you're cramping my style," she said, and looked at her poor innocent babe. Before she could continue, someone pounded at the door. They could hear the butler's raised voice. But at that instant, Sabrina sensed Karsten and that he was in trouble. Handing Jason to Aram, she ran out into the hallway just in time to catch Karsten before he collapsed. She gently let him glide to the floor. After putting Jason down, Aram squatted to help. Sabrina, seeing fluid oozing from him, held Aram back. "Don't Aram. Don't anybody touch him."

"But what's the matter with him?"

"I don't know. Karsten, can you hear me?" She put her ear to his mouth and faintly could make out that he was asking for Miri.

Just then Jason crawled near, and seeing Karsten, made for him.

"Lucinda, please get him," Sabrina said quickly. Then, seeing the servants staring at Karsten's alien appearance, she said, "Aram, have the hallway cleared. There is nothing they can do."

After the servants left, Aram said, "But there has to be something. We can't just stand around."

"Stand free. Don't touch him or me. Lucinda, please sit down on the floor and see if you can hold on to Jason." After Lucinda settled herself with Jason in her lap, Sabrina explained, "I'm going into a trance now to contact Miri. I have done this before."

Sabrina sat down on the hallway floor, away from everybody and went into a trance, her mind searching for Miri. She almost had her when a bouncing energy-ball nearly made her lose contact. But she held on to Miri's mind, sending that Karsten was on Madras and in trouble, and for her to come and please bring Jason along.

While Sabrina mind-searched for Miri, Jason bounced in Lucinda's lap and burbled, "Miri, Miri," then, simply disappeared, leaving Lucinda staring open mouthed at her empty lap. She gave a cry of alarm and looked up at Aram. But before he could say something, Miri suddenly appeared in the hallway, carrying Jason.

"Here, have your green-eyed monster back," and handed Jason to Sabrina. Then she bent down to examine Karsten.

Sabrina held on to Jason and looked at Lucinda. "I'm sorry. I hope it didn't frighten you too much. Now you know why

I can't just leave him with anybody." Squatting down beside Miri, she asked, "What's happening to him?"

"Don't know. Lara should be here soon, then we can beam him up to the Peregrine and take him to the Antares. Thalon, I hope, will know what to do."

Suddenly there came a chuckle from the corner behind them. Rising slowly from the floor, astonished Sabrina asked, "Sabot?" After taking a deep breath, "What brings you here?"

"A bouncy ball of energy whooshed past me. I couldn't for the life of me figure out who that could be. So I followed it here." Bending over Karsten, "Oh my," he said, tut-tutting, "We have a small problem here."

"You know what's happening to him?" Sabrina asked, while holding on to a squirming Jason.

"Oh yes, I know. And I can help. Miri, you stay and help Sabrina with this energetic baby so she can go to this tea tomorrow. I will go with Karsten. It's about time I get together with Sargon."

Miri's communicator beeped. "Miri," she answered.

"This is Lara. What's going on?"

"You need to beam Karsten and . . ."

"Oh, I don't beam up. I don't like that at all," Sabot said and disappeared.

"Miri," came Lara's agitated voice. "Who's that monk?"

"A friend of Sabrina. He says he knows what's the matter with Karsten and can help him. So, beam Karsten up because I need to stay here. Sabrina needs a babysitter."

"What do you mean babysitter? Can't she get someone else?"

"No. I don't think anyone could handle this green-eyed stinker of hers. I'll tell you all about it when I get home."

"Okay, beaming up Karsten. Lara out."

When Karsten suddenly disappeared, Lucinda gave a cry of alarm. Sabrina looked at Aram. "She doesn't know about energy transportation?"

"No," Aram said. "The Madrians are keeping this knowledge from the ordinary people. I don't know why. Probably has something to do with not wanting their superior culture diluted by alien influences," Aram said cynically.

"Oh Lucinda, I'm so sorry. I bet this was the most extraordinary day in your whole life."

"You can say that again," she answered, trying to regain her composure. "You do this all the time?"

"Oh yes. It's quite common where I come from," Sabrina told her, hoping to sound reassuring.

"I'm sorry we frightened you," Miri said when suddenly Jason disappeared from Sabrina's arm to reappear in Miri's. "Now you cut that out," Miri told him, trying to stymie the babbling. "I wish you were less exuberant. But with a mother like that," giving Sabrina a pointed look, "I guess you can't help it." Miri hugged him and then held him up in the air, wriggling his body back and forth, which naturally drew a round of happy giggles from him. "How much have you found out?"

"Thalon informed you?"

"Yes. He opted to stay on the Antares waiting for you to come back."

"I have most of what I need. Tomorrow at this tea-party, I'm going to meet Ras al Khazim and see what I can elicit from him."

"You're going to rifle his files?"

This was an old phrase Sabrina used when reading someone's mind.

With an aggrieved expression Sabrina looked at Miri and said, "How can you accuse me of something like that? I thought you were my friend."

Chapter 4

At Aram's suggestion, Lucinda and Sabrina arrived at the tea-party after it already started and the introductions were over. This was the accepted way for a temporary consort to participate. She was never introduced. Naturally, Sabrina didn't feel bound by Madrian customs so she wriggled her arm though Aram's and asked sweetly, "My dear, will you introduce me to your friend?"

"Pius Algoron, meet Mary Sandor. She has come to visit me for a while."

Sabrina and Aram had agreed not to use the name Sabrina or Hennesee in case Ras al Khazim might remember it from hearing Sarah talk about her.

"I'm pleased to meet you, Miss Sandor," Algoron said politely. He looked at this young stately woman with the green eyes and honey-colored hair and wondered who she could be.

Before Aram could say more, Sabrina ignored polite protocol and immediately got to the point and asked, "How is Silvan?" She stopped and without a blush said, "I apologize, my condolences. I'm sorry I should have done that first. But I'm kind of curious. No one at the Academy seemed to know what happened to Silvan."

"I accept your condolences. After my wife died, I sent Silvan home to my people."

"Aren't you from Aritani? You're far away from home, "Sabrina said.

"How did you know?"

"I have met people from your home-world before. I recognized your accent," she told him. Naturally, she had already scanned his surface memories.

"I see," he said dryly. "My tour here is over. I'm going back home as soon as my replacement arrives."

"Do you remember a Sarah Thalon?"

Algoron looked at her a little startled. His eyes quickly drifted over the crowd. They found Ras al Khazim and lingered for a second.

There was a touch of a smile as Sabrina followed Algoron's glance and also noticed al Khazim's unobtrusive look, giving away his curiosity to know who this beautiful woman was. He was trying to figure out what relationship she might be to Aram Valdor ra Sandor.

"Yes, I remember Commander Thalon," Algoron finally answered.

"Oh," Sabrina said and then smiled. "Let's call her Sarah for short, without the rank."

"As you wish."

"Sarah told me that Silvan ran some tests for her?"

"Yes. And I gave them to the Ambassador," he said, looking at Aram.

"We greatly appreciate your, . . ." Sabrina was interrupted by Algoron warning her that Ras al Khazim was approaching.

"I wondered how long it would take him." She smiled at Algoron, "Lets ignore him." She took Algoron's arm, and slid her other arm through Aram's and led them off.

Algoron chuckled. "I wouldn't want to cross swords with you," he acknowledged.

"Literally, or figuratively?" Aram asked. He knew of Sabrina's excellence in both.

Algoron just smiled.

"Don't you think the ambassador from Acheron and this young woman make a handsome couple? I wonder who she is. His wife is said to be off planet." Sabrina heard a women whisper and grinned at Aram. "You'd better introduce me as your daughter-in-law or something like that," Sabrina told him.

"But that's not correct anymore," Aram said, leaving Algoron mystified.

"Well then, we better say that Acheron's kin ties are not easily explainable."

"I think that would be a better ploy," which he had to use immediately after Algoron left. They were approached by an older gentleman.

"Greetings, Ambassador. How are you this beautiful afternoon?"

"Doing very well. Thank you, Sir."

"How is your lovely wife?"

"Lady Thalia has been unexpectedly called away . . ."

"And this is why I have to content myself with her husband," Sabrina told him with a dazzling smile.

"Now Mary!" He nearly said Sabrina. "May I introduce Ridan? He is the curator of the museum here. This is Mary Sandor. She is a relation of Thalia."

"Oh, I see. You are related?" There was a slight frown as he looked at Sabrina's honey-colored hair and sea-green eyes. If he read anything more into it, he was too tactful to say.

"Oh yes." Sabrina told him. Noticing the frown, she smiled. Because of genetic damages, the people of Acheron have very little skin pigment, and their hair is mostly a silvery white and their eyes a watery light blue. Pretending naive enthusiasm, she said, "You know, this is such a lovely tea-party. Do you have parties like this very often?" She gently edged the gentlemen toward the refreshment table while continuing with, "I have only been a short while on Madras and there is so much to see and to learn."

"Oh, it's not good for pretty young girls to get to serious. It disturbs their digestion and gives them headaches."

"Are you serious?" Sabrina asked, taken aback by his apparent sincerity.

"Yes. It is a well-known medical fact that their delicate disposition does not lend itself to arduous studies."

"You don't say." Sabrina pulled an amused face and gave Aram a quick glance. "You always learn something new," she conceded. "Would you two gentlemen please excuse me for a moment?"

She filled a plate with delicacies and a cup with tea to take to Lucinda who sat demurely in a corner of the room.

"Lucinda, thank you for your patience," Sabrina said by way of an apology. "I don't think this party is very entertaining for you. But here are some refreshments." She held out the plate and cup to her.

Lucinda gracefully took the cup and plate. When she raised her eyes, there was a slight twinkle. "Oh, it's not too bad. Naturally, no one will acknowledge me. It is always interesting to watch people, for a little while. But, I'm ready to leave when you are."

"It won't take long. Oh, I see Aram had found someone else to talk to. So, I'm going back to Ridan since he is still standing by the table. This should give Ras al Khazim an opportunity to approach me."

Sabrina returned to the table to get refreshments for herself.

By that time Ras al Khazim would no longer be denied an introduction to this exciting newcomer.

It was not necessary for Sabrina to read his mind. His whole posture broadcasted that he was going to check out this female and see if she was approachable.

Oh you horny bastard, Sabrina thought. As he came up beside her, she managed a smile.

"Ridan, how can you be so selfish and keep such charming company to yourself?"

Ridan bridled slightly with a sharp "Ah!" He felt loath to lose such a delightful and attentive company. With an acerbic voice he said, "Ras al Khazim, may I introduce Mary Sandor?"

"Sandor?" Ras asked surprised.

"She is related to Aram Valdor ra Sandor."

Ras was silent for several seconds thinking if she's a relation, she would probably be chaperoned. His interest vanished. Ras al Khazim spoke to her only in the briefest manner, but it was enough time for Sabrina to rifle through his files. What she gathered astonished her. He was a very complex man, subtle, even tender, and then capricious and cruel. No wonder he held such fascination for Sarah. Ras, in his way, still loved Sarah, but was infuriated by her thwarting his efforts to subdue her. She also discovered something about a monetary loss that Sarah's disappearance meant. There was an Orion in the background. She gained the names of the child sellers; especially the woman who had been startled by Davida's eyes. There was a connection with the services rendered by Lisa Abramas' boss. The name Lyra held a painful memory. As she probed deeper, she nearly gasped. The poor child committed suicide rather than endure his constant and often very painful demands on her.

The two gentlemen were surprised by Sabrina's abrupt departure. She only said "Excuse me," and with a curt bow went back to Aram.

"Aram, I gathered what I need. I will take Lucinda home with me and look up a Lisa Abrama. Respond to the accusation of Ras al Khazim. I will go back to the Antares and talk with Thalon. We will develop a strategy before I come back again to Madras."

Chapter 5

Lisa Abrama looked up from her desk and through the glass door. A tall woman, walking with an assured stride came toward her office. Wonder what she's after, maybe a concubine for an inopportune husband or to adopt a baby? You never know what these rich and spoiled women want. I hate them, Lisa thought, they can be so unreasonable.

When the glass door opened and Sabrina walked in, Lisa rose from her chair and came around the desk with an air of confidence. "Good afternoon. Would you like to be seated?" Lisa pointed to an arrangement of chairs around a small table.

"Thank you. You are Lisa Abrama?"

"Yes, Lady . . ."

"My name is Sabrina Hennesee. I need to ask you some questions."

"What can I help you with?"

Acheron's fashion did not only have roomy trousers, but also roomy pockets. Sabrina reached into one of them and brought out a small recorder. To Lisa's uneasy look she set it on the table and turned it on.

"Lisa Abrama, do you remember a Sarah Thalon?"

Lisa's face fell and her assured composure evaporated. She drew a deep breath before answering. "Yes, I remember Sarah Thalon. A nice lady. I hope the service I rendered was satisfactory."

"And what was the service you rendered?"

"I functioned as her chaperon."

"At whose request?"

Lisa paused for a moment. "A client named Ras al Khazim asked me if I would accompany Miss Thalon on several occasions."

"What reason did he give when asking for your service?"

"He wanted to become acquainted with Miss Thalon."

"Miss Thalon did not request your service."

"No.

"What were your instructions from Ras al Khazim?"

Lisa began to squirm and looked defiantly at Sabrina. "I'm not at liberty to give out confidential information."

"Lisa Abrama, your instructions were to prevent Miss Thalon from learning too much about certain Madrian cultural practices. Ras al Khazim instructed you not to enlighten her about them. Am I right?"

Lisa rose to go back to her desk, but halted when Sabrina said, "You need not press the call-button. He is already on his way."

Lisa looked toward the door as the owner of the establishment strode into the room. "Miss Abrama," he asked curtly, "are you having difficulties?"

"No Sir. Miss Hennesee is inquiring about the instructions Ras al Khazim gave when he desired a meeting with Miss Sarah Thalon."

"Miss Hennesee, we don't . . ."

"Aw cut the bunk," Sabrina said icily, but it didn't sound as well in Galactic as it did in English. "Let's quit beating about the bush. I know what kind of an operation you run here. I know about Lyra and Nala. I know about Ras al Khazim's instructions, and the deceptive contract he had Miss Thalon sign. You secured the document, and you arranged for the small ceremony. You were in on the duplicity."

"Miss Hennesee, I don't like the accusations you are making." Pointing toward the door, he said, "I want you to leave, now."

"Your name is Rason, right?"

"Yes."

"Okay Rason, let's do this another way." Sabrina did something she had never done before and hoped never to have to do again. She brutally invaded his mind and then recoiled at what she found. She brought some of his most deep-seated memories of hate and fear to the foreground.

Rason gripped his forehead with both hands and groaned; the pain was sharp and tearing. Staggering backwards he groped for a chair as he looked horrified at Sabrina. When he tried to speak, his lips wouldn't move.

Sabrina looked at him expressionless and handed him a deposition already written. "Read it and then sign it," she told him.

With shaking hands he took the document and began to read.

The deposition only went into his dealings with Ras al Khazim. When he finished, Rason put his signature to it, then gave it to Lisa Abrama who also signed after reading it.

Sabrina told Lisa to make two copies, one for Rason and one for herself.

Sabrina took the original. Retrieving the recorder she rose to leave, noting the heavy sigh of relief from Rason.

"Lisa, come with me!" Sabrina suddenly said, sharply.

Once they were away from the office, Lisa asked why she wanted her to come.

"Lisa, he would have beaten the hell out of you as soon as I was out of sight." From Lisa's stricken face, Sabrina knew she was right. "Come with me. You need to give me another deposition. I have notified the ambassador from Acheron, and he will have a lawyer waiting for us. After that, wait for another hour, then go back. By then, your boss will have concluded a business deal and be in a better mood."

"You know all this will get me into trouble."

"You've been in trouble ever since you stayed to work for Rason. You know he is dishonest. He deals in what I call slavery. But then, you only work for him. That should be a mitigating circumstance."

Lisa made a sour grimace, then said, "Answer me one question, what did you do to him?"

Sabrina said, "I pinched him where it hurt," and left it at that.

Back at Aram's house, Sabrina introduced Lisa to Aram and to an associate of Mister Solon, the lawyer Aram had advised her to use. After that, Sabrina went to relieve Miri of Jason.

"I'm glad you're back," Miri told Sabrina. "This kid of yours wants to disappear all the time. I think he's practicing wish-craft. He zeros in on you, and there he goes. I had to go after him twice."

Sabrina laughed as she picked up Jason. "Did you give Miri a hard time?" she asked. Jason was so happy to see her he gurgled. "That what I thought. You were a naughty boy. Sorry Miri. Give me ten minutes, and then we should be on our way. I know you're worried about Karsten. So am I. I hope he's all right."

She returned to Aram's office where Mister Solon's associate had taken Lisa's deposition. Aram and Sabrina also signed it.

39

Sabrina, before leaving, gave Aram a brief outline of what she had accomplished and instructed him again to answer Ras al Khazim's charge. Once that was done, she gathered her few belongings, and with Jason on her arm, she and Miri went to board Spitfire.

Chapter 6

With Jason secured, and before Sabrina could engage the special effect, Miri began to moan. Sabrina froze for a second and slowly turned around. Miri looked ghastly. She had broken out in a sweat; her pores were oozing a sweet-smelling fluid.

"My god Sabrina, what's happening to me?" Miri cried out as she wiped her forehead. Terrified, she looked at the moisture on her hand.

"Miri, hold on. Okay?" Sabrina told her. "I'm engaging the special effect now. So, close your eyes."

As Sabrina keyed in the effect and destination, she wished fervently that Sabot would still be on the Antares. As the effect took over, it was in no time that the Antares loomed before them.

"Antares, this is Captain Hennesee. I have an emergency. Have Captain Thalon and Sabot meet me in the hangar-deck."

"Relaying your message. Anteroom depressurizing. Dock at your discretion."

When Spitfire came to a halt in the hanger deck, Sargon stood with Logan on his arm and two medics beside a gurney, waiting for the door to open. With Jason in his hammock-sling slung across her shoulder, Sabrina just cleared the steps when Sargon thrust Logan at her. "I'll take care of Miri," he told her and waved for the two medics to follow him inside Spitfire.

Sargon only gave Miri a cursory look. As soon as she lay down on the stretcher, he hurried off behind the medics.

Sabrina looked at her two sons, one sleeping and Logan bouncing on her arm. He was bubbling over for joy at seeing her. But Sabrina felt frustrated; she was hampered by the two babies.

"You can't have everything, Logan, remember that," she told her son, while he repeated over and over "Mommy is home; my Mommy is home."

She hugged him tightly, and kissing him on his cheek, she told him, "Yes Sweetie, I'm home. I'm here. Let's go."

At least now, she had a place to go home to.

After she settled in and the boys were off playing, she called Sickbay. When the phone was answered she said, "This is Sabrina, is Sargon still there?"

"This is who, and who is still here?" responded a very confused voice.

"Oh dear," Sabrina sighed, then, said, "This is Captain Hennesee. Is Captain Thalon still in Sickbay?"

"Yes Ma'am. He is still here."

"Ma'am?" Sabrina said. "Oh never mind. Get him on the phone."

It seemed only a second until a voice said, "This is Captain Thalon."

"It's me, Sabrina."

"What did you do to my yeoman? I have never seen anyone look so confused."

"Let's not bandy. How is Karsten and Miri?"

"You wouldn't believe me if I told you."

"Sargon," she said, her voice rising.

"Well, come down if you can," he said and hung up.

Sabrina looked frantically for a babysitter who could handle Jason and Logan. Finally Kara answered.

"Kara, just for a little while," she begged. "I just want to run down to Sickbay. I should be back in no time."

"Okay, I'll settle for no time," Kara teased her.

When Sabrina arrived in Sickbay, she immediately zeroed in on Sabot. "What's happening?" she asked him.

Sabot had the most cherubic smile on his face as he looked up at Sabrina. "We may see the creation of a new species," he told her, delighted.

"We are what?" Sabrina asked, dumbfounded.

"Don't ask such stupid questions," Sargon chided her.

As Sabrina inched her way toward the gurney, she perceived a gigantic cocoon. When she touched its outer shell, it felt dry and leathery.

"Okay, what's it gonna be, moth or butterfly?" Sabrina asked, tartly.

"Probably neither," Sargon told her.

"This is Karsten?" pointing at the cocoon.

"Yes, and Miri."

Sabrina looked at him as nonplussed as he had seldom seen her and chuckled.

"We don't quite know what's going on, but Sabot says that since they are symbionts, their metamorphosis has to be synchronal."

"Those are a lot of big words that tell me nothing," was Sabrina's aggrieved rejoinder. Suddenly, her eyes fell on an individual she had never seen before. He was close to six feet, his lavender coloring almost matched Lara's, and he had tawny eyes and straight black hair.

"Do I pass inspection," he asked.

"Are you related to Lara?"

43

"Thank God, no. She's enough just being Miri's friend."

Sabrina looked back at Sargon with a raised eyebrow.

"This is Tinian, he's Miri's mate."

Sabrina looked at Tinian and then at the cocoon. "Interesting," she said. "When all this is over, do we know what the result will be?"

"We don't know. I doubt there will be an immediate change. It could be a month, weeks, days, who knows," Sabot told her. "Why are you in such a hurry?"

"Because I promised Kara to be back in no time," Sabrina told him. "She's babysitting the boys."

"We'll keep you posted as soon as we know, okay?"

"Thanks Sabot. I'll see you later."

*   *   *

Sabot's vigil was entering its ninth week when he called Zoe and Tinian to Sickbay. Also Sargon and Sabrina came, and they all stood silently in a circle around the gurney, but at a discrete distance. Suddenly, there was a loud crack, and the cocoon split down the middle. A spindly arm reached up and pushed the covering away. Soon, a head appeared.

"Karsten!" Zoe exclaimed.

It seemed to be Karsten. He looked with an uncertain expression at the gathering, and then looked back down into the cocoon. Soon Miri's head popped up at the rim of the casing. Her expression was as uncomprehending as Karsten's.

Sabot stepped up and pushed the upper part of the casing out of the way, then motioned for Sargon to stand beside him.

"Sargon, I want you to mind-meld and bring them back to the present. They haven't forgotten, but the recollection of their former life is like a shadowy thing on their minds.

When Sargon stepped up to the gurney, he gently took Miri's hand in his. "Miri," he said in English, I'm Sargon. We are friends. Do you mind if I put my hand to your forehead?"

Miri's gaze was still without recognition, but she gave consent.

Sargon's hand rested lightly on her forehead and again he called her by name. Then, controlling the rate and intensity, he brought her recent memories to the forefront first before touching on her early horrifying nightmares.

"I remember," Miri suddenly said.

Sargon then went to Karsten. "We are friends and your name is Karsten. Will you allow me?"

Karsten's memories came quick and certain. He looked at Zoe and then at Miri. "Oh my goodness!" he said.

"It wasn't a dream then?" Miri's voice cracked. "Oh, that's one hell of a thing to have happened." Then she looked at her belly. "Don't tell me," she said.

Sabot began to chuckle. "You're pregnant, aren't you? You should be happy."

"I would be, if it were Tinian's. But it's Karsten's."

Karsten gave Zoe a whimsical look. "Do you mind, greatly?"

"Not if it means that now you and I can have children."

"I think this wasn't so much a metamorphoses, then a transformation into a reproducing adult."

Everyone looked suspiciously at Sabot, but he seemed to be in earnest.

"You mean I just came out of my childhood?" Miri said, indignantly.

"Why get mad?" Sabrina chimed in for the first time.

"You stay out of it. I remember you, you . . . boy, I'm glad you're here too," she finished. Then pointed at Sabot, "But I don't remember you."

"You should. He's been sitting here like a hen hatching this egg."

Sabot gave Sabrina an exasperated look. Before he could say anything Sabrina added, "He was the only one who knew what to do." Turning to Sabot, "Why don't you explain who you are and where you come from? And how come I'm always bumping into you when I need help the most."

"As you know by now, my name is Sabot," he said, looking at Sargon and then at the others. "I was given an assignment, and Sabrina seemed to be someone I'm bumping into all the time. My concern are the Mir. My mission is to take them back to their universe. It seems that Sabrina's participation is somewhat indicated. I don't know all the ramifications. We will just have to play it by ear."

Turning to Miri, Sabrina asked, "Isn't Sabot the guy you talked to when you so mysteriously disappeared off the Trefayne?"

Miri looked a little lost. "Oh!" she said, then laughed. No Dear, he's not."

"Well, I'm trying to figure out how he fits in. Like I said, he keeps popping up at the most auspicious times," Sabrina said.

"The only thing I can say is, that I was assigned here," Sabot defended himself.

"That's all very nice," Miri said, "but it still doesn't explain anything."

"If you're finished with this serious discussion, I think I'd like to get out of here and into a shower." Karsten spoke up for the first time.

"Good, you need one, you're a stinker," Sabrina told him.

"Girl, I'm out of childhood. Now it's time you treat me with more dignity," Karsten demanded.

"That should be interesting to see," Sargon remarked.

Chapter 7

Four weeks later, there was a meeting of all the administrative personnel of the Antares. When Sabrina entered the briefing room, everyone was already assembled.

"I know I'm not late and I got here before you told me to be here," she quipped.

When the laughter died down, Sargon said, "We perused through the mountainous literature you left us with. It's very interesting to see all the changes you wrought."

"I like the one about house-rights," Karsten chimed in as he sat next to Sargon, smiling like Cheshire the cat.

"Now, ladies and gentlemen," Sabrina intoned dulcetly, "that is something you can't pin on me. It was Kamila's idea," and she gave Kamila a pointed look.

"Well, as I remembered, you were not too averse to the idea, Sabrina ra Thalon."

"No, but I tightened it up a little."

"Let's get back to our agenda," Sargon interrupted. "We agree on the major items of your charter, and after a vote, we will have the laws enacted. But why we want you here, Sabrina, Aram has responded to Ras al Khazim's charges, and we now have a court date."

Sabrina finally sat down and gazed at Sargon and then Sarah. "I have a brief here and a plan on how we should proceed."

Then looking at Sargon she stated," I get the impression that you have a greater motive for this trial."

"Yes. What happened to Sarah should never happen to anyone else. Give me your brief and I will work with you on it. I looked over the evidence you gathered, and it looks good. Sarah, do you mind going back to Madras?"

"No. It won't bother me in the least. I would like to confront Ras al Khazim and lay his manipulations and some of the Madrian practices open to scrutiny. I was pretty sick when I left Madras, but I have put most of it behind me."

"Good. Ayhlean, I want you to outfit Scout II. I need this done by tomorrow. Aram's message only reached me an hour ago."

"Scout II? How many people are you taking?" Sabrina asked.

"We have to pick up Joran and Marlo from Galatia. I have a directive from Lahoma for him to go to Madras and set up a trade agreement. Then, there will be you with your two offsprings. We have to take Nala because she is needed on Madras. Then we have Sarah and Davida, Joshi, Benjie and Chiara . . . and we have to detour to Khitan to get Chantar and Sirtis. She had an engagement there she was loathe to miss. Karsten will come along as an interested party."

"You haven't mentioned the court date."

"Three days hence."

"Ah! They are hoping we won't make it."

"That's about what it sounds like."

Sabrina, Yoshi and Benjie helped Ayhlean in readying Scout II, and before leaving, Sargon and Sabrina went over its engines. By mid-afternoon the ship was ready with Spitfire in its hold and they set out.

Their first stop was Galatia to pick up Joran and Marlo. Sabrina was operating the transporter, and after they materialized, Joran came off the platform and ran to embrace Sabrina, kissing her heartily on the mouth.

"We're going to have a baby," he told her ebulliently.

Sabrina had never seen him as exuberant as he tried to swing her around. "We are going to have a what?"

"No silly, Marlo is going to have my baby."

"I thought that was what you meant. Congratulations." Then looking at the radiant Marlo, she said. "I'm very happy for you. Joran, you remember the fortuneteller at the fair?"

Joran was at a loss. "What are you talking about?"

"I went with you to a fair and was called a scandalous woman for it, and you don't remember?"

Joran began to laugh. "Oh, yes, I remember. She told me that I would have children."

Suddenly the com came on. "Are we finished with the family reunion?" It was Sargon's voice.

"Yes Sargon," Sabrina replied, her voice sounding happy over the com. "We can proceed now. We have the two and a half people on board."

Sargon laughed. "Congratulation Marlo, Joran. Five minutes, and I will engage the special effect."

"Best you get to your cabin and lie down. Do you know what to do?" she asked Joran.

"I'm familiar with the drill," he told her, his face still beaming.

* * *

It was early morning when they arrived on Madras, two days before the court date. Aram, over Sargon's not too vigorous protest, had made his house available to them.

Pointing to the children, "You are not going to have a quiet moment with all of us here," Sargon told him

"Don't worry; I hired extra staff. It is not often I get to see you and Chantar. How's Sirtis?"

"The baby's doing fine and so is Chantar. We just picked both up from Khitan. It's not often that an artist from another world is invited to perform for the Chirons."

"Hi, Aram, your butler quit yet?" Sabrina queried, as she came through the outer door into the vestibule. Logan was holding onto her overdress, but Jason let go of Sabrina's hand, and crawled toward Aram.

Aram bent down. "Hi little fellow, remember me?" Aram asked, wagging his chin. "When is he going to walk?" he asked Sabrina.

"He's already hard at trying. He would love to keep up with Logan," Sabrina told him and dropped her duffle bag to retrieve her son.

By then, everyone had begun crowding into the hall.

Chantar came toward Aram. "Hello Uncle. I hope you know what you're letting yourself into," she said, her smile aglow.

"Being a mother becomes you." Turning to Sargon, "I have never seen her so radiant," he said.

"I thought that was the Sargon effect," he complained. "Now I will have to share the spotlight with Sirtis."

Sirtis, almost a year old, was drowsing restfully on her mother's hip, sated from an earlier breakfast. She only grunted when Aram picked her up.

"Black hair," Aram said. "A nice change from the silver white. What color eyes does she have?"

"They are tawny. Thanks to Sargon's genes, we now have some coloring."

Davida walked up to Aram, "My sister," she said, pointing to Sirtis.

Aram smiled down into Davida's dark face, saying, "I guess we won't get away from those cat eyes".

"They are tiger eyes," Davida protested.

"Yes, you're right, and they are very beautiful," Aram placated. "Is this Nala?" he asked, pointing to a fourteen-year-old girl. He remembered her as a frightened little waif.

"Yes. Hasn't she grown nicely?" Sarah asked, with her hands on her ward's shoulders.

"Yes, she has, and she is quite pretty. I can see why you're proud of her." Then he turned to Yoshi. "Nice to finally meet you." Aram clasped his hand. "I naturally know Benjie. Well, there is Chiara." He hugged her with his free arm. Then arching an eyebrow at Sargon, "Where's Joran?"

"We left him and Marlo asleep on the Scout."

Their greeting was interrupted by the butler announcing, "Breakfast is served."

Shortly after breakfast, Sabrina went upstairs to the room assigned to her and the boys to retrieve her attaché case. She was just spreading the papers out on the dining room table when the butler entered, announcing that a Mister Solon was here to see his Lordship.

Aram told him to show Mister Solon into the dining room.

Mister Solon turned out to be a very short and slim man with a receding hairline.

"Mister Solon, please excuse the dining room, but this table has the largest flat surface to spread out the papers."

"No excuse needed, Lord Aram. I often work off my dining table for the same reason."

"May I introduce Sabrina Hennesee? She's the lawyer who is going to handle the case."

Mister Solon looked surprised. Sabrina appeared much too young to be a qualified lawyer, on top of the fact no one had told him he would be working with a woman.

"Ahem," he coughed delicately, "I could work the case by myself."

Aram's mouth quirked, but his voice was solemn when he assured Solon, "You will find Miss Hennesee quite an able attorney. It was she who put this case together."

"Mister Solon," Sabrina said, "if you please, would you sit next to me. It will be easier for us to discuss and to look at the papers."

"Ahem . . . if you say so."

Mister Solon edged around the table, and careful of the crease in his trouser legs, took the chair. He was about to ask to look at her summary when the door opened and Chantar entered. Mister Solon, who had just leaned back in the chair suddenly sat up and to Sargon's amusement, slowly rose from his seat. Sabrina, sitting next to him, felt his heart skip a beat. He was instantly enchanted by Chantar. There was an intense femininity about her to which men readily responded. But there was also an arresting strength showing in her face.

"Mister Solon, may I introduce my friend Chantar Bahrain ra Sandor."

"I am charmed, my Lady," Mister Solon said and swallowed so hard it made his Adam's apple jump.

"I am pleased to meet you Mister Solon. Sabrina, the reason I came is we can't find Jason. He disappeared on me."

Sabrina using her telepathic link, searched for Jason. "Chan, he is in his favorite place, the kitchen, getting stuffed with cookies by the cook."

"Oh thank goodness, I'll get him," she turned and was about to leave when

Sabrina said, "No need; Joran is bringing him."

Within two minutes, Joran walked in, carrying Jason.

"Want your cookie monster back?" he asked Sabrina, brushing crumbs from the front of his shirt.

"I guess I better keep him with me. He's getting sleepy anyway." Sabrina reached for a long shawl. "Come, help me wrap him in," she told Joran.

Jason, securely strapped to his mother, and being full of cookies and milk, went contently to sleep. Sabrina sat down with Jason in her lap and commenced to explain to Mister Solon the evidence she had gathered, and the tactics she was going to employ.

"Very impressive," Mister Solon admitted grudgingly. He looked at Sargon, who sat across from him, "I noted that you and Miss Hennesee have more in mind than just to thump Ras al Khazim across the knuckles."

"Of course, Mister Solon," Sargon agreed. "This is why I invited representatives from the Planetary Alliance to watch the proceedings. It is to prevent anything like this happening to another unwary woman. Madras has not been very open with an explanation of its cultural idiosyncrasies."

"Madras has the right to pursue its own destiny without undue interference from any other world," Mister Solon said severely.

"I'm in total agreement with you there," Sargon said in all seriousness. "But, when it causes entanglements such as the one we are trying to unravel, it becomes a necessity for pertinent laws to be explained."

"If you could apprise . . . ?"

"The lady involved will explain it herself," said the soft voice of Sarah. She had come in unheard, carrying Davida. But as soon as she was through the door, Davida squirmed to be let down, then, ran to Sargon to be picked up.

To Sarah's amusement, Solon had half risen out of his chair and stared in astonishment at her. Never before had he seen anyone with such dark skin and it took him completely by surprise. "Miss?" he asked hesitantly.

"Sarah Thalon, and sitting in her father's lap is my daughter Davida. She is also a plaintive in this case."

"How so?" Solon asked astounded.

"Ras al Khazim's intentions toward her."

"I see. Would you be so kind to give me a concise rundown on all the incidences?"

Sarah looked questioningly at Sargon for instructions.

"Sabrina is your lawyer here," he told her.

"But she does what you tell her."

"Since when," Sargon rejoined.

"When it's important you two collaborate." When she looked at Sabrina she noticed the arched eyebrow. "Well?" Sarah asked.

"Let's give your deposition," Sabrina told her, and pushed the recorder toward her.

"Okay," she told Sabrina, then began. "I'm Commander Sarah Thalon, Chief Medical Officer of the Worldship Antares. I was advised to come to Madras to fulfill an Alliance requirement to obtain a diploma from an accredited teaching hospital. I was here for five years.

"When was the first time you met Ras al Khazim?" Mister Solon asked.

"Ambassador Aram Valdor ra Sandor asked me to meet with him at the office of the president of the Academy."

"Miss Thalon, was this the first time you met Ras al Khazim?"

"Yes, Mister Solon."

"When did you next meet Ras al Khazim?"

"To me, at that time, it seemed by chance. He invited me to a faculty tea."

"Did he introduce you to the faculty members?"

"No, Mister Solon. Instead I met Lisa Abrama. She became my chaperon on other occasions I met Ras al Khazim."

"How did he propose to you?"

"He asked me to become his wife."

"Are you sure he said wife?"

"He used the word I understood to mean wife. We spoke in Galactic."

"He never used the Madrian word?"

"No. If he had, I would not have understood it."

"You don't speak Madrian?"

"No. The language in Port City is Galactic."

"Now we come to the child."

"The child is without a doubt Captain Thalon's. You can see for yourself if you compare their eyes. Also I told Ras al Khazim that I could not marry him because I was pregnant."

"And his answer to this was?"

"It wouldn't matter. He would accept the child."

"Did he give any reason for his generosity?"

"No. I thought he would accept the child because he loved me."

"Miss Thalon, you're very naive."

"A generous word for stupid."

"No. I don't think its stupidity, but naivety about men."

"You can say that again."

Mister Solon only gave her a reserved look, and continued; "Now we come to the child. He had no knowledge that it was Captain Thalon's child you were pregnant with?"

"No."

He gave her a searching look. "Whose child did he think it was?"

"He thought it was Meshab Ashlan's."

"You had a relationship with Mister Ashlan?"

"No. He caused me to get drunk and then raped me."

Mister Solon gave a short, controlled cough. "You did not have a consensual relationship with Mister Ashlan?"

"I was drunk at the time," Sarah stated with some embarrassment.

"Ahem, do you . . . forgive me . . . get intoxicated often?"

"Mister Solon," Sargon interrupted, "I can attest to Miss Thalon's sobriety. I have known Sarah for over thirty-three years, and I have never seen her inebriated. She only drinks sparingly. I think it was the combination of the wine and liqueur."

"Yes, I read it. This is a lethal combination to guaranty drunkenness. What did the woman say when she saw the child?"

"She spoke Madrian. Nala translated it later for me."

"And al Khazim?"

"He said," You stupid fool. You ruined everything."

"Did you know what he meant?"

"No."

"Did Lieutenant Hireyoshi kidnap you?"

"No, of course not. He came to my rescue."

"All right. This shall do for now. Thank you Miss Thalon." Turning to Sabrina he said, "I will find the laws pertaining to this issue and supply you with the pertinent codes."

Mister Solon then rose and took his leave. As the door closed softly behind him Sarah said, "Going over all this, I feel like such a fool."

"Now, Sarah, you're nothing of the kind," Sabrina told her sternly.

Chapter 8

The court session was to begin at nine o'clock. Sabrina had Yoshi ready and looking sharp, dressed in his alliance uniform. As they walked into the courtroom, every head turned. Ras al Khazim sat in front beside the prosecutor. He never so much as glanced at Yoshi.

Mister Solon rose to meet Sabrina who was decorously dressed in her Acheron outfit of slacks and overdress. She greeted Mister Solon in a quiet voice and after introducing Yoshi, both sat next to him.

Fifteen minutes late, the three judges walked in. Sabrina's eyes instantly fell on the first judge, an elderly gentleman, bent and stern. There was an aura of sadness about him. Unabashed, she read his mind and knew he was an honest and decent man. The second judge was younger, around fifty. He was heavy-jowled with a broad nose and full cheeks. His small, round eyes were deep-set in his faintly ruddy face. Sabrina smiled. He had the look of a man who enjoyed good living. The third and presiding judge was seated in the middle and of a different kind of mettle. He was tall, well groomed; he had a hawk nose and close-set gray eyes. When Sabrina rifled through his files, she abruptly stopped and became more thorough. She found that the outcome of the trial had already been determined, but she also discovered something to threaten him with. Something he would do anything for it not to be revealed.

As the judges settled in, the door swung opened again. It opened in such a way that everyone turned around to look.

Sargon and Chantar paused, standing between the two doors. When Sargon saw he had everyone's attention, he walked sedately to the chairs assigned to the Antareans and took his seat in an unhurried manner. Also, everyone's eyes were drawn to the children. Sargon carried Jason, since he was the only one outside of Sabrina who could contain his exuberance in using his wish-craft. Chantar carried Sirtis, and Nala followed, hiding behind Sargon. Last to come in was Karsten with Logan on his arm.

"Quite a procession," Mister Solon whispered to Sabrina.

"He planned it that way."

"Did you see Ras al Khazim's reaction?"

"I don't think he knows yet who that is."

A gong sounded and the stentorian voice of the bailiff rang out, announcing that the court was now in session.

As the charges were read, Sabrina beckoned Karsten.

"Karsten," she said, as he squatted beside her chair, "I want you to take Spitfire and find your pirate friend for me."

"Why? What's up?"

"The outcome of this trail is already a foregone conclusion. The presiding judge is in cahoots with Ras. But the judge has a secret he wouldn't want anyone to know. So, tell your friend about a Judge Wolther of Madras, and ask if he would appear in court. With that, I think the verdict will swing our way."

"Okay, I'll see if I can find him."

"Pray for a miracle, Karsten."

Karsten went back to tell Sargon and handed Logan to him.

Sargon gave Karsten and the two boys in his lap a long-suffering look, but Chantar came to his rescue by handing Sirtis to Nala, and she took Logan.

Since she could not see behind her, Sabrina followed the transaction with her PSI awareness and had a hard time suppressing a grin at Sargon's annoyance.

At that moment, the judge asked how Yoshi was going to plead as Sabrina's attention turned back a fraction too slow.

"Who is representing the accused?" the presiding judge asked in an acerbic tone of voice.

"I am, Your Honor," Sabrina promptly answered

He looked surprised at Sabrina and then at Mister Solon. He scowled contemptuously at Sabrina, saying, "I hope we don't have too many distractions from an incompetent female who fancies herself to be a lawyer,"

Only her eyes narrowed, but her voice sounded unruffled as she said, "I beg the court's indulgence."

"You won't get much of that from me."

"So noted."

"Well, how does your defendant plead?"

"Not guilty, your Honor."

"Wouldn't it expedite matters if he would admit his guilt?"

"There can be no admission of guilt when there is no guilt . . . your Honor."

"Well, let's get this nonsense underway."

Ras al Khazim's lawyer, a Mister Rama rose. "Your Honor, my client Ras al Khazim, who comes from an illustrious family of Madras, claims that this defendant named Yoshi . . ."

Sabrina rose quickly. "Exception, your Honor!"

"Now what?"

"My client is Lieutenant Omi Hireyoshi."

"I only have his name as Yoshi, your Honor."

"Your Honor," Sabrina asked respectfully. "Then admonish my worthy opponent to amend his record."

"So ordered. Now let's go back to the charges."

"This Lieutenant . . ." When Sabrina half rose from her chair, he amended, "Omi Hireyoshi is charged with kidnapping Sarah Thalon of the household of Ras al Khazim."

"This is a serious charge," the presiding judge agreed. "Give us the specifics of what transpired?"

"Ras al Khazim states that this individual barged into his apartment and forced Sarah Thalon to follow him."

"Do you have any witnesses?"

"No, Your Honor."

"Then you have no witnesses to call?"

Sabrina rose. "I have a question for my esteemed colleague. I would like to ask him if the name Sarah Thalon is a Madrian name?"

Mister Rama turned to Ras who shrugged his shoulder. "We are not cognizant of the origin of the name."

"The judge turned toward Sabrina. "Miss Hennesee?"

"The name comes from the Worldship Antares. Sarah means lady or princess in an ancient language. The name Thalon means falcon. Miss Thalon's name means descending from the royal lineage of the house of Falcon. Will you, Mister Rama, please explain how a lady from such an exalted family came to be found in the house of a man such as Ras al Khazim?"

When Sabrina sat down, she received an electric spark from Sargon that felt like a thump on her forehead. She knew she had overstepped her bounds and felt relieved when she sensed this amusement.

Mister Rama looked nonplussed at Sabrina and then at Ras al Khazim. "Your Honor, Sarah Thalon was an intern at the Academy's hospital, and in that capacity, my client made her acquaintance."

Sabrina rose. "Your Honor, we would like to expedite this small matter. I think your Honor has more pressing things to attend to. To do so, with your permission, I would like to question Ras al Khazim."

"So granted, if it will hurry up this farce. The charge is that the defendant kidnapped Miss Thalon from his apartment, what is there to discuss?"

"Your Honor, I would like Lieutenant Omi Hireyoshi to have his day in court. I think you were informed," Sabrina said, and pointed up to the gallery and at the back of the room. "that we have representatives from the Planetary Alliance present here. Also, the news media is covering the proceeding." Then in a solemn voice, she added, "We would not like to give these representatives the wrong impression about Madrian justice."

"Ras al Khazim, please take the stand," the judge ordered. Sabrina could sense the judge becoming worried and less pleased with al Khazim.

"State your name for the record," Mister Rama asked him

"Ras al Khazim." he said in a quiet voice, while glaring at Sabrina. He finally recognized her. She had been introduced to him by Aram Valdor ra Sandor at the tea party.

"Thank you. As we heard a moment ago, you met Sarah Thalon as an intern at the Academy's hospital. Are you very involved with the students at the Academy?" Sabrina asked.

"No, Miss Thalon was introduced to me by the Ambassador from Acheron."

"Would you tell the court the reason for this introduction, since you, as you stated, are not in any way involved with the students at the Academy."

"Miss Thalon had suffered some persecution and I was asked to look into it."

Sabrina turned to the presiding judge. "Your Honor, to expedite this farce, I would like al Khazim to be excused for a moment so I can call another participant in this travesty."

"Whom do you wish to call? I hope you understand that the court is giving you great latitude."

"I appreciate the court's forbearance. I would like to call Meshab Ashlan to the stand."

There was a slight stir from Ras al Khazim as Meshab strode down the aisle.

It had been with great difficulty to persuade him to appear in court. He was now married and had a practice. He did not care for the notoriety, or the embarrassing revelation. But his little son, now two years old, had suffered from a malady. There seemed to have been no cure for it. It was Sargon who persuaded him to come and the incentive was the healing of his child.

When Meshab was seated, the presiding judge turned to him. "Are you here of your own free will, Mister Ashlan?"

"Yes, your Honor."

"There was no incentive given for you to come?" He specifically asked because he had heard from other sources of the cure of the terribly debilitating skin disease his son had been suffering from.

"Yes, there was. Captain Thalon healed my son. I'm coming out of gratitude and to rectify something I did I'm not too proud of."

"Then in some way you're coerced, if only by gratitude?"

"No. Captain Thalon took care of my son before he made any proposal to me."

64

"We will let that stand for now. Proceed, Miss Hennesee?"

"Meshab Ashlan, as not to be redundant, you will acknowledge that you know Sarah Thalon; that you had sexual relations with her. Now, in your own words, tell us how this came about."

"I made a wager that I could bed her anytime I chose. I proceeded to make her drunk, and then raped her."

"Thank you. I know that was difficult for you to admit, and we appreciate your candor. Now tell the court one more thing. Was Sarah Thalon a whore as she was called on campus?"

"No Ma'am. Sarah was a virgin. She is a sensitive woman and an excellent doctor who cares very much about her patients. What I did to her was unforgivable."

"Thank you Meshab Ashlan. Now, I would like to call Lisa Abrama."

There was a stir from the back. A note was passed to the bailiff and given to the presiding judge.

"We are informed that Lisa Abrama is deceased. She is said to have committed suicide."

Sabrina stood frozen. "Oh no, I should never have let her go back," she muttered to herself.

For the first time Armand, the stern looking judge whom Sabrina judged to be an honorable man, spoke up. "Miss Hennesee, you seemed to show great concern for this witness."

"Yes, your Honor. I have some damaging evidence from her about her employer. I would like to ask the court for a recess so I can look into this matter. I don't believe it was suicide. Miss Abrama, by talking to me, may have jeopardized her life. I would like to ask the court for an adjournment."

Sabrina was also worried about Karsten finding his friend the pirate, and this was a maneuver to gain more time. The deposition she had from Lisa Abrama would have been enough.

The presiding judge pounded his gavel. "Court adjourned until tomorrow at eleven o'clock."

Outside the courtroom, Mister Solon took Sabrina aside.

"Miss Hennesee, is there a need to explore Miss Abrama's demise?"

"No, Mister Solon, she is not needed. It was to give Commander Karsten more time."

"A necessary ploy, then," Mister Solon nodded

Chapter 9

It was next morning, and two hours before the court date, when not far from the courtroom a make-shift nursery had been set aside for the Antareans since they brought their children along. Sargon, standing with his hands braced against the doorjambs asked, "Everyone here?" When he got an affirmative, he continued, "I have ordered food to be brought in."

The food arrived, and everyone sat where they could find a comfortable spot to relax with their tray. While they ate, Sarah, who had not yet appeared in the courtroom, was updated by Sargon on what had transpired so far.

"He never asked if I might be here?" she asked incredulous, looking at Sabrina. "He couldn't be that oblivious of the fact that if I'm here, his whole case falls apart."

"Maybe he doesn't quite understand where you come from," Nala said.

"You might have a point there. Did he recognize you?"

"No, I don't think so."

Turning to Sabrina, Sarah asked, "What do you think?"

"What I know is that Judge Wolther and Ras are in cahoots. The outcome of the trial is already decided, and you are to be handed over to Ras al Khazim, since you were never released from the so called contract. The two thought to use Yoshi as a lever. They are well aware that this could go on his record. The two hoped that it would scare us into complying.

By now, I think Ras knows quite well where this case is going. I bet he wishes he never opened that can of worms. He's getting scared."

"He thought he could get me back?" Sarah asked incredulous. "What a fool! So you think he's scared? Suit's him right!"

"No Sarah, as you know this case is not only about you and Ras el Khazim. Sargon is using it to prevent anything like this from happening to someone else. And there is more going on than just your so-called abduction. I hope Karsten finds his Orion friend."

"What's he got to do with it?" Sarah asked, looking at Sargon.

"He has knowledge I need, and a great surprise for Wolther," Sabrina answered instead.

"Ah well, it will go as Sargon wishes anyway." Sarah commented, suspecting that he had a large hand in the planning.

"Why will it necessarily go as Sargon wishes?" Chantar asked, putting Sirtis down on the floor.

"There is an old saying, Chantar, that everything goes as God wills, but on the Antares, it's as Sargon wishes," Sarah said in a mock-fatalistic voice to Sargon's amusement. Then she reached behind her for the bag that held her guitar. "Let's have some music before I get morbid."

Sarah passed out pages of a ballad for which Kamila had written the lyrics and Sabrina set to music. It required several singers. Sarah began with her mezzo soprano. At the second line, Chantar came in with her soprano voice, followed by Sabrina's contralto. Suddenly there was a baritone, and everyone looked surprised at Sargon. This was the first time they had ever heard him sing. Then there was another surprise when Karsten picked up the melody and sang tenor. No one knew he was back.

"Well if that doesn't beat all. I thought I was due for a court date and I walk in on a concert." When the music flagged, "Sing on, sing on my dear people," Karsten's Orion friend said. "This is so much more pleasant than what I'd envisioned."

But his entrance had the opposite effect. Everyone stopped and stared. Orions are without a trace of hair. Their skin is pure white and their heads round.

Davida, who had been seated, playing with blocks, rose and looked astonished at the Orion. Pointing, she said, "Moon."

At first, no one caught on what she meant. Suddenly, Sargon began to laugh. "I'm sorry Yafo, an unfortunate comparison." Then he explained what she had implied.

"It could have been worse," Yafo grumbled, and laughed with the rest of them. Then he caught sight of Sabrina. "My beautiful lady who aimed a potshot over my bow," he scowled.

"Ah, but Mister Pirate, it was expected. I only tried to get your attention. Come to think of it, I could have blasted you right out of space. Look at it this way; you owe me your life."

"Is she always like this?" Yafo asked.

"Worse," Karsten warned him. Looking at Sargon, "How are we doing? Is Sabrina riding roughshod over the court?"

"She's having it her way. Watch and see."

"We have five minutes to court time," Chantar reminded them.

"What do you want me to do?" Yafo asked Sargon.

"For right now, keep Sarah company. I will send Nala to get you. I only want you walk in toward the end. And I want you to make sure the presiding judge, whose name is Wolther, sees you."

"Ah, Wolther, I know the gentleman very well. And I have a bigger surprise for him."

"That' what I'm counting on," Sabrina told him.

Mister Solon's head peeked in. "We have to . . ." he stopped abruptly when his eyes fell on Yafo and then Karsten. Trying to ignore their alien looks, he swallowed hard. "Court will be in session in five minutes," he finished, his voice suddenly off key.

*   *   *

When the Antareans entered the courtroom, the associate judges were already seated. Five minutes later, the presiding judge floated in with his robe billowing behind him. He had just ended an argument with Ras al Khazim and things didn't look so good anymore. This hearing had turned into more than just an abduction. It had dawned on him that Madras was on trial, and their private habits were being put under scrutiny. His mien was forbidding as he turned to Sabrina.

"Miss Hennesee, I hope this hearing is not going to be dragged out."

"No, your Honor. I hope to wrap it up this afternoon."

Looking at his monitor, He recapped it with, "The last witness, a Miss Abrama, we were informed is deceased. So call your next witness."

"With your indulgence, your Honor, I have two depositions here. One is from Mister Rason, Lisa Abrama's employer, and the other is from Miss Abrama."

Sabrina walked slowly up to the podium and gave two copies to the presiding judge and two copies to each of the associate judges. Before taking her seat, she gave two to Ras's lawyer and asked Mister Solon to read the originals aloud.

Mister Solon began by reading the deposition Rason had signed with Lisa Abrama. It was a description of the deception played on Sarah. Lisa Abrama's deposition was about Lyra and Nala, and the contract to sell Sarah's baby.

Wolther was breathing hard. "These are monstrous accusations," he raged. "This . . ."

"Miss Hennesee," Amand, the associate judge, interrupted for the second time, "I have noted that you are well-prepared, but I really don't think this is all about an abduction."

"No your Honor. It's about a deception practiced by, well, we will only name Ras al Khazim."

"I guess you will have some more surprises, so I will let you continue."

"Thank you, your Honor." For the first time Sabrina smiled. "As you heard from Lisa Abrama's deposition, Ras al Khazim had arranged for a woman named Zenta, to handle the inconvenience of a little girl child named Davida Thalon."

For the first time Ras' lawyer protested, "Your Honor, this is all hearsay. There is no evidence that this transpired."

"Oh yes there is," Sabrina affirmed. "I hope you're not loath to accept the testimony of a child."

"The child, Davida?" Mister Rama asked.

"No, the now fourteen-year-old Nala. She was present when the deal was made between Ras al Khazim and the woman Zenta."

"We will accept her testimony," Judge Armand said before the presiding judge could say otherwise.

Nala rose slowly from her chair and gave Sargon a pleading look. She was afraid to look at al Khazim. Sargon gave her a reassuring pat and moved aside for her to walk down the aisle.

She walked very slowly. When she looked at the judge, she sidled up to Sabrina and wouldn't budge.

"Your Honor, this child is clearly frightened. Would you allow Captain Thalon to stand with her?"

Again Judge Armand spoke up. "As long as he does not coerce her in any way or manner."

Sargon rose, and taking Nala by the hand, led her to the witness stand. She swore to tell the truth and then was asked to state her name.

"My name is Nala Thalon."

"Since when?" asked Mister Rama.

"Since I came to the Antares."

"May I interrupt to clarify?" Sabrina said.

"Go ahead," Judge Wolther told Sabrina, "before I am again overruled by Judge Armand."

"I would like to ask Ras al Khazim if Nala is his daughter or a member of his family."

"She is not," Ras al Khazim answered.

"Is she your ward?"

"No, she is not."

"Is she your property?"

"No, of course not."

"Then Nala belongs to no one but herself, is that so?"

"I guess you might say that."

"Okay, then, Nala Thalon, tell us where you were and what you overheard." Judge Armand encouraged her with a brief smile.

Nala swallowed, then, her hand stole into Sargon's. "I was in Ras al Khazim's study when he made the deal with Zenta."

"You are not mistaken about what was said?" Mister Rama asked.

"No Sir. Ras al Khazim said that as soon as the baby was born, he wanted Zenta to come and take it away. They agreed on a price. He would pay her five hundred Krones, and then he demanded half the selling price."

"What happened when Zenta saw the baby?" Sabrina asked.

"She screamed, devil's eyes, she has devil's eyes. You see, Davida has Captain Thalon's eyes, and Zenta had never seen eyes like that before."

Mister Rama rose, "Captain Thalon, this means that this baby is your child?"

"Yes, Mister Rama, Davida Thalon is my daughter."

"Let's have Nala continue with her story," Sabrina interrupted. "Nala, tell us how you came to be in Ras al Khazim's home on Campus?"

"Zenta took me. When I got there, Lyra was already there and she was very scared. One evening when he came home, I ran into a guest room and hid in the closet. But suddenly the door opened and he came in with Lyra. Lyra was begging him please don't hurt me over and over. He just said you silly child, you better shut up. He undressed and then," Nala paused and looked to Sargon before continuing. He made Lyra take off her clothes, too. He laid down on the bed and there was this thing . . . sticking up and he made Lyra sit on top of it. When he pushed her down on it, he grunted real loud." Nala stopped and her lower lip quivered. "Lyra screamed and screamed." Nala winced and closed her eyes for a few moments. "But he only turned over and made more funny noises. After a while, he got up and went to the bathroom. Lyra lay on the bed, whimpering. When he came out again, he only looked at her and told her to clean up. One day he came home to the mansion, and asked for Lyra. But Lyra saw him and ran out of the house," Nala's eyes closed tightly and a tear rolled down her check. "She ran right smack into a big truck, and she was dead. Then one night he

73

asked Azara to bring me to Sarah's apartment. Sarah, I didn't know her then, was at work and not supposed to come home until late that night. He was making me do the same thing he made Lyra do. But suddenly there was a door closing and he got up and left. Next morning, Azara told Sarah that I was her niece and would be staying with her for a while."

"Then there was that other night. He made me go into that room again, and it hurt and I screamed and he slapped me. Suddenly the door opened and the light came on and Sarah stood there. I was so afraid because I thought she would be mad at me, but when he jumped at her, she slammed him right into the wall and then punched his face out," Nala said with audible satisfaction.

"Then Sarah took me to the hospital and had me sewn up, and she had her baby there, too. When the nurse asked my name, Sarah told her it was Nala Thalon," she said proudly.

"A very enthralling story," Mister Rama said. "But only a child's story and, it is her word against that of Ras al Khazim."

"Oh no, it is not," Sarah said, coming though the door as if on cue. "I believe I'm Miss Hennesee's next witness."

Ras al Khazim blanched and half rose from his chair. "Sarah," he whispered and sat down heavily.

"And who are you?" asked the presiding judge.

"May I introduce Doctor Sarah Thalon, Chief Medical Officer of the Worldship Antares," Sabrina said.

"An impressive title . . ."

"And the lady earned every bit of it," Sabrina interrupted him. "She is the lady Lieutenant Omi Hireyoshi is supposed to have abducted, your Honor," she said with a slight ironic bow.

Mister Rama rose. "What would you call it if someone broke into your apartment and abducted your . . ."

74

"Wife?" Sabrina finished for him. "Or, wasn't she his wife? Would you please enlighten us as to the precise description of their relationship?"

"Miss," Rama put the same emphasis on Miss as Sabrina had on doctor. "Miss Thalon is a temporary consort to Ras al Khazim."

"I want to ask a question of Aram Valdor ra Sandor." When Aram rose, Sabrina asked, "How did Doctor Thalon introduce Ras al Khazim?"

"Doctor Thalon always introduced him as her husband."

"Did Ras al Khazim ever correct the misstatement?"

"No. He did not."

"Thank you Mister Ambassador. I have a document here," Sabrina said, holding it up. "Could you tell me what kind of document this is, Judge Armand?"

"In appearance, this document resembles a marriage contract," Judge Armand told her, as he glanced at it.

Walking up to the bench, she asked, "Would you please read it."

Judge Armand put on his glasses, then, took it from her. As he began to read, he looked up in surprise. "This is written in an ancient script. This language is no longer in use; most people can't read this. This is a short-term contract designating a Miss Sarah Thalon as a temporary consort. It says that should a child be born during the term of the contract, and proven to be Ras al Khazim's, the child will pass into his family. At the end of the contract there is no compensation for Miss Thalon's services. This is a very callous and one sided arrangement. All the benefits are on Ras al Khazim's side."

"Judge Armand, you stated that very few Madrians are now able to read this ancient writing style. Would you expect a so-called out-worlder to be able to read this?"

75

"Assuredly not. I only learned to read these ancient manuscripts as a law student."

"Then, if Ras al Khazim told Doctor Thalon that this was a marriage contract, she would have no way of knowing that it was not a marriage contract."

"No, she could not have known."

Turning to Sarah. "Doctor Thalon, do you speak the language of Madras?"

"No, I do not. Ras al Khazim and I always spoke in Galactic."

"So, you could not read this document and relied on Ras al Khazim to tell you its purpose.

"Yes. I did."

"Doctor Thalon, you told me that you can substantiate Nala's story?"

"Yes I can. I walked into the room and Nala was sitting astride Ras al Khazim. I had to take her to the hospital because of the substantial damage done to her vaginal area. She was only twelve years old."

"You also stated that you called the Starship Explorer for help. You called the Explorer from where?"

"The Space Command Center of Madras. I asked the communications officer, Lieutenant Tejur, to help me and to enter it in his log-book."

"Did you reach the Explorer?"

"Yes. The Explorer was commanded by a Captain Murasaki. But immediately Lieutenant Hireyoshi came on screen and I told him that I needed help urgently, and to be picked up."

"What was your emergency?"

"Ras al Khazim threatening Davida."

Incredulous, Sabrina asked, "He threatened an infant?"

"We object!" Mr. Rama interjected.

76

"So do we, to the threatening of an infant. To keep this brief, when Lieutenant Hireyoshi appeared in Doctor Thalon's nursery, he was holding a weapon. But unknown to Ras al Khazim, he was also recording the rescue. Would you activate the screen, please?" she said to the bailiff. "The judges will be able to view it on their monitors."

The monitors showed Ras al Khazim holding Davida by her heels over his head, and Yoshi's voice telling him that he had a weapon and would shoot if he, Ras, did not put the baby down, Do it now, and do it gently.

Over the murmuring voices, Sabrina was heard to say that she hoped no one would equivocate over the meaning of the action shown on the monitors.

The gavel banged for several minutes before silence could be restored. After order was established, Judge Wolther banged his gavel one more time and said, "We will concede the necessity of Miss Thalon calling for help. We will also concede that there was no abduction . . ."

"Your Honor, I have one more witness. He came a long way to testify. It would be a pity to have him come all this way for nothing."

"Call your last, and I mean, last witness."

"I call Captain Yafo from the Orion Hegemony."

When Sabrina mentioned his name, Judge Wolther's body shifted abruptly as if to flee. His face was chalky as he stared with dead eyes at Yafo striding into the courtroom.

Yafo, ignoring protocol, walked up to Sarah. He paused and looked her over. Then, he ran his thumb down her cheek. "You're right, she would have brought a pretty penny," he said loud enough for everyone to hear as he looked at Ras al Khazim.

The courtroom was again drowned by an uproar. Sargon rose, and facing the audience, held up his hand. Everyone hushed instantly. "Judge Armand, ask Judge Wolther or Captain Yafo what happened to your daughter."

There was a strangled cry from Wolther, followed instantly by a rap from the gavel. "This court will come to order! Miss Hennesee, I will hold you in contempt of court if there are any more disruptions. My judgment is that the defendant is innocent of the charges and the court is dismissed."

"Oh, we don't want to be too hasty," Judge Armand said. "Captain Thalon, what about my daughter? She disappeared about seven years ago and my wife died of a broken heart."

"Judge Armand, why don't you ask Captain Yafo?" Sabrina said.

"Captain Yafo is an Orion and they are notorious liars. I don't think anyone will be so foolish as to take his word . . ." Judge Wolther hissed through his teeth.

"Maybe not the word of an Orion, but would you take my word?" A young woman came through the open door, and walked down the aisle. She appeared to be in her early twenties.

Sabrina who stood next to Judge Armand could hear a choked gasp and then his whispered, "Jasmine?" For a second he stood motionless, and in a broken voice said, "My child, my daughter," and hurried to her.

"Papa," Jasmine cried, "oh Papa, I thought I would never see you again."

Tears ran down his face as he embraced her. "Oh my god, my daughter, my daughter," he said over and over, holding her close to him.

He looked at Sabrina, "How did you find her?" he asked with his tear-chocked voice.

"I didn't. Captain Thalon found her through Yafo." Sabrina felt a stirring in her mind which she had attuned to Judge Wolther to keep track of him and perceived that he was about to take flight. "Judge Wolther, this trail is not yet over. There is one more witness."

It took a monumental effort to show a semblance of calm. He glared at Sabrina with malevolence. "I have already declared the defendant not guilty, what more do you want me to do?"

"To hear Jasmine Armand's story."

"This court is adjourned."

"No! This court is not adjourned," the Kadiff of Madras said from the balcony. I would like to hear Jasmine Armand's story. Please, Miss Armand?"

"Judge Wolther raped me when I was sixteen. Because I would not keep quiet about it, he kidnapped me and after repeated indignities, later sold me to what he thought was an Orion slaver. Captain Yafo might be a pirate, but a pirate with a conscience. He took me to a school for young ladies, and I grew up there."

"There goes my reputation," Yafo muttered into Sabrina's ear.

"What we have heard here is a monstrous outrage," the Kadiff said, "Be assured that my office will look very carefully into all these charges. Judge Wolther, I'm having the police place you under arrest."

Before the bailiff could act, Wolther fled the courtroom through a back door.

While a search ensued, Sabrina stood off to one side and suddenly stiffened. Her eyes went swiftly over the courtroom. "Quick, take the children out of here," she told Sarah and Chantar, Don't ask, just do it," she urged when Sarah hesitated. Sabrina approached Judge Armand, "Please, quick, follow Miss

79

Thalon," she told him and shepherded him and his daughter toward the exit.

Sabrina went to look for Sargon and found him standing in the back of an alcove. When she walked up to him, her eyes fell on a stranger standing next to him. The stranger leaned lazily against the wall, inspecting his fingernails. His skin appeared tanned, and he looked of an indeterminate age. He had a slim figure, and his eyes were of a dark color and almond shaped. Her first impression of him did not predispose him in her favor.

"Sabrina, may I introduce Mendes."

"Sargon," she said, ignoring Mendes. Sargon stiffened at the same time as Wolther's agitated emanation impinged on them both. "Come quick," she told Sargon and grabbing him by the sleeve, pulled him along.

As they stepped over the threshold into the courtroom, they saw Ras al Khazim leaning against the rail talking to his wife. Renara sat with her face turned away and with her eyes cast-down; her whole body language bespoke of total rejection. Just then Wolther burst through the back door and ran up to Ras al Khazim. He pushed him and screamed, "This is all your fault, you greedy over-sexed son of a bitch!" Then he brought a gun from under his robe and shot Ras al Khazim.

Sargon started to rush into the room, but Sabrina, catching his sleeve, held him back, shaking her head. There was another bang, and Wolther fell to the floor. "It is better this way," she whispered

Sarah, hearing the report of the weapon, rushed in. Sabrina followed her as she bent down to Ras al Khazim. She only looked at him, and then at Sabrina. "He's dead." Her voice was matter of fact. Sabrina was glad she didn't hear any emotion.

Then Sarah went to Wolther. He was just barley alive. "All women are bitches," he croaked. "It's all their fault."

"No, it's not their fault, it's yours. The only thing you have any business judging is yourself."

He gave her one long poison-laden look then his eyes fluttered, then closed.

Sarah shuddered and thought, if looks could kill.

The court was never dismissed, but everyone filed out. When he Antareans met at the room set aside for them, Sarah grabbed Sabrina by the arm. "Did you see Renara al Khazim?" she asked. "What an experience for her to have to live through. Did you know that she was every day in the courtroom?"

"Yes. I saw her intently watching the proceedings. But I don't think Ras's demise bothered her very much."

"What do you mean by that? You know something I don't?" She gave Sabrina a shrewd look. "Have you been rifling her files?" Sarah asked, suspiciously.

"How do you know about that?"

"I told you a long time ago that I'm not as stupid as you think."

"I never thought you were stupid."

"Quit sidetracking. What did you read?"

"Renara has already gone to the elders in the family. She provided them with proof of Ras's loose living and his spend-thrift ways. They were especially upset with him for using children for his aberration. What I gleaned from Renara, was that the elders have already decided on his demise. The humiliation of all of it being made public sealed his fate. But then, Wolther did the job for them."

Chapter 10

The Antareans met back at Aram's house. When Sabrina walked into Aram's reception room, she was delighted to see Algoron.

"Surprised to see me?" he asked.

"Frankly, yes."

"You presented an excellent case, but I don't think it will alter the women's situation here on Madras."

"Is that why you send your daughter back to your home-world?"

"Yes. Things were all right as long as Marsala was alive. But now, I have no intention for Silvan to marry a Madrian."

"Having married a Madrian yourself should have given you a special insight into their culture."

"It did to some extent. But remember, we lived in Port City. Marsala was a history professor. She wrote a treatise on Madras's history for her doctorate, which primarily touched on the women's issue. When she handed it in, it was not accepted, but the professor, a historian, gave her suggestions on how to rewrite it."

"What was her theorem?"

"The historical events influencing the women's status on Madras."

"And her conclusion?"

Algoron looked at her and smiled. "You wouldn't believe it if I told you."

"Try me."

"Initially, Miss Hennesee, it began over a protest about a dress code. Fashion, according to the prevailing religious persuasion, had gotten out of hand. Women were showing too much flesh and were causing moral decay. Their next attack was aimed at working mothers, accusing them of abandoning their offspring to daycare centers. This was stated as the cause of juvenile delinquency, mothers not being at home. They talked about family-values; that mothers should be the caretakers of their households. That was the beginning. Many women did respond to this calling from the pulpit, but slowly, their rights eroded. Laws were enacted to take their rights away, until they had none. It was said that women are to be protected; they were under the protection of their husbands. Soon they were not allowed to hold property. Fathers are now the sole custodians of the children. Then, women were not allowed to walk the streets without being properly covered and escorted by a chaperon. They receive only a minimal education, that is why Silvan was educated in Port City and so was my wife."

"That is not a very pretty picture," Sabrina said.

"No it's not. It was not always so. The Madrians have a very . . . what we would call, advanced civilization. Or should I say, had. The dominant religion became the state's religion. Their religious book is now the foundation of their laws. This church is a fundamentalist church. It had frozen all free thoughts and advancement in science. Only their particular brand of scientific knowledge is allowed to be promulgated. I want to tell you, I am glad to go back to Aritani."

"Is your world that much different?"

"Yes. Women and men are equal. Women and men hold high offices." With a whimsical smile he added, "We don't have a state religion. Marsala was looking forward to go home with me. But . . ."

"I'm sorry; again, my belated condolences."

"It's all right. How is it on your world?"

"My world is a ship. On the Antares one gets what one earns. There is no gender differentiation." Then she smiled. "Do you know on the Antares I'm addressed as Sir when I'm at work?"

"And your work is?"

"I'm second in command."

"And who is first in command?"

"Captain Thalon."

"But he is a male."

"It's not gender; it's age. He is older than I."

"Mister Algoron, what has she been telling you?" Sargon asked, as he and the stranger she had been so briefly introduced to, joined them.

"She is telling me that you are first in command only because you are older," Algoron told him, amused.

"Age and command has its privileges."

"Uh-huh. Am I getting the boom lowered on me?" Sabrina asked.

"No. Just to remind you that you won't have it all your way. To change the subject, I think I introduced you to Mendes?"

"Yes, briefly."

"Mendes has information about Elisheba."

"Do you?" Sabrina asked eagerly, and for the first time she looked fully at him.

Mendes gazed back at her with a set of inscrutable eyes that reminded her of Ayhlean's, and then adjusted the sleeves of his impeccable fitting suit. He brushed at a nonexisting fleck of dust. With a languid tone of voice he said in English, "Captain

Thalon asked me to inquire into her whereabouts. She left the Doran during its first lay-over at a space station. Since then, she has changed to several different ships. That's why it has been so difficult to trace her. Right now she is on a liner . . ."

"What's a liner?" Sabrina interrupted.

"It's a civilian-run interstellar ship."

"Looking at Sargon, she asked, "Like an ocean-liner?"

"Sort of."

"What is she doing there, Mister Mendes?"

"She's a housekeeper, or cabin keeper. She cleans cabins," he clarified.

"What a waste of an education," Sabrina remarked.

"What a waste of what education?" Sarah broke in, as she joined the group.

"Mister Mendes says he knows where Elisheba is," Sabrina informed her.

Sarah's eager face turned to him. "You do? Where is she?"

"Would you believe, she's cleaning cabins on a space-liner," Sabrina told her, visibly outraged.

"Oh God!" Sarah exploded and hissed through her teeth. "Why did she leave? Ras's explanation never made sense." When Sabrina suddenly looked uncomfortable, "You know why she left!" Sarah accused her. Grabbing her arms, "Sabrina, you better tell me why she left in such a hurry."

Even more uncomfortable, Sabrina stared at her. "It was because of Ras."

"I figured that much."

"He told her that, because of your advanced pregnancy, you agreed he could have sex with her . . ."

"Whaaat? That's utter nonsense! I never . . . He never . . . I don't know what to say."

"The night she left, he broke into her bedroom and made advances toward her. She knocked the crap out of him, threw her things together, then left in a hurry. I think she didn't want to hurt you, or, was afraid you wouldn't believe her, or something like that."

"Oh god, oh god," Sarah said, grinding her teeth.

"Sarah, your disturbing Davida," Sabrina told her.

Davida and Logan were asleep on a couch, and Jason was already tucked into his carrying sling.

"I will keep Captain Thalon informed on her movements. I have an agent following her. As soon as I know more, I will send a message to the Antares," Mendes told Sarah.

"Thank you, Mister . . . Mendes?" Sarah asked. "You don't know how relieved I am to know that she's at least alive." She turned toward Sargon," Of all the damned, stupid things she could have done," she exploded. "Why . . . why . . . oh drat," she said, slicing with one arm through the air, "it's no use . . . aw, shit!"

"Are you finished emoting?" Sabrina interrupted. "If you are, you can come home with me."

"What do you mean?"

"I have a ship."

"How did she get a ship?" she asked Sargon.

Sargon only shrugged both shoulders, ignoring her. He told Sabrina, "You take Sarah and the kids. I'll take Scout II. Yoshi is due on the Explorer. Chantar, Benjie and Chiara want to go back to Acheron, ditto Joran and Marlo, so Karsten is taking them in the Aurora. I guess that should do it."

Mendes had been watching silently, his eyes wandering from one to the others with a puzzled look on his face. When he turned to go with Sargon, Sabrina heard him say, "Are you related to all of them?"

"No, of course not. They were all orphans and some have adopted my name because they couldn't remember their own. Some have adopted the name of the woman who raised them. Like Benjie, he took Sabrina's name. Yoshi retained his own."

"And the children?"

"You mean, my children? That was only a one-time gratuity," he told him with a broad grin, enjoying the memory.

Sabrina wore a sour face when she noted Sargon's satisfied air.

Chapter 11

It was good to be home again, even if it meant taking command of the Antares. After their return, Sargon just simply disappeared and Sabrina knew Chantar had gone home to Acheron.

Several years passed, until one day, Sargon simply breezed in onto the bridge. Sabrina finished instructing a young ensign on the control panel of the forward sensors before she looked up. Since he was in uniform, she asked, "Are you taking command?"

"No." He turned to Chandi, "Lieutenant Hennesee, take the bridge. Sabrina, come with me."

After the doors to the lift closed, she was about to ask what in the world he wanted, when the doors on the opposite side opened. He led her to his office and let her enter first.

When she stood at attention, he said, "Why don't you sit down?"

"I don't know. I get that ominous feeling you're about to spring something on me."

"Oh. I have a little job for you."

"I knew it."

Sargon chuckled. "Now, that's no way to talk to your commanding officer."

"No Love, I'm still in command."

"That's just a minor formality. You remember Mendes?"

"Yes of course."

"I want you to meet him on Sarpedion. Since you have Spitfire, it should only take you a day or so to return."

"And the boys?"

Sargon assured her that he could take care of her boys, now aged nine and eight. He handed her an arm-bracelet with, "There's a micro-chip underneath one of the stones."

When she looked at him with a raised eyebrow, he made a face in response. "I know it's not the latest state of the art. Even outdated technology comes in handy, sometimes."

"Oh, it's gonna be a spy mission?"

"Sort of. You only have to give the bracelet to Mendes; that's all."

"And then I can come back home?"

"Yes."

"And you need to send me for this?"

"Well, I could send someone else, but they'd have to borrow Spitfire." Sargon arched an eyebrow at her, knowing the answer. If she could help it, Sabrina never let anyone else use her ship

And that settled it.

* * *

Once Sabrina landed on Sarpedion, she hailed a taxi at the spaceport and gave the driver the address Sargon had given her. Mendes lived in a high-rise, twenty stories up.

After she rang the bell, she watched as the door opened slowly, and suddenly a shot rang out and Sabrina found herself pinned to the floor with Mendes on top of her. Mendes had seen the gunman the instant he opened the door and pulled Sabrina down. After he was sure the gunman had left and it was safe, he pulled Sabrina into his apartment.

While shielding Sabrina, Mendes made a curious discovery. Being a touch-empath, he hated even the slightest physical contact with people. The only ones he didn't mind touching were Sargon or Lara. Even Miri, he only touched if necessary. Most emotions he gleaned, were, at the least, distasteful. But Sabrina's, although strong, were without guile. His contact with here was pleasant, a very rare occurrence.

"Do you always bring your henchman with you?" he asked her testily, falling into English. He recognized her immediately from Sarah's trial.

"Sure, I like standing in the doorway to be shot at. Who was he anyway?"

"I guess just a friendly visitor. Now, what do you want?"

"Want?" Sabrina asked, her voice rising.

"Yes. Why are you here?"

"Of all the damned ingrates I've met, you take the cake."

He straightened up and looked down at himself. "Should I be pleased? Just look what you did to my trousers! The crease is crushed and they are all wrinkled now," he complained in his grating, nasal voice, and glared at her with undisguised disgust. "Brandon!" he called, "I need a fresh pair of trousers. Will you put them out for me?" Turning to Sabrina, "Now what in . . . well, what brings you here?"

Sabrina cast him a smoldering look. "Captain Thalon asked me to give you this," she said, handing him the bracelet.

He took it from her, only using his thumb and index finger.

"It's not poisonous," Sabrina told him caustically

"You never know," Mendes said musing and studied the bracelet. "Have you had breakfast?"

"No. I just came to deliver this. Now . . ."

"Not so fast. I can use you . . ."

"I'm not here to be useful!"

He ignored her outburst. "Tonight, there's a social, and I think it would be a good idea if I had someone to go with me. Do you have something to wear to a social?" Looking at Sabrina's coveralls, "I guess not," he answered his own question.

The valet came in. "Breakfast is served, Sir," he announced.

"Thank you, Brandon. Put another plate on."

"I said I was only here to deliver the bracelet."

He gave little heed to her protestation and walked into the breakfast room. When she didn't follow, he came back into the entrance hall. "I'm serious. I need you. After breakfast we have to go shopping. You have to look at least presentable going to this affair."

Sabrina looked at him, nonplused. His nasal affectations and lazy sounding voice grated on her nerves and she was looking forward to getting away from him.

When he arched an eyebrow, Sabrina relented and joined him for breakfast. Mendes was silent throughout, deep in his thoughts, while playing with the armband.

Watching him for some time she finally said, "You're going to eat, aren't you?"

He slowly raised his eyes to her, then, began to eat in a preoccupied manner.

* * *

Going shopping with Mendes was a memorable experience. Sabrina had never met anyone as fussy, arrogant and sometimes downright rude to her or even the sales personnel.

Within an hour, they had gone to numerous shops, but none of the dresses appealed to him. At the last store, he had the poor salesgirl so flustered she nearly brought the same dress twice. By the time he finally made a selection, Sabrina was on the brink of rebellion.

He insisted that Sabrina try it on again. The dress clung tightly to her body. She looked at her reflection. "What in the world are you trying to make me look like, a tart?" But inwardly, she admitted to herself, that she liked the way it flattered her figure,

Mendes' glassy stare was icy enough to wither a more sensitive soul. He looked at her with complete disregard and responded with one demoralizing comment, "Indeed."

His magnificent unconcern made Sabrina blink.

"Now we need shoes."

"The shoe department is in another section," the salesgirl informed him.

"Well, tell whoever is in charge to bring whatever we need here," he said, airily, and waving her off, dampened the girl's hopeful expression.

While the salesgirl went off, Mendes elegantly crossed his long legs and leaned back in his chair with an uninterested air, drumming his fingers on the armrest.

Sabrina looked at him with renewed dislike.

Selecting the shoes, thank god, took less time. Their next stop was a hairdresser. Again, Mendes proved himself a fussy perfectionist. To Sabrina's unheeded sigh, he took the comb away from the operator.

"No, no, no," he said, "that won't do. This hairdo won't go with the personality she's supposed to affect," and he demonstrated how he wanted the hair done.

Sabrina was totally out of her ken with someone like him and tried to tolerate his eccentric behavior. When they left the hairdresser she was still deciding if what she felt was amusement or anger.

*   *   *

For the social, Mendes wore black, silky, close-fitting breeches and matching tunic. As they entered the reception room, all eyes turned toward them as he sedately walked in, his arm linked with Sabrina's. They had arrived rather late.

During the early part of the social, both mingled within the crowd and Mendes introduced her as Sappho. Later she whispered in his ear, asking "The courtesan?"

His lips quirked into a smile.

As she moved through the crowd with him, Sabrina tried to assess him. He was not as tall as she, and had a lithe body. His skin was tan and it seemed to have a red tinge to it. Also, his face was asymmetric and the skin looked as if it had been pulled tightly over his skull.

"Do I pass inspection?" he suddenly asked her.

"I don't know. I'm not quite sure about you. What am I supposed to do here?"

"Enjoy the social. Let's try the food."

The food was arranged buffet style. As they moved from dish to dish, a tall and fairly young looking woman approached Mendes.

"Hello Mendes, what a pleasure to see you again."

Her words didn't match what Sabrina was reading. The stranger had been startled, and her surprise was anything but pleased.

Mendes' eyes widened, and one corner of his mouth crooked into smile. He snorted slightly. "Ah, Elvita, I didn't think you would be missing me."

"Now Mendes, you shouldn't say such things. What brings you to this pleasant gathering?"

"You my dear. I brought you a bracelet." Mendes reached into the pocket of his tunic and took out the bracelet, offering it to her.

Elvita took it between her thumb and forefinger with the same distrust Medes had shown. "If I had known," she said, "I wouldn't have worn this bracelet," and pointed to the one on her arm.

"Well, now you have two," Mendes told her, unmoved.

Some of Elvita's deportment bothered Sabrina so she did something she hated to do, she rifled her files. Oh my word, she thought to herself. She's a double agent, working for the Altruscans. I wonder if Mendes knows.

Later that evening, there was a recital. The baritone was just bearable. Immediately following the recital, they left the party. Before entering the taxi, Mendes turned to Sabrina, "Can you take me to Daugave?"

"Right now?"

"Yes."

"But my things?"

"Brandon will have them waiting for you at the Space Port."

*   *   *

As Mendes had said, Brandon was waiting under the wings of Spitfire with her belongings.

When Sabrina hesitated, Mendes snapped, "Get going, girl."

"I don't know if you'll like riding in my Spitfire?"

"Why?" he asked. When she didn't answer, he said, "Well?"

She had hoped to get rid of him. "I don't like being this close to you. You drive me nuts. So during the flight, you keep your mouth shut," she told him bluntly. Now, having said it, she felt better. Here, she had the upper hand, her territory, plus she was getting back at him for the way he had treated her.

Mendes only grinned.

Sabrina settled herself in the pilot's seat and pointed for him to sit at the auxiliary station, then called the tower. When she received permission to lift off, she started the ignition sequence. Turning to Mendes, "By the way, that woman, Elvita, she's a double agent."

"We've suspected her for some time," he told her as he watched the craft taxi to the take off point. Before lifting off he said, "What's in the bracelet is adulterated information. Just true enough for the Altruscans not to suspect it."

"What are you doing at Daugave?"

"Reporting in."

After Spitfire cleared Sarpedion, Sabrina turned back to Mendes. "Now, you need to keep you eyes wide open, I wouldn't like for you to miss a thing," she told him.

As an answer he tilted the chair back and closed his eyes. The last thing he heard before the effect took over was a disappointed, "That darn blabber mouth," meaning Sargon.

Once she established orbit around Daugave, Mendes in his irritating voice said, "Okay, after you beam me down to headquarters, you can go home."

Chapter 12

Sabrina had recently come off duty and was just stepping out of the shower when the house phone rang. She was instructed to report immediately to the small briefing room. She gave the sarong she had laid out a rueful look and decided to slip into her baggy sweat suit instead.

When she strode into the briefing room, her eyebrows rose and she stopped short for a second as her eyes fell on Commodore Doeros sitting next to Sargon. Also, Serenity the Arachnid from the planet Coronis was present in her human form. Serenity could assume many different forms, including, looking human, but without human feelings or emotions. To her silent what's up query, Sargon's face remained blank and unreadable, giving her no indication of why she had been summoned. She pulled out a chair and slowly sat down at the oblong table.

Commodore Doeros' demeanor clearly showed his annoyance as Sabrina sat down before being asked. Her overt disrespect always nettled him. There was a scowl on his face as he cleared his throat. Pushing a manila envelope toward her, "Captain Hennesee," he said arrogantly, "these are your orders with explanations for you to read. Captain Thalon has volunteered you for this mission, vouching that you are amply qualified."

Sabrina shot a glance at Sargon and then at Serenity since Doeros' comment had not been very enlightening. But as always, the Arachnid was utterly unreadable. Also Sargon's mind shields were tightly closed. Since she could not elicit any information that way, she asked in her most reasonable tone, "Is there more I need to know, or can I leave to read this?"

Serenity's obsidian eyes looked emotionless at Sabrina, but there was a little twitch to her mouth, which in her case might go for humor. "We thought for you to return to Earth to collect the data we need to see if your home planet is ready to join the Federation of Planets," she said in English, a language Doeros was not familiar with.

"Maybe you'd like to know what happened after we left." Sargon injected.

She looked at him. Her first thought was, but the boys. She hadn't planned on leaving them, not until they were older, and ready to leave her. So, the only reply that immediately came out of her mouth was, "But what about Logan and Jason?"

"I am very confident of my capability to look after them. Then, they're shortly joining the Academy, so they would have moved away from home anyway."

For the young Antareans, it was mandatory to become part of the Cadet-corps after their fourteenth birthday. The cadets lived in an area which at one time contained Sabrina's first home on the Antares. It had been expanded to include a wide plaza surrounded by school buildings and dormitories. Also, there was a hotel on a tree-lined street with shops. The park was still there, but much smaller. It was the only recognizable place from old.

"But I would be here for them to come home over the weekend."

Switching back to Galactic, "You want to take the job, or not?" came Sargon's curt question.

Sabrina contemplated it, but only for a moment. "You'll take care of the boys?"

"Of course."

"Okay, sounds good."

When she received an uncomprehending stare from Doeros, Sargon interpreted. "She has accepted."

*   *   *

Sabrina had barely entered the vestibule of her home when she was waylaid by her two sons.

"Dad said you're going away," Logan accused her.

"He already talked to you?"

"He did."

"Mom," Jason said, pushing on her shoulder so she had to face him," do I have to move over to the Academy?" His voice was petulant, and there was a dark scowl on his face.

"I don't know. Sargon said he would take care of the two of you while I'm gone."

"I hate it when you go off," Logan said explosively. He always reacted agitated when Sabrina was away from the Antares. There were still deep feelings that had left scars from the time he was an infant when Sabrina had to withdraw her presence to shield him.

"Logan, the mind touch will be there no matter how far I'm away," she assured him. "The only time I have withdrawn from our connection was to protect you. I think you're old enough to understand. I don't like to leave you, but I know Sargon will take good care of both of you."

"Don't you let anything happen to you," Jason growled at her.

Sabrina tousled Logan's jet black hair, and then Jason's auburn mop. When a pair of amber cat eyes, and a pair of green eyes looked earnestly into Sabrina's sea-green eyes, she chuckled and drew them into a tight embrace.

Just then the door opened and Sargon came slowly into the vestibule, his eyes on Pegasus flying up toward him from the tiled floor. Pegasus was Sabrina's house symbol.

When he saw Sabrina and her sons standing in the vestibule, "You haven't read your orders yet!" he accused her.

"No, not yet. I was waylaid by these two. Jason is worried that he has to join the cadets."

"If he tests out ready, I don't see why not. He and Logan could be together."

"But I could stay here with Medea looking after me."

"We'll see," Sabrina said while watching Sargon. "Is there anything you want to talk to me about?"

Looking at her he said, "Couldn't we go somewhat farther into the house, maybe?"

Sabrina was staring at him, her green eyes wide. "Oh, of course, how remiss of me," she replied with the ghost of a smile.

Sargon knew that was not it. He had several times barred her from entering his place when he had guests, or just returned from a mission. She was just paying him back. Grinning, Logan naturally understood. He knew his parents well, and sometimes joined in the game they were playing with each other. With some of this Jason was left out not having Logan's PSI abilities. But he did have other gifts, like Miri's disappearing trick, with which he had led his mother, or Sargon, on some merry chases.

99

Sabrina guided Sargon to chairs set under the peristyle which was formed by Doric columns surrounding the inner court. In the center of the court was a pool, and at the far end stood the statue of a little boy perpetually relieving himself into the water. Long ago, Sabrina had caught the then two-year-old Logan imitating the statue and taken a film of it.

The opposite wing was still empty, except for the far side which Joran, his wife Marlo, and daughter Margali, occupied.

They were barely seated when Tomar, acting as Sabrina's butler, brought a tray with lemonade. "I think something to drink would be in order," he said officiously.

Sargon had discovered him with his wife Medea, and Lantos the gardener, at the slave markets of Anshar. Sabrina had upbraided him on his callousness of buying human beings. Sargon's answering remark had been, "How could I have freed them otherwise? Do you want me to send them back?"

Later, after digesting Sargon's news, she had called Tomar, Lantos and Medea into her living-room and told them that she had no desire to keep servants, but they were welcome to join her house. There had been only one relapse and Sabrina warned them if they thought of themselves as servants, she would send them back to Anshar. Tomar and Medea had taken her admonition serious. Since then, he and Medea had commenced bossing her, especially when both thought she was remiss in taking proper care of herself.

After Tomar left, "Same question," Sabrina said.

"Like Serenity said, your mission is to see if Earth is ready to join the Alliance. But what I came to ask you is, while you're on Earth, try to find Elisheba. I have hired people to search for her. The last I heard is that she might be living in the vicinity of Haifa. She is reported to be married and that her husband is a member of a very orthodox Jewish sect. I have very bad feelings about all of this. I can't explain it," he said when Sabrina raised a questioning eyebrow. "I want her found. She must have a choice either to stay, or to come home."

"I see," Sabrina said, and again in her mind she saw the redheaded elfin face of Elisheba. There was still a lot of guilt associated with that mission. It had dire consequences for Elisheba, and in her mistaken belief, she felt she had failed Sargon. She left the Antares, first to stay at Sarah's, and now it seems she'd gone to live on Earth.

"Another thing," Sargon's voice broke into her thoughts, "I wish you would stop baiting Doeros."

"He's not my favorite Commodore," she grumbled.

"What'd she do?" the boys wanted to know.

"She has bad manners," Sargon said, dryly.

"You ought to spank her, then," Jason said, with a mischievous sparkle to his eyes and a wide grin on his face.

"Oh no me boyo," Sargon told him, reading his mind and grinning back. He locked eyes with Jason, "I know you would like for me to get into trouble, to get back at me for sending your mother away. Nothing doing, kiddo."

"When does she have to leave?" Jason asked, ignoring Sargon's stare, and the accuracy in reading him.

"She has a week to get ready and to help the two of you get settled in at the Academy.

Chapter 13

Sabrina stood with her face pressed against the porthole and watched Earth come into view. The small passenger shuttle approached the Space Station which had been built long ago by the Altruscans. The Cartel believed it was a safe haven for them should war break out on Earth. Sargon, then known as Jim Thalon, had with the help of Sabrina's parents and a young man named Roger, moved it beyond the Cartel's reach.

The steward standing behind her touched her on the shoulder. "Miss Hennesee, we will be docking in five minutes. An ambassador named Keleb will meet you at the Space Station."

"Thank you."

After the shuttle docked, she was escorted by the Captain to the reception area.

"Ambassador Keleb is from the Altair system," the Captain informed her. "He has been in contact with the Earth government from the beginning. He helped in evacuating the people from the planet during its turbulent episode, and worked with others to organize its resettlement."

Sabrina thanked him again.

The file Doeros provided contained only names for her to contact. It did not tell her anything pertinent about Ambassador Keleb or any of the other people. There was a brief comment on the current governmental set up on Earth, and a historic summary from the time of the upheaval to the present. There were also several access codes to computer files. She surmised that she was to gather her own unbiased information, then submit her findings in writing to the Coordinator of the Alliances Council.

The man waiting for her in the station's reception area was impressive. His wide shoulders and snow white hair gave him the look of a patrician, but his face became wooden when he saw Sabrina coming toward him.

The Captain introduced her. "Ambassador Keleb, this is Mary Hennesee, the representative from the Worldship Antares,"

"I'm glad to meet you, Miss Hennesee." He greeted Sabrina with deep solemnity, standing stiff-backed, inclining his head a fraction. "I would like to reiterate that your mission has to be kept secret. We can't upset the sensibility of the Earth people by informing them that they are to be scrutinized by aliens. I will work closely with you in formulating the proposal. General Dehner from the Air Academy will be your contact. He graciously offered his home. I worked with him for many years and have found him to be very professional and personable."

"I will reside in a private home?" Sabrina asked, astounded.

"Yes, we thought it best. I hope it will be agreeable?"

"I don't think it will present any insurmountable obstacles," she told him with a slight smile and shrugged her shoulders.

Keleb's attitude baffled her. He was too reserved, too unbending, no humor. When she rifled through his memories, he was all he represented himself to be. All his credentials and who he said he was, was easy readable, but still, her gut feeling irrationally told her that she didn't like him.

*   *   *

It was early the next day when Ambassador Keleb came to pick up Sabrina at the Station's hotel. She had seen little of the Space Station, and it seemed she wasn't going to see much of the terminal on Earth either, or its people. After disembarking from the Shuttle, the Ambassador hustled her into a waiting air-car, and while they sped toward their destination, Keleb briefed her on the Earth people.

Sabrina had the distinct impression that he had never been apprised of her origin, and she had no intention of enlightening him.

The air-car landed at a housing complex which reminded Sabrina of a Pueblo with its self-contained units designed to offer maximum privacy. Each unit had recessed porches and a small garden planted on the roof of the unit below. Stairs and narrow walkways led from unit to unit.

After they rang the doorbell, they were greeted by a tall man with graying hair, hazel eyes and a pleasant smile.

"Miss Hennesee, welcome to my home," he said, extending his hand. His grip was firm, although gentle, as he held Sabrina's hand in his.

The formal Miss coming from Dehner, whom she instantly liked, did not sit quite well with Sabrina. It must have shown in her face because Dehner shot a questioning look at Keleb.

Sabrina chuckled. "Sorry, most people just call me Mary," she glibly told him.

Dehner looked her up and down and wondered why someone so young would have such an important job. His impression of Sabrina was of a youngster. To him she appeared to be between twenty to thirty years old.

Inwardly, Sabrina smiled, knowing the impression she gave. She had just turned sixty-one.

Keleb coughed impatiently, then, said. "I'm sorry, but I have to leave. Appointments, you know." He said his goodbyes and asked that his regards be conveyed to Mrs. Dehner.

Both, Dehner and Sabrina were glad to watch him fly away in the air-car.

"Not much on protocol," Dehner said to cover his obvious relief at Keleb's departure.

Just then Martha Dehner came down the hallway. "I thought I heard the doorbell," she said to her husband, then saw Sabrina. "Come, let the lady into the house and quit standing on the doorstep," she admonished her spouse. Mrs. Dehner appeared to be dressed to go out.

Sabrina instantly liked her. She was slightly rotund and exuded a warm personality. Motherly, Sabrina thought.

When General Dehner pick up her meager luggage, her duffle-bag, "Is that all you have with you?" she asked. When Sabrina nodded assent, "Poor dear," Martha exclaimed, "We need to go shopping. You need more things to wear."

"Thank you Mrs. Dehner, I would like that."

"Call me Martha. That Mrs. Dehner just doesn't sit right with me. I'm sorry, I have to leave. The Academy just called me; I'm to substitute. They're short on teachers again."

"I can teach," Sabrina felt compelled to say.

"Do you?" Martha asked surprised. "Are you accredited?"

"No, sorry I mentioned it. I have no credentials which would be accepted here."

"What can you teach?'

"Engineering math, and also language."

"English?"

"No, Galactic."

"Oh, that's interesting. The faculty was talking about that language some time ago. It would be important if we were to join the Planetary Alliance."

"Is there much talk about this Alliance?"

"Oh, everybody thinks it would be great if they would accept us."

"I'm hearing a small doubt in your voice. What makes you think it would not be feasible?"

"Well, we still have some eggheads around who don't like alien interference." Martha looked at her watch. "Kids can be late, but teachers, never."

After Martha left, Sabrina turned to Dehner. "Are there still eggheads around?"

"Yes. But the interference is subtle, through innuendoes. We can't put a finger on who's doing it."

* * *

The next morning, Sabrina woke up to sunshine streaming through her window. She had slept deeply and felt confused at first. Strange room, she thought as she looked around.

Aye, I'm on Earth and I'm Mary Hennesee. I'd better not forget that. In all her life, she had never answered to Mary.

Suddenly, there was a knock on the door, "Mary, are you awake?" It was Martha Dehner.

"Just a moment, Martha," Sabrina called out, hurriedly grabbing for her robe. She didn't know how Mrs. Dehner would react to seeing her in her birthday suit.

When she opened the door, Mrs. Dehner voice came from the kitchen. "Mary, how do you like your bacon?"

"Bacon? Real bacon?" she asked, walking into the kitchen. "I haven't eaten real bacon in ages".

"Of course, real," Mrs. Dehner answered. "Where have you been girl? Or shouldn't I ask?"

"Well, better not for the time being. I'm supposed to be hush-hush."

"Is that good or bad?"

Sabrina laughed. "Martha, give me time to sort things out, then I will give you an answer. Ooh, that smells good," she said, as she bent over the frying pan. And real coffee?"

"Absolutely. Really girl, where did you come from?"

"From a Space Station," Sabrina replied, straight-faced.

"And they don't have real bacon up there?"

"No. Hard on the pigs," Sabrina joked.

The morning passed amiably with a nice chat in which Sabrina asked most of the questions. She queried Martha mostly about the people, the Air Academy, and the present Air Force.

After Martha and Sabrina cleared the table and put away the dishes, Martha asked, "How would you like to go to the mall right now?"

"I would love to," Sabrina replied, enthusiastically.

The mall proved to be an enormously large and tall building packed with shops, restaurants and offices intermingled with apartments. It was a city within a building. Everything was sound proof and solidly built. Sabina noticed the numerous recreational areas around the building. Martha told her there was a golf course, several ball parks, tennis courts, swimming pools, and a large park with a children's playground, or just for walking.

Sabrina felt great walking. Being confined in a ship with not much to do, she almost became claustrophobic. The Antares was spacious, or when she was on a Starship, she was too busy to mind. Being only a passenger had been the most trying experience.

She and Martha had a good time together. Sabrina bought several dresses, some jewelry, as well as other necessities at Martha's instigation. Later, they rode the elevator up to a restaurant and sat out on the terrace for lunch. When they arrived back home, General Dehner was impatiently waiting for them.

"Martha, you're supposed to let me know if you're flying the coop; especially with Mary. We can't let anything happen to her."

"You're the only one who knows the scenario and script," Martha replied to the reprimand. "If you would tell me what's up, I could make better decisions about what and what not to do."

"I think I can take care of myself, General," Sabrina assured him, trying to smooth over the situation.

"I don't doubt it," he said, and gave her a cursory look. He had noticed her assured walk and her poise. To contradict all this, she appeared to be young, and there was this feminine and vulnerable look about her which he suspected might be deceiving. "But you see, I have my orders," he said, turning to Sabrina. "Sensible or not, I have to follow them. And please, call me Robert. Being called general in my own house is just a little too formal."

"Okeydoke," Sabrina replied.

Both, Martha and Robert broke into laughter.

"Where did you pick that up?" he asked.

"Oh, I don't know. A friend of mine uses it," she told them, thinking of Miri.

*   *   *

On Sabrina's third day on Earth, Dehner came home at noon with a camera. He took Sabrina's picture.

"That's for your ID," he explained. "I got you a job at the Academy."

"Oh, I see. So, you went over someone's head?"

"Several of them. You can start Monday."

"Two days to get ready?"

"Too soon?"

"Nope. That's just time enough to work out a lesson plan. What did I get?"

"You said you can teach Galactic. Also, they need a substitute for a math class. We forged your papers. My mother would turn over in her grave if she knew," he added whimsically.

"Aw, your mother would do no such a thing," Martha replied. "She was the most unconventional woman I ever met."

* * *

Two days later, Sabrina walked into her class of six students. Most of the kids seemed to be in their early twenties. She suspected they had been hastily assembled. With relief, she noted a blackboard on the wall. She liked boards; they made explanations easier.

"Good morning," she greeted them. "My name is Mary Hennesee. You can call me Miss Hennesee." She gave them a sweeping glance. "How many of you really want to learn Galactic, and how many of you have been ordered to come here?"

Two raised their hands.

"Explain."

One of the girls stood up. "I already have too many classes, and with this language class, I have an overload."

"I surmise you can't get out."

"No. It was an order."

"What's your grade-point average?"

"I got a three-point-five."

"That's not bad. If I tutor you, would that help?"

"If you could, that would be great."

"And you?" she asked the other hand-raiser.

"Do you know engineering math?"

"Sure do."

"Great, that would help if you don't mind tutoring me, too."

Sabrina went to the board. Swiftly she wrote; I, you, he, she, we. they, and are, in English and than in Galactic. Then she pronounced each words in Galactic and after that, erased the words in English. Pointing to herself she said "I", and pointing to a student, she had her pronounce the word you. She went around the class giving everyone a chance to get a feel of the words before she added more \such as here and there and other pronouns, articles and a few nouns and verbs.

Close to the end of the hour she said, "Okay, you have thirty minutes to write a simple sentence, using the words you have learned; you can leave as you finish. You two stay and we'll figure out a time that's convenient to meet."

She graded the papers as they were handed in and also set Tuesday afternoon as the time for tutoring. Half an hour later she left to sub for the math class.

Most of her math students were mechanical or aeronautical engineers, and according to the book given to her, should have completed calculus and be ready for partial differential equations.

When she entered the class, everyone was present. She stepped up to the podium and looked out at them, noticing only one third were girls.

"My name is Miss Hennesee and I'm your sub. According to my notes you should know all about calculus. Let's see if your professor is right."

Her teaching style was new to the students. Instead of standing on the podium lecturing or writing on the board, she sat on the edge of her desk and had the students answer their own questions. She began by asking a question, then, asked why the answer was right, then, recapped what made it right and where to go from there. Her style of teaching involved the participation of every student, and thirty minutes before the time was up, she handed out questions for a quick assessment. Several students came up before leaving to comment on how quick the time had flown by, and to ask whether she would be here tomorrow.

Chapter 14

Teaching at the Air Academy gave Sabrina access to an extensive library and computer network. There were newspapers covering the reconstruction after Earth's upheavals, the rebuilding of certain cities, and information regarding the new laws enacted at the time, as well as personal stories of heroism. Only a few books touched on the turbulent years around the turn of the century. Sabrina still remembered the earthquakes, the tornadic winds and floods. On her flight back to Earth, she had familiarized herself with the data accumulated by the Planetary Alliance. Slowly, she pieced Earth's history together from the time she had left to the present.

During those turbulent years land had disappeared and new land had risen. The climate had changed dramatically in many parts of the globe. The whole societal structure had changed, and new words had been added to the English language.

In her younger days, to her parent's consternation, Sabrina acquired the very annoying knack of breaking into other people's computers and literally rifling through their files. Under Sargon's training, she became even more proficient at computer technology. Working at the university, and under the guise of writing an important government paper, she had gained unlimited computer access. Since the library was open late, especially during finals, Sabrina could be found far into the night, raiding computers and gathering data. She also wrote a program to help her sift through and correlate the information.

A Naval station on the West Coast aroused her suspicion. Personnel with certain qualifications were being assigned there. A small airplane factory had secret government orders, and priority for certain and otherwise difficult to obtain items.

Also, in the library she found the book Jonathan had written, and checked it out. As she read it, Jonathan's personality came through in his writing style with his great insight and understanding of people. Reading through his pages brought her parents alive for her. She began to understand and realize how much they had been involved in checkmating the Altruscan conspiracy, and why they had been assassinated. She learned about the existence of the Cartel, their drive for power and total disregard of other people's rights. In the end, she found herself forgiving her parents for dying so horribly and leaving her an orphan.

* * *

One day, after her math class, Sabrina stepped out into the hallway and saw Martha coming toward her.

"Hi Mary, how does lunch sound?"

"Now that you mention it, I think that would be great since I'm finished for the day."

"I'd like to introduce you to a few of my friends, if you don't mind."

"That's just what the doctor ordered," Sabrina remarked.

"Why Mary, are you ailing?" Martha asked solicitously.

"Don't try so hard to be too humorous."

At the cafeteria, three elderly ladies hailed Martha.

"Hi, we thought you missed the cafeteria and just about decided to go looking for you. It was you who invited us, remember?"

"I had to wait until Mary finished her class." Turning to Sabrina, "Let me introduce my friends. This is Christy, Nancy and Caroline."

"Hi Mary, "Christy said, "Martha talks a lot about you, and since you're new, she thought you needed some friends."

"Thanks, Christy, friends are always nice to have."

"Martha never mentioned where you came from?" Caroline asked.

Sabrina grinned, "I lived for a long time on the Space Station," she said, with one eye cocked at Martha.

"She had a devastatingly boring life," Martha commented, her face bland and guileless.

"Well, you came to the right place, then." Nancy giggled.

The bantering went back and forth while they ate lunch. Suddenly Sabrina saw an opening to ask certain questions her research was not capable of answering. Nancy just mentioned the time when the Earth rumbled last week. "It registered only 4 point on the Richter scale, but still it scared everyone."

"How much do you remember about those horrible days?" Sabrina asked.

"Mary, I really don't like to think about them," Christy said. "If it hadn't been for those spaceships, no one would have survived. I remember when I felt like the world was crashing down on me, a small spacecraft came swooping in and picked me up."

"Yep, at first the soldiers fired on them, that was before people got angry and stopped it. It was a crazy time." Nancy's whole body shook, the mirth gone from her face. "But what really angers me is to think how stupid people were in those days."

"What you mean by that?" Sabrina asked.

"I don't know how much history you had," she said, looking at Sabrina. "How old are you? Between twenty-five . . . thirty?"

"Well, you're close," Sabrina said, amused.

"You remember anything that happened after the cold war?"

"No, not really," Sabrina lied.

"Probably not, I guess you were too young. During the cold war and the wars afterward," Nancy continued, "nations stockpiled atomic and biological weapons. Those facility and storage areas were destroyed by the earthquakes. What do you think happened to all that bio stuff? It was released into the air, killing thousands and thousands of people. And those were the lucky ones! The neurological damage was unbelievable."

"Yes," Christy said, "I remember a pregnant woman dressed in old rags with most of her mind gone. She would huddle in doorways; you couldn't get close to her. People stopped by and gave her food. One day, I was just going home when I saw her in the middle of the street moaning and crying. She held people at bay who wanted to help her. Her water suddenly broke, and as she squatted down she gave birth to something that was beyond words. People fainted. Some just turned away and threw up. A doctor finally arrived at the scene and gave the woman a shot to calm her down. Then he scooped up the birth and wrapped it into a sheet someone had brought."

"There were many birth defects and still going on, "Martha said quietly, "Many babies are stillborn."

Now Sabrina understood the sorrow she sometimes felt emanating from Martha. She had lost her babies.

115

"They poisoned the whole damned Earth, you know," Nancy said vehemently. "You know, there are areas which are literally hot and will be for thousands of years. The radioactive waste, guess what happened to that? The ground is radioactive, including the ground water. There's no life in those areas; it's appropriately called the Dead Zone. And then the toxic waste! How could those people have been so stupid, is beyond me."

"It wasn't stupidity," Caroline said passionately, her fist coming down on the table. "I can tell you in two simple words what it was. It was unadulterated greed! They were so busy creating all those weapons and preparing for war. And it wasn't just us. There were other nations. Then they were so busy making money. No one ever asked the simple question, what if? What if there was never going to be a war? What were they going to do with all the accumulated atomic weapons and radio-active waste? They were obsessed with making those damned bombs. It never occurred to them to figure out how to destroy all of this if it wasn't needed. It was the same with the industries. They never figured out what to do with the waste; they buried it. It's not whether they had any brains; they just failed to use them. They all played the money game, the political game, the executive game. Games and games, you just name it. They created the games, made up the rules, then, began to believe it was real. They played to the hilt. They never carried the thought beyond the games, they never asked, what if." When she stopped, she was shaking, with tears coursing down her face. "I'm sorry, Mary, I guess this isn't a very cheerful lunch," she said, and pushed her plate away.

Caroline's outburst had drawn a crowd. Sabrina scanned them and felt anger emanating from everyone.

"We had to clean up the mess they made. They never thought of that either," a young man said.

"I'm sterile because of their stupidity," a young girl said furiously.

"You can't imagine the knowledge we've lost," added an elderly professor. He was over ninety and the oldest teacher on campus. Sabrina looked curiously at him. "There are not many of us old people around, most having died during all the turmoil. If it hadn't been for the extraterrestrials, we would have had to start from scratch," he told her.

When Sabrina left the cafeteria she felt very subdued. What she had heard was Acheron's story, a story of devastation and survival. She also knew that during the upheavals, spaceships came in and literally plucked people off roofs and treetops. After the Earth became quiescent, they were brought back. Many of the young people were born on those ships. Maybe that explains their eagerness to get back to the stars. They championed joining the Planetary Alliance.

*   *   *

This was Sabrina's last day; school would be out until fall. She had befriended many of the young people at the Academy. The kids reminded her of the ones born on the Antares. They were open, enthusiastic, and she found them to be very intelligent. Working with them lessened her feeling of homesickness. And now, she had to decide what to do next.

After three days of idleness, Sabrina became restless.

"You don't have a very still behind," Martha accused her.

"Nope, I don't like it when I have nothing to do."

"I can see that. Why don't you travel?"

"I have already considered that. I only need to decide where to."

"How about checking out the West Coast?" When Sabrina raised a questioning eyebrow, she added. "Well, it's not the West Coast as it used to be, but there is a huge bay area and a Naval Station there. It's one of our bigger cities with a wonderful variety of people to meet.

"You are a gem, you know. I think I'll take your advice."

Sabrina had already decided on the West Coast so she could investigate the Naval Station, but gave Martha the credit for mentioning it.

Martha again took her shopping and advised her on what style of clothing to take along. While Sabrina was packing her duffle bag, Martha walked in just as she folded her Antarean uniform.

"What kind of uniform is that?" Martha asked, suspiciously. "I haven't seen anything like it before."

"Just a little thing I wear once in a while."

"I gather you're not going to tell me."

"Not yet. There will come a time when I can let you in on it."

"Oh well, I'm only the General's wife," she said in mock resignation and slumped her shoulders.

Sabrina laughed. "Believe me, there have been lots of times when I felt just like you. Nobody would tell me what was going on when I knew something was brewing."

Martha came over to finger the material. "I've never felt anything like this either. What's the meaning of the orange stripe?"

"To tell me apart from someone else," Sabrina wisecracked.

"Then there's more to you than meets the eye."

"Is Martha badgering you?" Dehner's voice interrupted. They had no idea how long he had been listening. "Mary has a job to do, and the less people know about it, the easier it will be for her. That's the only reason we're trying to keep it quiet."

"But she wears a curious uniform. Have you seen one like that before?" the unquenchable Martha asked.

Dehner walked over to look at it. "No rank?"

Sabrina smiled, and in answer ran her fingers along the small, thin orange insert on her collar.

"Hmm, I see," he rumbled, and looked at his wife," doesn't tell me anything either," he told her.

"Our Mary is definitely a mystery," Martha quipped.

Chapter 15

At the end of the week, Sabrina boarded a plane and flew to the West Coast. Much of the topography had changed. Looking down from above gave her a feeling of just how devastating the destruction had been. Massive stretches of land were devoid of people.

Arriving at the West Coast, she went through the normal steps of acquiring a taxi and renting a room. The hotel she chose was closest to the beach.

It was late afternoon, when donning her swimsuit; she sauntered down to the waterfront. There were small restaurants along the shore. Most of the people sat outside, under umbrellas, sipping drinks and . . . milkshakes!

Sabrina hadn't had a real shake since she left Earth. So getting one was the first thing on her agenda. Sitting outside the restaurant with her bath towel draped across her chair, she observed the people lying on the beach, some alone, some in pairs, some smooching, or just walking by. It was interesting to see their relaxed attitude. Not much different from what she remembered. Later in the evening, after having dined, she went for a stroll along the beach when, suddenly, someone hollered, Sabrina!"

Astonished, she turned. "Ian McPherson!" she called out, and ran into his outstretched arms for a tight hug. Then her eyes fell on a boy standing beside him. He seemed to be around fifteen or so.

"Oh, you haven't met Charles. He adopted me, or I him. I don't really know which way it went."

"Hi, Charles. I'm Sabrina."

"I know. Ian talks a lot about you."

"Does he now." Sabrina scrutinized Charles closer then asked, "Aren't you an American Indian?"

"Seneca," he told her proudly.

"I see." Turning toward Ian, "What in the name of whatever are you doing here?"

"I'm working at the Naval Station, training pilots. Why are you here?"

"I'm not here. I'm Mary Hennesee for the duration of my stay. I'm interested in having a look-see at that Naval Station. You think you could get me in?"

"You're not Mary Hennesee, your Mata Hari," Ian replied sotto voce.

"What's your script?"

"Seeing if Earth is ready to join the Alliance."

"Uh. Big script?" Ian asked.

"I don't know yet."

"In the mean time, are you set to have some fun as well, Mary, darlin?"

Sabrina gave him a long look. "We are not on the Antares, right?" Then followed up with a big grin, "I'm not adverse at all to having fun."

"There's a small bar where most of the fly-boys meet . . . and some of the astronauts."

"Are they still called astronauts?"

"It sounds archaic, but that's still the name. How does right now sound?"

"Fine by me. How about Charles?"

"He goes home, right?"

"Do I have to?"

"If it were anything else but that bar. Why don't you find yourself a friend and cruise the beach."

The bar was a small affair . . . intimate. As they entered, Ian was greeted by a group of pilots.

"Hey," they hollered, and waived for him to join. "Come and introduce us to that dish."

"Men haven't changed," she mumbled into Ian's ear.

"Not much. They still like to show off and act like big boys." Ian walked up to the table, "This is a friend of mine," he introduced Sabrina. "Her name is Mary Hennesee, and she' mine, so keep your mitts off."

"Hey, you're not very generous," one of them complained, seemingly a bit under the weather.

"Mike, you knock it off," Ian warned.

But the guys turned out to be nice, and Sabrina enjoyed herself. Most of them were young men, training to become pilots.

"Want to come on base tomorrow?" Ian asked, after they exited the bar an hour later.

"Yes, I would like to look at the airplane plant. Then I'd like to see one of your planes, if that's possible?"

Ian stood at attention, "Yes, Sir," he said and grumbled, "I thought you were on a holiday."

"Only sort of."

*　　*　　*

The next day, Ian was waiting for her with a Jeep at the main-gate of the base.

"Come, climb in. I'm in a hurry. I have to test fly a new type of plane. Wanna fly with me?"

"What a silly question. Of course I do."

They drove for quite a while, because the airstrip was at a considerable distance from the main base.

The plane sitting on the tarmac was a fighter jet.

A whistle escaped Sabrina and her eyes lit up. "Wow!" she said. Jumping out of the Jeep, she went around the plane, "That's one sleek baby." Turning to Ian, "Why is Earth building fighter jets?"

"We still have Altruscans around," Ian explained.

"What do you mean, around?"

"Well, they intermingled with other races, and so are hard to tell apart from the regular guys. That's the reason given for building these fighter planes. I don't really know where the requisitions come from. The news media is screaming for an investigation."

"I should think so," Sabrina replied, while inspecting the fuselage. "The design is beautiful. How does it fly?"

"Climb in," Ian invited her.

"You naturally got permission for me to fly with you?"

"Are you kidding! If they knew, they would put me in jail."

Once they were in the air and out over the ocean, Ian contacted the tower. "This is Ian McPherson; I'll be coming in and out on your radar. Just wanting to let you know I'm out here."

"Okay, Mister McPherson, we'll keep you in mind," the tower answered.

Through all this Sabrina had remained silent.

"You can talk now," he told her the moment communication was closed.

123

"Mister McPherson?" Sabrina asked.

"Well, Mary Hennesee," putting the accent on Mary.

"Okada put you up to this?"

"Yes. He doesn't like all this sudden, military build up. He told me to nose around. Weel now lass, hang on to yer hat."

To Sabrina's delight, he put the plane through its paces. Climbing up and plunging, rolling, and abruptly switching direction. Just as they were skimming over the top of the water, Ian began to buzz a submerged sub which had shown up on his scanner. Sabrina leaned forward, watching intently.

The sub slowly emerged and the communicator came on. "What in the hell are you trying to do?" a harsh voice demanded.

Ian switched to visual, wanting to see the captain's face.

"Sir, this is a test flight and I'm only putting the plane through its paces," Ian said, his voice expressionless. Suddenly, the angry face of the captain came on screen. Sabrina received a jolt. She barely had the presence of mind to keep her gasp from becoming audible.

Ian apologized profusely and veered off. Once they were back in the Jeep, Sabrina pulled his face toward her and gave him a sober look. "Ian," she said, "I'll eat your dirty socks, but that captain was an Altruscan."

"Are you sure?"

"I said I'll eat your socks."

"Better question, how did you know?"

"My hackles rise when I just get in the proximity of one. Ian, my survival depended several times on being able to spot them. What are you planning to do?"

"By taking you up and buzzing that sub, I think I'll get a reprimand. That will be a good opportunity for me to quit and report to Soltec."

"Why not Keleb?"

"Because, I'm not too sure of that one. I like Soltec; he's one of Sargon's friends."

"Before you quit, I'd like to get into that plant. There are so-called secret government orders to build more of those cute planes we just flew."

"How do you plan to do that? They don't let civilians in."

"Well, maybe you could get me coveralls with captain's bars."

"Why only a captain's?" Ian asked with a lopsided grin. "You know this is the Air Force. Captains are not that high on the ladder."

"I don't want to overdo it."

"Would you trust me enough to be alone with me in my bachelor officer's quarters?" Ian asked, as he draped his arm across her shoulders.

At first, Sabrina looked startled. Then her eyes crinkled and she began to chortle. "Ian, I'm not responsible for your hormonal surges," she told him, reading him well.

His answer was a sour look. He would have liked to have known her in the biblical sense. She was beautiful. She stood over six feet tall with a beautifully proportioned body. She had lovely honey-colored hair, and he liked the way it fell straight across her cheeks. As he looked into her incredible sea-green eyes, he shook himself. "I hate mind readers," he growled.

Sabrina shrugged her shoulders, her amusement clearly showing in her face. "Let's go, before the captain of that sub radios back, and you're persona non grata."

*   *   *

Ian shared his B.O.Q. with a captain who was about the same height as Sabrina. Going to his roommate's closet, he pulled out a set of coveralls. When Sabrina put them on, they sat a little tight on her. Her curves hadn't been measured in.

They rode by Jeep to the hanger's main entrance and she and Ian marched right in. Ian spotted one of the engineers and hailed him, "Scott, the wings need more support to stabilize them. When I veered off, there was too much give. Otherwise, it's doing fine. Let me show you where the supports ought to go." Ian talked fast to keep the engineer's attention on him so Sabrina could stay in the background.

Ian walked over to the nearest plane and Sabrina followed close behind. As both men disappeared under the wing, Sabrina used her PSI ability to scan the work crew.

The men working in the hanger seemed to be all right, nothing more complicated there. They were normal human beings. But, as she scanned the manager, the reading she came across was similar to Keleb's. There was the work knowledge, some normal personal memories. But again, they were more on a monoliniar plane. Missing was the multifaceted personality humans exhibit. Also, lacking was a sense of humor. It was as if his personality had been programmed similar to that of an android. But he was no artificial life-form. He was flesh and blood. It puzzled Sabrina, but there was no more time for her to figure it out, because Ian came out from under the plane.

"Captain," he said to Sabrina, "I know you're in a hurry. I'm grateful to you for giving me time to look at this," pointing at the plane. "Thanks, Scott. I know you'll give them my recommendation. I have to leave or Captain Bates is going to be late."

"What did you get?" Ian wanted to know after they sped off in the Jeep.

"Funny reading from the main office."

"Funny, how? Come on girl, don't make it so suspenseful."

"Same type of reading I get from Keleb. I got his surface memories and knowledge about planes. No deep personal memories about childhood, or having been in love, and no sense of humor."

"I see. What are you going to do about it?"

"It's a little bit too early in the game yet, Ian. I will go back to General Dehner in case Soltec wants to contact me. Tell Soltec to keep tabs on me. I might need him."

"Short vacation, Lass," Ian said.

"Well, I'm supposed to be on a job anyway, but I'm glad I ran into you."

They parted, and upon her return to the Dehner's house, it was already early in the evening and she found that Martha had gone to visit a friend. Robert Dehner was home alone and surprised by her early return.

After exchanging cordial greetings, Sabrina invited him to go for a walk. Several blocks away from the house, Sabrina took a device from of her purse and ran a body scan. "Well, that's good. You're not bugged," she told the flabbergasted general.

"What in the hell is this all about?"

"Robert, there's something going on, and I have to get to the bottom of it. Can't tell you until I talked to Soltec."

"You know you can contact him through Keleb."

"How well do you know Keleb?"

"I've known him for a long time," Robert replied, cautiously.

"Did you notice anything strange the last couple of times you met?"

"Come to think of it, yes. He seemed unusually reserved. He has a routine going with Martha when he comes to our house. But it has been absent for some time. As you know Martha is a great cook, and he likes her cooking. He's been a frequent visitor for dinner."

"And last time, he didn't?"

"Well, the last time I thought was because you were here; maybe he was in a hurry. He has done that before, too."

"I see," Sabrina said, playing with her bottom lip.

Dehner kept his eyes on her, but she made no further comments. When they returned to the house, there was a message on the answering machine. "Mary, this is Soltec. I just learned that you were back. I know this is short notice but I'm having a small dinner party at my house. Call me back if you can attend." He gave the number to call.

She immediately returned the call. "Sir, I received your message," she told him, "and your kind regard inviting me to your party."

"I will have you picked up in half an hour. Will this give you enough time?"

"Plenty of time."

In half an hour Sabrina was ready and waiting. Soltec personally picked her up. "General, would you like to come too? I see you are all by yourself."

"Of course, I would love to."

They drove off, and before entering his house, Soltec told Sabrina, "I got Ian's message. Are you sure?"

"Yes, Soltec, I am. The armament buildup is ordered by the Altruscans."

There was a not-so-kosher exclamation from Dehner, but, before he could voice a comment, Soltec held up his hand. "Not now, I'll brief you later." Turning back to Sabrina, and to

Dehner's complete bafflement, Soltec said, "Now I wish I had someone with Thalon's ability to read people's minds."

"You're not able to mind-read?"

"No. I have no PSI abilities."

"Who would you like to have scanned?"

"Keleb."

"Why?"

"Some of his close associates noticed some odd behaviors."

"I see. Let's join the party. General Dehner, would you like to take my other arm?"

"I always prefer lady's requests to orders, much more fun."

As they entered, there were eight people scattered around the living room.

"I'm sorry for the delay, but I had to invite my friend here when I heard she was back in town," Soltec apologized.

The dinner was exquisite and the company pleasant. Sabrina made her rounds and was introduced to everyone. She carefully scanned Ambassador Keleb's memories. Since she had only met him that one time after coming to Earth, she had no prior knowledge regarding his past. He displayed no reacting to her scanning, so she delved deeper into his mind. He also had no PSI abilities. She was slowly sipping her wine, when she almost choked. "Sorry," she gasped and coughed. "It went down the wrong way. Soltec, would you mind . . . if I stepped into your study until . . . I catch my breath?"

"Of course, Mary. Come, I'll take you." He led her solicitously from the dining room. "You can quit coughing now. We are out of ear shot."

"Sorry . . . this is real," she could barely say . . . "a few seconds."

Soltec went to get a glass of water. "Now, what brought on this coughing fit?" he asked, watching her closely.

"You won't believe it, but Keleb isn't Keleb anymore. Something or someone is superimposed over his personality."

"Soltec blanched. "You must be kidding!"

"Nope."

"How do you know?"

"I found no childhood memories of Keleb. Whoever the leading persona is, is well-briefed and coached, and I think by the Altruscans. So we can be certain that they are still here trying to take over this planet. Especially now since it is sparsely populated, they could gain control much quicker. Also, they're trying to prevent Earth from joining the Alliance. You need to check and double check where all the orders for the new fighter planes and ships come from. I talked to the young people here, and they're great. They can't wait to be part of the Alliance."

"That's the feeling we have too. But there were so many incongruities we didn't understand. That's why Thalon suggested having you come here. He warned me to be aware that trouble always follows you. I don't know what he meant by that, and I still don't."

Sabrina laughed. "He was referring to my tendency toward finding trouble if trouble fails to find me, as I have done here. So what are you going to do?"

"We need to find the conspirators. Can you help us?"

"I don't think so. The Altruscans know me. I have had several run-ins with them. There's bound to be one who would recognize me. Also, you can't use Miri or Lara for the same reason. I don't think they know Ian. By the way, where is he?"

"On the Space Station since he resigned. The Captain of the sub you two buzzed called in a report complaining that Ian gave his girlfriend a ride in one of the new fighter planes. He said that Ian used unsound judgment to impress his girlfriend."

"Yes, I guess it was the captain who called in. By the way, he is an Altruscan," Sabrina added.

"So Ian said. But we already know from Lara that they intermixed with other races to become less noticeable."

"Since I'm still on vacation, what would you say to my visiting the Space Station? I could find out what's going on there. Also, I would appreciate it if you could have a ship available for me." At Soltec's raised his eyebrow, she added, "Well, it only has to be a little one. I'd rather have my Spitfire, but it's on the Antares."

Chapter 16

As Sabrina boarded the Space Station, she was searching for Ian when an unknown presence invaded her mind. Turning around, she glimpsed a small alien with a mottled, cinnamon-colored skin. It seemed to be short-sighted. The eyes squinted as it walked toward her.

"Sabrina," it mind-sent, "I have come to meet you. If you wish, you can scan my mind," he sent to her, also he corrected her thinking of him as an 'it'."

"I don't think I'm a match for you," she sent back. "Do you communicate only through mind-link?"

"Yes, I do not use speech." He quickly explained why Ian wasn't there to meet her, and that he was instructed to take her to a ship stationed out in space. He also gave his name as Basra.

Basra and Sabrina boarded the small shuttle Soltec had procured for her, and they flew out to a triangular ship hovering in deep space. On board, Sabrina was met by Soltec. As he approached, she ran a mind-scan.

He chuckled, realizing what she had done. "I'm glad to see you're cautious; we already had some nasty surprises."

"Basra's discoveries?"

"Yes, it's why we sent for him. Basra's people have a long acquaintanceship with Earth. They have been the designated watchers for millenniums."

"All those old UFO stories?" Sabrina asked.

Basra chuckled, "Yes," he sent. "We had your people going for a long time. Your scientists and military were always trying to disclaim what people had seen."

"What have you discovered, Basra?" she asked, using her voice.

"It's an old story," Soltec answered, instead. "Years ago, when you were still a child, I believe, humans discovered the Altruscan's presence, and tried at least to checkmate them."

"Yes, with the help of Jim Thalon, as he called himself then," Basra sent to both Sabrina and Soltec.

Sabrina perked up, "Jim's friends?" she asked.

"Yes, there was a very courageous man; his name was Jonathan Wright . . ."

"Jonathan?" Sabrina murmured.

"You knew Jonathan?" Soltec asked.

"Yes. I didn't like him very much then, because he disrupted my life. I believed at that time he was the reason my parents had become secretive, excluding me from what they were involved in."

Soltec contemplated her for few moments, "Hennesee," he said. "Among Jonathan's friends was a couple named Brook and Noel Hennesee."

"Those were my parents, Soltec."

"Indeed. It looks like you are completing their job. At that time, a Cartel tried to gain control over the world's markets. The Altruscans aligned themselves with members of that Cartel, also gave them advanced technological knowledge. Some of the Cartels members survived with the Altruscans help; and they are again at their old game.

"I guess we could change my script," Sabrina said.

"Change your what?" Soltec asked.

"My job description."

"I think I get your meaning," Basra sent.

Sabrina laughed, and nodded to him. "Mind reading can get you in trouble," she told him. She suddenly smiled. He had sent her a warm and sunny feeling. She gently touched him on the arm to let him know that she had received his gift.

"Let's go to a lounge down this passage," Soltec suggested. "I have a gentleman waiting there. His name is James Ashley."

"Ashley?" Sabrina asked surprised.

"Bret Ashley's son."

"Oh Soltec, I also knew Bret Ashley. It seems such a long time ago."

When they entered the lounge, a man, probably in his late seventies rose from an easy chair and came toward Basra with outstretched hands. "Basra my friend," he exclaimed. "I didn't think I would ever see you again. How have you been?"

"I have been well," Basra told him, using speech. "I think I have a surprise for you," pointing toward Sabrina. "Do you remember your father talking about Noel and Brook Hennesee?"

"Yes, he was very fond of those dear people. I think my father almost married the mother of one of them."

"That was my grandmother," Sabrina informed him.

"Your grandmother?" he asked surprised.

"I'm Noel's daughter."

"You're what?" James Ashley stared at her.

At first Sabrina wondered at his reaction and his look of incredulity, then, began to laugh until she ran out of breath. She had aged very little and looked only to be about thirty years old.

"Sorry, living out in space can do strange things to you."

"I think I'd like to go your way a bit," he said, looking appreciatively at her.

"So, the Cartel is still actively pursuing its old goals?" Sabrina supposed.

"Yes. I think with your help, we can put it out of business," Soltec said.

"I surmise you have definitive plans?"

"No, Sabrina, not really. We have to play it by ear. Thanks to you, we now know who's behind all the weapons build up. It will be up to you to find all the Cartel members."

"See, we have already rewritten your script," Basra was sending her. "General Dehner can open some doors for you. You will be introduced into high society. You think you can handle that?" Basra sent feelings of confidence toward Sabrina.

"I appreciate your message of confidence," she told him. "Will you be my back up?" she asked Soltec.

"No, there is someone else I want you to meet. He is unknown to anyone. He has never been in this sector before."

"You've pricked my curiosity."

Without warning, a door slid aside and a scholarly looking gentleman entered. He was as tall as Sabrina with jet-black hair and dark piercing eyes. Sabrina sensed danger and felt the hair on the back of her neck prickle. She gradually shifted her weight to one foot and readied herself for any action.

"Sabrina, this is the gentleman I was talking about. He will be accompanying you wherever you go," Soltec told her.

"Basra, I don't like his vibes," she urgently sent.

"I noticed," he sent back, undaunted.

Sabrina began a gentle mind probe, but hit a barrier so dense she winced and quickly pulled her feelers back. "Sir," she said, "to be able to trust you, would you please lower your mind-shield?"

For the first time since he entered the room, he considered her; his mind penetrating hers with ease. He mentally recoiled when Sabrina slammed her own barrier down.

"Since you insist," he said. "Normally, this is not done with someone not of my people. But as we need to have complete trust in one another, I think it would be expedient."

He slowly let his barriers down, and Sabrina gently began her probe. He was a scholar and from a people who showed almost no emotions or feelings. The Chirons she had previously met, controlled their emotions, but admitted to feelings. This entity had none.

"I see you are familiar with the Chirons. Your emotional control will be of great help in our daily dealings. Also, I see you are a mutant. It took great courage to do what you have done. We will work well together."

"Then you are agreeable?" Soltec asked Sabrina.

"Yes, it is agreeable," she told him.

"Sabrina, your new script is that he will be your mentor. You will travel with him and seek out the members of the Cartel to neutralize them."

"How does General Dehner fit in here?" she asked Soltec.

"He will introduce both of you into society. He is an old friend of the current President. We will go from there to see who else you can meet. Like I said, we will have to play this by ear."

Suddenly, Sabrina let out a gasp. "I know you. You're Sabot."

"We have met?" he asked, astonished.

"Yes. You appeared to me several times dressed as a monk."

There was a puzzled frown on his face. "I don't think so," he said and the puzzled look increased. He put his hand to his

136

eyes and stood motionless for a time. "Yes, I see, there was a meeting; the Trefayne."

"It was on the Trefayne I saw you for the first time. Why is it you don't remember?"

He gave a deep sigh. "When I take on form, and this time human, some of my memories are not clearly transmitted. I apologize for not remembering you," he said, and for the first time smiled, then frowned at her puzzled look.

"Sabot, when I met you for the first time, and later, there was a feeling of warmth about you. But when you walked in just now, the hackles at the back of my neck rose."

"Right now, I'm a different personality and you will have to get used to it," he said with finality.

*　　*　　*

"Did you know I picked up a temporary duty assignment?" Robert Dehner grumbled while he and Sabrina sat in Martha's sunny kitchen eating breakfast.

"I expected it," Sabrina said.

"Then you know more than I do."

"You don't seem to be too happy about it."

"Martha isn't included."

Halting buttering her toast in mid-motion, Sabrina considered him for a moment. "Oh, I see. I don't think it will be a long absence," Sabrina assured him, empathizing with his dislike of being away from his wife and his home.

"Now tell me, what is this all about?"

"Your superior will need to instruct you. There's little I can tell you otherwise," Sabrina told him and took a bit bite out of her toast. Over the crunching of the crust she heard the door open, and turning around, saw Martha slowly coming into the kitchen.

"Mary," she said aggrieved, "what are you doing spiriting my old man away from me?"

"Martha my love, if I could help it, I wouldn't do this to you."

"I wish you wouldn't be so mysterious."

"I know. It's a pain not knowing. I have the same disposition; I want to know."

"That only means you're placating me, and I won't be filled in."

"That's about the gist of it. Why don't you come and sit down? Here, have a cup of coffee."

Taking the seat and the offered cup, Martha sniffed, "If you weren't so likable, I could at least be mad at you. Now finish your breakfast; you have a plane to catch."

"We still have three hours, Martha. There is plenty of time," Dehner said. He and Sabrina were to fly to Virginia Beach where the Nation's Capitol was now located.

"Whatever happened to Washington?" Sabrina asked.

"The Potomac overran the land in a wide swath and to top it, there was a hurricane. Everything was flooded and blown down. There's little of the city left."

Looking at his watch, Dehner continued," We are to meet the President at two, then, we should know more what this is all about. Unless, you already know?" He shot a pointed glower at Sabrina.

My dear Robert," she said, "I might know, but I'm not always in a position to inform you. I wish I could. But it is vital that only very few people know. My safety and your safety might depend on it. That's all I will say about this. I hope you respect my situation."

"Robert, I think we have been put in our place," Martha said dryly, but there was no rancor in her voice. "Sorry Mary. We like you and are curious about you. There's so much mystery surrounding you. You don't talk about your family, or where you came from."

"Some day I might be able to do that, okay?"

Robert patted Martha's hand and said, "Fair enough?"

*   *   *

Robert and Sabrina took a private plane to Virginia Beach. After they landed, a staff car met them at the airport, and took them to the new seat of government.

"President is just a title we have kept for sentimental reasons," Robert informed her. "Now, it's more a job than a position of authority. He is just one member of the World Management Commission. This Commission is the governing body, which is an expansion of the United Nations. But there are some who would like to go back to the old order."

"I see," Sabrina said. Both were silent for the remainder of the ride. Robert leaned back in the seat and fell asleep, while Sabrina became absorbed in her own thoughts.

To Sabrina's surprise, the President's office was in a large building that looked like any other office building. They were met in the foyer by an aide and rode in the elevator up to a suite on the third floor. When the door opened, the President himself met them.

"Welcome, Miss Hennesee. Hello Robert."

"You two knowing each other will make things somewhat easier," Sabrina said, genuinely pleased.

"We went through the Air Academy together and grew up in the same neighborhood. By the way, my name is William Lennert. Please don't call me Mister President; Bill will do."

"I won't if you tell me not to," Sabrina said, smiling at him. He was tall and burly, with a head of bushy white hair, and very penetrating, hazel eyes. "Have you been briefed?" she asked Lennert.

"Yes, Soltec laid out your script for me. He said you and your mentor should be introduced into, as he put it, high society. Only the job description of your mentor has been left open for you to decide."

"I think that was more on the order of politeness than consideration," Sabrina said, not being swayed in the least.

"Now, Robert," Bill Lennert said, "what you're going to see here, not even Martha must know. I know you two are close. I also know Martha, and I like her very much, and I don't want anything to happen to either of you. Would you please follow me into the next room?"

When Bill, or William Lennert, opened the door, Robert let his breath out with a gasp. Sabot was an imposing figure with his stern, austere demeanor. He was dressed all in black.

To lessen the tension, Sabrina commented, "Sabot, with all due respect, you look sinister."

"That's only your conscience or perception which would envision me thus," came his indifferent reply.

"Robert, this is my mentor, Sabot. Your job is to introduce us at the party tonight."

"So I've been told," Robert grumbled.

"This evening is to be a gala event. The only part I dislike is the woman giving it. She literally elbowed her way into society, a real scandalmonger. Probably a nasty piece to boot," William Lennert informed them.

Dehner showed clear signs of unease. But he was more concerned about Sabrina being in Sabot's company than the woman giving the party.

Sabot saw the reluctance. "Mary will be in safe company with me," he assured him. "I think she appreciates your concern, but she is very capable of taking care of herself."

Dehner didn't like having his mind read so easily and physically retreated.

The air was getting tense in the room. To defuse it, Sabrina turned to Bill Lennert and asked, "Will you be also at the party?"

"Oh, I wouldn't miss it for the world," he assured her.

"Are you prepared to give a rendition of your talent?" Sabot asked.

"As you know I can," Sabrina replied.

Turning to Dehner and Lennert, Sabot told them, "You will have a treat tonight. Mary will play the piano for us. Will you also sing?"

"I think we will move with the flow," she replied, offhandedly.

Later, Lennert and Dehner accompanied her and Sabot down to the foyer and out to a waiting taxi. "I will meet you, then, at the party," Lennert said, as he handed Sabrina into the cab. He and Dehner went back up to the office.

* * *

When Sabrina entered the ball room, the talking stopped and all eyes turned to her. She was dressed Grecian fashion, her hair piled high on her head. For the first time, she also wore heavier makeup than she preferred. Sabot, walking beside her, wore what Sabrina remembered in her mother's time was called a Nehru jacket, made of a silver-gray material.

President Lennert left his group and came toward her. "My dear Mary," he said, "you are simply ravishing."

Sabrina laughed. "You know how to warm a poor girl's heart," she teased, taking his arm to be introduced.

"Ambassador Soltec, I think you would enjoy the company of Sabot, while I introduce everyone to our Mary," Lennert said, and shepherded Sabrina into the crowd.

During the evening, someone asked the hoped-for question in light of Sabot being introduced as her mentor. It was the hostess, an older woman with several gold chains dangling on her meager bosom, and her long, claw-like fingers were loaded with rings. The fine hair on the back of Sabrina's neck rose when the woman approached with an ingratiating smile. A careful mind-touch said, Altruscan. Sabot, who was in constant mind-touch with Sabrina, received the message.

"Play your part," Sabot's sent, his voice sounding in her head.

"My name is Artea," the hostess introduced herself. Then with syrupy sweetness asked, "What is your mentor teaching you my dear, some obscure religion?" Artea closely watched Sabrina's expression as she spoke, already calculating how she might use her for her own gain.

"Oh no," Sabrina assured her, smiling just as sweetly. "He is furthering my career in music."

"Do you sing or play an instrument?"

"Oh, I do both."

"What do you play?"

"The piano of course."

"Ladies and gentlemen, this gorgeous creature says she can play the piano," Artea suddenly announced overly loud and in a high pitched, shrill voice. Artea harbored a hatred for anything beautiful and talented, and as always, it aroused her animosity. Only because of many secrets gleaned from indiscrete former lovers did she still enjoy her position in the Altruscan hierarchy.

Sabrina had already read her mind. The decision not to antagonize her came after a quick mind-plea from Sabot, asking her to play along. Only to Sabot was the minute shrug of her shoulder perceptible as Sabrina let herself be led to a piano.

First, she played several pop songs from her era, and then a rendition of America the Beautiful. Everyone stood and sang as she played.

President Lennert came up to the piano. "Thank you Mary. That was truly beautiful. It's one of my favorite songs."

Before she could answer, his aide stepped up, "Sir, there is a phone call for you."

The President returned shortly, "I'm sorry Mary, but I have to cut our evening short. I must go back to my office."

"Oh, but she can't leave now," Artea interjected. "Everyone is enjoying her performance. Let me see. Why don't you and your mentor, as you call him, stay here for the night?"

That was just what Sabrina and Sabot had hoped for and graciously accepted Artea's offer.

*   *   *

The following morning, Sabrina was standing bare in the middle of her bedroom when Sabot walked in. He knew she was not dressed, but it never occurred to him not to come in.

Having her servants spy on them, Artea knew just when to enter. Her cold, hard eyes roved over Sabrina's body. Dripping honey, she said, "Mary, you look absolutely marvelous," she

143

exclaimed. "Have you ever thought of becoming a model?" She ran a modeling agency as a front, enslaving girls to become escorts to adventurous men; especially Altruscans. She knew just the man who would go for a looker like this Mary; and that would be another feather in her cap.

Sabrina reading Artea's flitting thoughts transmitted them to Sabot. He cringed. Remaining civil, Sabrina declined her generous offer with, "That is very kind of you, but I'm interested in becoming a concert pianist."

"But dear, I can help you with that, too," she assured Sabrina. "I entertain many people from the music world. If you ever want to change your teacher, I can arrange that, also." She gave Sabot a poisonous look. "With a teacher, I know you wouldn't have to pay by doing favors." She had totally misinterpreted Sabot's presence in Sabrina's room.

Even Sabrina cringed mentally. At first, she had been surprised when Sabot entered her room, but immediately realized that he was not in the least affected by her nudity. It meant nothing to him. She understood from Artea's meddling mind that she believed they had slept together.

A gong reverberated through the house.

"They have finally betaken themselves to ready breakfast, those useless servants," Artea muttered under her breath, but still audible enough for Sabrina and Sabot to hear.

"We will join you in a moment," Sabrina told her.

The moment she left, Sabot tuned into Sabrina's mind and sent, "I looked through her papers last night and found some of the people we are looking for. She only collects what is hurtful to others."

"I surmised that," Sabrina told him while getting dressed. "She is what we call a blackmailer. Those are very nasty people. Did you get what she was implying with her offer?"

"Yes, she wants you to be one of her marketable goods."

"Very aptly put. Another thing, we need to communicate verbally once in a while, or someone will suspect what we are doing."

He looked at her thoughtfully. "I hadn't thought of that. Talking telepathically is second nature to me, but I know you have a good point there." Unexpectedly, Sabot went to the phone and called a taxi. At Sabrina's questioning look, he sent, "There is no more to gain from here today. We will depart. She will contact you later when she thinks you can be useful to her."

Sabrina went to Artea and profusely apologized, blaming their abrupt departure on Sabot's choleric temperament.

*   *   *

Sabot had rented an apartment for the duration of their stay and commenced, true to script, for Sabrina to practice on the piano. At first she enjoyed it, but later accused him of tediously adhering to it.

"Is there something you would rather do?" he asked, astonished.

"Yes! The sun is shining, the birds are singing, and I am sitting in this apartment messing around with a piano," she complained. "There is a beach close by, and a whole ocean of water."

"I guess I'm remiss. I don't understand humans very well, yet."

"How come your memories only begin when you took on your present persona? Do you remember nothing of your earlier appearance as Sabot? I know you are nothing like Keleb, or even Miri or Lara."

145

"No, I have not been taken over by another personality. I surmise Miri and Lara are friends of yours. Also, someone named Sargon. Do you know his real name?"

"Only of his being the beginning and the end of his people; that is how he interprets it."

"He will fulfill this prophecy."

"There is someone else named Cassandra. She predicts that I will be Sargon's demise, and she hates me for it."

Sabot sat in silence for a while, then, said musingly, "Cassandra is neither human nor animal. Sargon and the one you call Karsten, have created a body for her."

"What is she, then?"

"She is this thing she calls a 'worm'. She is a part of the worm, but separated because of the two men. She is very dangerous. She adores Sargon and Karsten, but feels great animosity toward you. So it would be wise to stay away from her."

"Are you telling fortunes?" she asked teasingly. "I thank you never-the-less. I always feel very uneasy when I'm close to Cassandra. So, I was not just imagining it. Now if you can tell me about Miri and Lara."

"Miri is a good friend, but Lara is a law unto her self. She is no danger to you. Like you, both are mutants, as also is Karsten."

"And Sargon?"

"Your life and his are intertwined. This one will fulfill his destiny as it was prophesied, but not as it was interpreted."

"What made me think of Miri is the way you disappear. But your way is different," she added slowly, trying to sort it out. "Miri becomes something else when she does her disappearing act, but you I think, raise your vibrations."

"You are very observant."

"Would you let me experience how you do this?"

Sabot gave her a long and appraising look. "I think it could be done," he finally said. "Come close to me and we'll see if you can feel what I'm doing."

Sabot stood close behind her, their bodies touching. Sabrina immediately recoiled. "You're hot," she exclaimed, surprised.

Sabot looked at her, his eyebrows raised. "Yes of course, my temperature is several degrees above yours."

"Well, I didn't know. Let's get back to where we were," she said and then chuckled.

"Some more of your jocularity?" he asked, while putting his arm firmly around her waist. "Recall exactly the room next to this one." Moving along with his mind, she felt peace and serenity emanating from him. Also, to her incredulity, Sabrina found no opposite in his nature, no good or evil, hot or cold, or even conflicting feelings.

"You need to stay with me and not appraise my disposition."

"Sorry," she sent and laughed. "Old habit."

Her mind again intertwined with his, and using her feeling nature, she followed him as he, for her benefit, slowly let his vibration rise. Suddenly, they both were standing in the next room.

"Do you understand?"

"Yes. But still, it is a bit disconcerting to disappear."

"You would need much practice with this, as with your piano lessons."

She bypassed his remark and asked, "Are you a member of the Planetary Alliance?"

"No. I came at Basra's request to combine my talents with yours to solve this situation with the Altruscans, so the Earth can join the Alliance."

"I noticed that you are not able to read minds as I do. I think you are a clairvoyant."

"You want me to tell you your future?" he asked.

She sensed that this was as close as he would ever come to levity and grinned at him. "No thank you, I have enough with daily management. Anything else would be more than I would care for."

"I will leave you for a while so you can frolic on the beach," he said, and disappeared right through the wall.

*   *   *

It was late that afternoon when President Lennert called.

"Mary Hennesee?"

"Speaking."

"Soltec said to invite you to an open forum. Some of my staff will be there."

"Does Soltec want me to look at some files?" she asked.

"That was the term he used."

"Okay, when shall I make my appearance?"

"It's tomorrow morning at nine. Can you make it?"

"Of course. I'll see you tomorrow then."

Chapter 17

Next morning, Sabrina put on a sensible dress, and as she arrived downstairs, she was met by the driver of a staff car. She told him she would like to arrive a little bit after everyone else. For her purpose, it was better to walk in when the room was full. She always counted on her first impressions.

When she entered, the meeting was already in progress as she'd hoped. She listened intently to the questions and answers, but could not understand why she had been asked to come here. There was nothing to discern. After the meeting, a casually dressed young gentleman approached her.

"Miss Hennesee?"

"Yes?"

"I have been asked to escort you for a second breakfast with the President."

"Nice of him. I haven't had my first one yet," she quipped.

As they entered William Lennert dining room, he rose. "Mary my dear, I'm so glad you could make it. For now, breakfast just for the two of us. We will be later joined by the Secretary of State. He advised me he has some urgent business to see to first, but should be here shortly."

Before Sabrina sat down, she took a curious gadget from her purse, and putting her finger to her lips, she made a circle, checking the room for listening devices. She pointed to a flower vase. "Mister President, I'm sorry to have to ask you to remove these lovely flowers. My allergies, you know."

"Oh, I'm so sorry. Of course I will have them removed," he said solicitously. He rang a bell and a gentleman entered. "Tom, would you please remove these flowers? The lady is allergic. This is Tom Miller. He takes good care of me." Bill Lennert smiled at his valet.

As Tom Miller took the vase away, Sabrina smiled at him, her eyes following him until he had closed the door behind him. She turned to Lennert. "I bet you have a leak. Things get out that were said in private?"

"Yes, that alerted us that something wasn't quite right."

"From now on, consider your quarters, or any room you enter bugged, and your valet is your eavesdropper."

"Miller?" Lennert asked, astonished. "But, he's been with me since I took this job two years ago."

"I think we should go according to script and eat our breakfast."

They were halfway finished when the door opened and the Secretary of State walked in. He was tall and elegant, with superb manners, but the conversation touched only on general topics. After breakfast, the Secretary of State invited Sabrina to a formal tea that afternoon hosted by his wife.

Slowly, over the next few weeks, Sabrina wound her way into Virginia Beach's Society and the international set. Most of the people she met were representatives of various governments, and she made it a point to converse with everyone. She was perceived as a good listener who enthusiastically asked questions about their countries cultures, including their views on joining the Alliance.

Sabrina soon seriously considered the invitations to visit their countries. Also, Bill Lennert introduced her as an aspiring concert pianist, and she was often asked to play. Sabot stayed very much in the background, but was in constant mind-touch with Sabrina. The introductions were mostly handled by the President himself. He had become her special champion.

*   *   *

Several weeks later, Sabrina was invited to sit in on a Cabinet meeting as a casual observer. She had already met several of the ministers, but the Secretary of Defense, a Mister Don Eton, was new to her. He walked in brisk and assured, followed by his secretary, a man who sat unobtrusively behind him. Sabrina's view of Mister Eton was obscured, so she decided to scan him after the meeting was over. The Secretary of Defense had a few new proposals, and as Sabrina listen to him, she found him to be sufficiently knowledgeable about the topics and technical terms in their discussion of a spaceship with a unique design. Some of the technology began to strike Sabrina as faintly familiar. After a series of detailed descriptions, she realized the modifications were of Altruscan design.

Once the meeting was over, Sabrina gave Lennert a prearranged signal to stop Don Eton. His secretary, a Mister Walton, seemed to be in a hurry, pointing to his watch.

"I'm sorry, Mister President," Eton said, "but as you see, Walton is trying to hasten my departure."

"That's all right. I only wanted you to meet a friend of mine. Mary, would you please come over here?" he called out, waving to Sabrina. "You see, she's giving her first concert at the Lighthouse Theater tonight, and I want as many people there as possible. You know, as an encouragement."

When Sabrina was introduced to Mister Eton, she almost missed his hand, staring at his secretary. He was Altruscan. The telltale gauntness was not there. He seemed almost chubby by comparison. But the fingers were longer than it was the norm for humans. And there were other signs, picked up mostly at a subliminal level, which told her what he was. Quickly she took a closer look at Mister Eton and scanned his mind. Mister Eton had been well briefed. Had she not discovered that Walton was an Altruscan, Eton would have slipped by her. There were no overt signs to tell her that his persona had been altered.

After they left, Lennert asked Sabrina, "What have you found out?"

"That the power behind the throne is an Altruscan."

"Not the Secretary?"

"No. That would have been too obvious. One can often maneuver better behind the scenes."

"We need to do something about this, and fast."

"Give me some more time. I need to find out how many infiltrators we have and where they have their headquarters. It won't take me long. I'll give you the information as soon as I have it." Then somewhat tartly, she added, "I didn't know I was giving a concert tonight."

"Well, it was the only thing I could think of in a hurry. We do have a concert tonight. So do come."

"Since I'm the object on display, I better be there." Sabrina told him, not too amused. She had made other plans to follow a lead she had gained through Artea, but they would have to be postponed,

*   *   *

When she arrived at her temporary home, Sabot and Soltec were waiting. "I'm glad both of you are here," she said. "I would like to move a little faster than we had planned. The way it looks, most of the major positions seem to be taken by the Altruscans. There's a lead through Artea. He's a business man. I think most of those left from the Cartel are changelings who are making a cautious attempt to infiltrate the top echelon of the government. We still need to find their headquarters."

"Slow down, Sabrina," Soltec told her. "We have not been idle. The business man you mentioned is still human. We talked to him. He knew something was wrong, but didn't understand what. After we explained to him about some of the incongruities he noted, he agreed to help us. It's a curious thing how you Earth people pull together if trouble is brewing from an alien source.

Sabrina only looked at him.

"Well, I struck out, I thought to get a rise out of you," Soltec quipped.

"Can we meet him?" Sabrina asked, totally ignoring his attempt at humor. "What's his name?"

"Neil Markham. And we have a date with him in forty-five minutes. You think you can be ready?"

Sabrina went to her bedroom to change clothes. Within five minutes she came back ready to go, wearing blue-jeans and a polo-shirt.

To her amazement, they were driving to a park.

"Why a park?" she asked.

"Less obvious," Soltec told her.

"More obvious," Sabrina replied.

"Why?"

"It might not be a person's habit to go to a park. So, his behavior would be out of the norm. You must always meet people in their customary environment."

"You should go on a lecture tour, Sabrina," Soltec replied, annoyed.

153

Turning to Sabot, "See, I didn't strike out," Sabrina told him.

"Oh, that's how you do it," Soltec said.

Suddenly Sabot said, "Soltec, you should never vie with an expert in irritating."

Sabrina looked with incredulity at Sabot. "Are humans rubbing off on you? I think you just made a joke."

Soltec laughed. "Thank you, Sabot. She got no less than she deserved, making fun of her betters." Soltec was saved from a retort from Sabrina; they had arrived at the park.

Neil Markham was tall with light brown hair, and a youngish appearance, quite distinguishable from the crowd.

In the back of Sabrina's mind a memory stirred. After she shook hands with him, the feeling of familiarity became stronger. She was unaware that she was studying his face.

Neil Markham chuckled. "Do I pass inspection?"

Somewhat discomfited, she withdrew her stare. "You said your name was Markham. You remind me of someone. Does the name Bret Ashley mean anything to you?" Sabrina asked.

"He was my grandfather." Neil told her.

"Oh, then he did have a daughter. I recently met his son. I guess that would make him your uncle." Sabrina said, and began to grin from ear to ear. "He once said he wanted a daughter just like me."

"That was a long time ago when he met a thirteen year old girl named Sabrina Hennesee who under the guise of helping did some unauthorized ransacking of his computer files. He used to talk to my grandmother about her." He looked at Sabrina in disbelief. "You couldn't be that Sabrina Hennesee," Neil Markham asked, puzzled.

"Space travel can do strange things to you," Sabrina whispered mysteriously, to Neil's confusion.

"Don't let her confuse you. She's just pulling your leg," Soltec told him reassuringly.

"Right now, I'm going by Mary Hennesee."

"I see," he said, comprehending.

"Why did you link up with the Cartel?" she asked him.

"To keep an eye on them. My grandfather joined them so he could manipulate their plots. He worked with Jonathan Wright and also your parents if you are 'the Sabrina' my grandfather talked so much about."

"Among the Altruscans, the name Sabrina is known and not very much liked. They would love to get their hands on me. So please remember to call me Mary."

Soltec gave Sabrina a sidelong glance for so quickly laying the cards on the table. Sabot smiled, knowing that Sabrina had already rifled his files. She had walked through Neil's memories which left nothing hidden. He was who he said he was. He was an honorable man. His involvement with the Cartel left a sour taste in his mouth.

"Thank you for meeting us," Sabrina told him. "We don't want to expose you to danger." She gave him her hand. "We may meet again in a more pleasant atmosphere, but for now you need to leave."

"What about the information I have?" he said, startled at being so rapidly dismissed.

"We already have all the information," Sabot reassured him. Mystified, Neil left, but paused several times to look back.

Suddenly sensing danger, Sabrina looked at Sabot, "We need to exit immediately. There's an Altruscan watching Markham. He hasn't spotted us yet, and he knows me."

"Keep on walking, "Sabot told her. "Tune into me and remember to visualize the living room, exactly."

155

All three faded out with no one noticing their unusual departure. Within the blink of an eye they materialized in the apartment.

"Now you've done it!" Soltec told Sabot.

"No, she would have discovered this talent on her own."

"Okay, quit talking like I'm not here. Is this because I'm a mutant?" Sabrina asked.

"No, it's because of Serenity's meddling." Sabot told her.

"Oh," said Sabrina, "I'm glad you enlightened me. Soltec, what makes you suspect me of being troublesome? I think that's what prompted your outburst."

"I did not have any so-called outburst," Soltec replied with a sharp sniff and a shake of his head. "I was warned by the highest authority on you that you're a mischief-maker." His eyes were dancing with barely contained humor.

"Ahem!" Sabot cleared his throat. "Please excuse me from this mutual admiration, and let's get down to work. Sabrina, have you gathered all the names, positions, and how the association works from Neil Markham?"

"Yes, I'll give Soltec a synopsis as soon as I can. More important, there will be a meeting of the Cartel Wednesday, next week."

"Good, that will wrap up the Mir."

Sabrina gave Sabot an astonished look.

"The Mir, as you know, are the Ovoid energy patterns. They have mastered a new ability and can now infuse themselves into other bodies without devouring them. Do you remember the ovoid on the Antares?"

"Yes, an innocuous slip of a girl," Sabrina groused.

Ignoring her temper, Sabot continued unruffled. "Remember me telling you about the Altruscan I lost?"

"How come you can remember all this of a sudden?"

"I have my memory back as your monk."

"But not his sweet disposition. You still look most sinister."

Sabot had to smile in spite of himself. "You see, Soltec, why it's time for me to leave? But let's go back to this Altruscan. He was on the planet where Sargon picked up the group of children and young people. This gave the Ovoid an opportunity to sneak unnoticed onboard the Antares as this insignificant slip of a girl, as you thought of her. The Ovoids, becoming enmeshed with the Altruscans, have taken on more of their traits. They also have distanced themselves from the hive . . ."

"What hive?" Sabrina interjected.

"The Ovoids have a hive-consciousness. These strays are experiencing individuality for the first time, and because of it, they are loath to return to their queen. This is the only reason they cooperate with the Altruscans."

"I see," Sabrina said slowly. "What happens when their bodies die or cease to be functional?"

"They dissolve the body and slip into another individual to take on his or her personality."

"Ugh," Sabrina said, shaking herself. "That is simply ghastly." She turned to Soltec. "I have seen it, and it still gives me nightmares. What are we going to do about it?" she asked Sabot.

"Basra has contacted their queen, and she has graciously agreed to meet us if we promise to return the strays to her. But Basra discerned that she has plans of her own. She was asked to return to her universe, but she prefers the experiences she is gaining here."

"What are we going to do about her? Can you imagine the danger she poses?"

"Basra and Sabot will deal with her," Soltec assured her.

Chapter 18

Wednesday, Sabot and Soltec arrived at the apartment, toting several curious looking contraptions.

"What are you going to do with those?" Sabrina asked, pointing to the bottles.

"My darling Sabrina, putting the genie back into the bottle, of course."

Sabrina's mouth gaped, "Huh? That, Sabot, was another joke you just made. And, aren't you getting to be a little impertinent. Darling?" she asked, but her eyes were dancing as she said it. She frowned as she walked around the bottles. "How in the world are we going to manage transporting these funny looking objects and getting them into a meeting?"

"Not to worry. Neil Markham is taking you to where the meeting will be held. More to the point, he's secretly stashing you in a room where you will wait until I arrive."

"And what happens then?" Sabrina asked, not able to contain her curiosity.

"That's for me to know and you to find out."

Sabrina's eyes rolled toward the ceiling. "God help us. If he's stays here any longer, he'll turn into a mischief himself."

"Yes, that has occurred to me. Now you see why I'm in such a hurry to bring all this to an end. But first, you are going to see an opera with Neil. I hope you will enjoy it."

"An opera? Why an opera?"

"Don't ask so many questions," Sabot said, testily. "Go and enjoy yourself."

Sabrina had no fear of meeting any Altruscan at the opera house because they had no patience with such foolery. Also, a long time ago she had discovered that most of them were tone deaf.

*   *   *

Sabrina shopped most of the afternoon for a gown. Neil came to pick her up dressed in tux and tie, and the moment she opened the door, she was greeted by a whistle as he eyes traveled appreciatively up and down her figure. His first comment was, "You're ready to go?"

Sabrina ignored the remark. As they descended the stairs, she asked, "What's this opera all about?"

"I really don't know enough to tell you. This is the premier, so it's a gala event."

Neil was right about that. The line of limousines seemed endless, rolling up to the entrance and discharging their passengers. The opera house was recently built in the grand style of the old European theaters. Steps led up to a peristyle and a wide impressive entrance. Inside, the great hall thronged with a festive crowd. Everybody who was somebody in Virginia Beach was present.

"Where did all the limousines come from?" Sabrina asked.

"Some enterprising individual collected all still existing limousines and cars; cannibalized some, and opened a taxi-service."

"Smart move."

"Let's go up to the first floor where the boxes are."

159

"A loge?"

"Just for this occasion."

Going up, the crowd thinned after the first floor. The box Neil rented was near the stage. As they entered, Sabrina noticed everybody busily craning their necks to see who was attending this performance. The noise was a constant hum. The auditorium was still brightly lit, so Sabrina suggested they stay in the background until the lights dimmed.

When the lights went down, the crowd hushed. The stage lit up, and the actors appeared vivid against a romantic scenery.

Later, Sabrina noticed that Neil's attention was not on the play. He was watching the people in the next box.

"Who are they?" she whispered, looking past him.

"What?"

"Over there," Sabrina pointed with her chin.

"Two of the men are members of the Cartel."

Sabrina turned in her seat. "But why are you staring at them?"

"One of them seems rather absorbed in the play. I didn't think it would interest him since it is rather too fanciful.

But that was not it. Sabrina was certain Neil was trying to imagine how it was done; taking over a personality. To cover his lapse, he quickly said, "I was supposed to let you know that the meeting is scheduled right here, after the performance."

She drew her brows down in puzzlement. "The meeting will be here? In an opera house?"

"Lots of people. And if they're seen, it's a good excuse for being here."

"I see." Sabrina leaned back in her seat and turned her attention back to the stage.

160

After the performance, Neil led her to a small room on the floor above the stage. "Sabot asked for you to wait here. The meeting will be in half an hour. I have to leave you to join them."

"Now?"

"Yes."

"What will happen? Do you know?"

"Sabot wouldn't say."

After Neil left, Sabrina situated herself comfortably in a large easy-chair to wait while easing into meditation. It was her habit never to go to any confrontation stressed. After a while Sabot's presence gently insinuated itself into her consciousness. He was standing behind her.

The first thing she asked him was, "Where are your bottles?"

"Strategically placed."

He strode past her and opened the door to check the corridor. It was still clear, but she heard voices floating up the stairs.

She stepped up beside him. "How are we going to do this?" She had no idea what he had planned. His mind was clamped shut against her probing. She tipped her head to see his face. "Am I to know what we," and she stressed the we, "are going to do?"

"In due time," was his enigmatic reply. His arm reached back and Sabrina found herself unceremoniously and with surprising ease pushed back into the room. He closed the door without it making the slightest sound.

"We will give them about ten or fifteen minutes for all to be assembled."

Sabrina leaned against the wall and listen with all her senses. Sabot seemed absorbed in his thoughts.

When his gaze shifted to her face, she felt a sudden surge of energy enveloping her. It was like being caught in a transporter beam. Both became incorporeal. Sabrina was held within Sabot's powerful mind, only able to move under his guidance. Instantly, both were standing unseen in the conference room.

There were ten men. As Sabrina scanned each, she transmitted the identity of the shape-shifters to Sabot. Only two were still human. One of them was Neil.

The men moved around, chatting and holding drinks. Suddenly, Sabrina felt an energy emanation from Sabot. To her astonishment, everyone in the room froze, except their minds. The horror emanating from them was almost palpable. Even Neil was not immune to the fear. The other human was petrified. Abruptly, Sabrina became solid and watched in amazement as the bottles popped in out of thin air.

Leisurely, Sabot picked up the first bottle and went to the first shape-shifter, tapping him on the shoulder. The touch, Sabrina sensed, somehow released the mind held image of the impersonated individual. To her shock and disbelief, the Mir collapsed into its primary shape, the ovoid energy pattern she was so familiar with. Sabot uncapped the bottle and there was a slight sucking noise as the ovoid was drawn into the container. Sabot quickly secured the receptacle.

After all the Mir had been secured, Sabrina, unsettled by the experience quipped, "Is that how the fairly tale of the genie in the bottle came about?"

"Child," Sabot said to Sabrina's absolute incredulity at being addressed in that manner, "I don't know about your childhood stories, but if you like, you can use your experience here and invent one."

"Sabot . . . !"

Sabrina's reply was stopped instantly. He changed, still discernable as a distinct entity, benign but distant, into a form that was all light and radiance.

"My work here on Earth is finished," his mind sent softly. "The ovoids will be returned, and Soltec's men have rounded up all the Altruscans. Earth will be able to chart her own course. You will be one of the architects, you and Neil, and others you will meet. Goodbye, Sabrina."

Sabot and the bottles disappeared instantaneously, and Neil and the other human were released from stasis.

Neil let out a gasp. "That was appalling." His face looked drained and overcome from the horror of witnessing the dissolution of a human form. The other man collapsed, the sheer terror of what he had seen starkly etched on his face.

Neil Markham went to him and extended his hand, "Come Alan, its over," he said and pulled him to his feet.

Alan Bean stared at him, his eyes wide. "What in God's name was that?" he said and gulped.

Sabrina refrained from replying, knowing no good response. She chose to listen, waiting for Neil to handle the situation.

"The Cartel is finished," Neil said evenly. "All of its members, except the two of us, are dead. Long ago, Henry Dixon, I don't know if you remember him, became involved with the Altruscans. Since then, they controlled the Cartel. After the upheavals, the Altruscan's plan was to replace all of us with shape-shifters."

"What are we to do now?"

Serious green eyes flickered over him as Sabrina studied the man before her. His face was still pale and the quivering lip showed a weak character. Probably because of this, he wasn't replaced by a shape-shifter.

"This isn't the time or place for explanations," she said calmly. "I think Neil should take you to a bar for a stiff drink. You could use one too Neil, and so could I."

*   *   *

After Sabot was gone, Sabrina availed herself of the invitations many of the representative of different countries had made to her. Meeting with the representatives in their native countries gave her a sense of their ideas and what joining the Alliance would mean to them. She had to correct many misconceptions. The hardest for many to understand was that being part of such a fast enterprise was not a forum to export their religions, philosophies or cultures.

Her last stop was to Rome to meet with one of the representative of what was now a United Europe. She had an open invitation from Maria Callander, Europe's delegate to the World Management Commission, Sabrina phoned her home to see if it would be agreeable to meet, and it was. The first time they met was at one of President Lennert's parties and they had become friendly, seeing each other several times outside the so-called social circle.

Sabrina presented her card to the butler at the door. He ushered her into a foyer, then asked her to wait. When he returned, she followed him into a library which served as an at-home office.

Maria Callander rose from behind her desk and came toward her with outstretched arms. "Mary, my dear, I hoped you would come to see me. Shelton, please bring tea," she said to the butler, then, led Sabrina toward two overstuffed chairs. "We will be more comfortable here. I'm delighted you've come.

Did you know that your debate at the last conference sparked a considerable and heated controversy?" Maria informed her.

"Debates are always good to clear the air and gain new insights," Sabrina said. "So, before the United Nation General Assembly convenes, I will meet again separately with the delegates of the World Management Commission, and we will go over the membership petition again, plus its entitlement, and restrictions."

"Do you know that there will be a first-time meeting with a representative from this Alliance, a Sabrina; I wish I knew how to pronounce her last name."

"Would you mind showing me this unpronounceable name?" Sabrina asked suspiciously.

Maria Callander wrote it on paper, and handed it to Sabrina.

"Of all the . . ." Sabrina exploded. "What an archaic way to spell Thalon." When Maria Callander looked bewildered at her outburst, Sabrina erupted into laughter. "I'm sorry, Maria. The name of the lady is Sabrina Hennesee. This archaic form of the name is pronounced Thalon in English, but it is very seldom used."

When the butler came in with the tea, it gave Maria Callander time to collect herself. "I think I deserve an explanation," she said, after the door closed behind him.

"Maria, my name is Sabrina Mary Hennesee ra Thalon. I was given an assignment to investigate certain anomalies here on Earth, and I surmise you have already been informed about the Altruscans interference, attempting to sabotage Earth's admission. My name Hennesee should tell you that I'm from Earth. It's an old Irish name. I have been given the honor of sponsoring Earth's admission into the Planetary Alliance if I find that you are ready to assume the obligation. My name

Sabrina is known to the Altruscans, so I could not use it. Very few know my middle name, Mary. Right now, I'm visiting here to get a better picture of how this world stands and I'm also updating history for my own erudition. Speaking with each delegate personally before the General Assembly convenes is another plan of mine." Sabrina sank back in her seat, balancing the tea cup in her hand and gave Maria a questioning look.

"That's a whole . . ."

"Can of worms," Sabrina finished for her.

"You have an interesting way of putting things. My brief here says that you are an Antarean?" Maria asked, nonplused.

Sabrina's smile was more of a grin when she casually said, "So it does. Maria, I was born on Earth, but grew up on the Worldship called Antares . . ." Any further explanation was interrupted by a discreet knock. The butler opened the door announcing Ambassador Soltec and a Mister Thalon.

Sargon and Soltec had barely crossed the threshold, when Sabrina's eyes were immediately drawn to Sargon. It took her a moment before she realized what was so startling. Sargon was wearing contact lenses to cover his amber eyes with their slit pupils. Her first memory of them was her first thought 'oh my god they are cat eyes.'

Soltec rushed in to greet Maria and was startled by Sabrina's unexpected presence. "Oh, you are here," he said, taken off guard.

"In the flesh," Sabrina replied, amused, looking at him curiously.

Sargon knew of Sabrina's presence, but had been remiss in informing Soltec. He tried to repress his laughter but couldn't. "Irrepressible as always," he told Soltec.

Soltec started to chuckle. "You're right. That's the word for her. Maria, my dear, I hope she hasn't given you a hard time?"

"No, she was just explaining the discrepancies in this dossier I have on her."

"Yes, please do, Sabrina Mary Hennesee ra Thalon," Sargon said mischievously. He was alluding to the arbitrary use of his name and the computer in Ayhlean's office, to amend her personal file.

Sabrina totally ignored his remark, instead asking in quick succession, "How are the boys? What's up?" She knew it was something serious, or he wouldn't be here himself."

"You remember Garth?" Sargon asked.

How could she not. She had been on a mission with Miri and Lara when Garth had captured her and put her through some of the most distasteful experiences in her life. In the end, she had humiliated him enough for him to be thrown out of the Altruscan space-force.

"What about Garth?" she asked.

"He and his daughter Merden have vowed your destruction," Soltec told her, "They are on Earth, looking for you. We have an idea about their current whereabouts. Could we impose on you to keep Sabrina with you until we clear this up?" he asked Maria.

Sabrina answered before Maria could. "My dear Soltec, being in Thalon's company has given you the wrong impression of me. I'm quite capable of taking care of myself. Right, my dear?" she said and walked toward Sargon. She raised herself on her toes, and, looking straight into his eyes, kissed him fully on his mouth.

Sargon showed no reaction and stood smiling down at her.

"I guess you bombed out," Soltec told her, sotto voce.

"No, she hasn't," Sargon told him regretfully. Cupping Sabrina's chin in his hand, he kissed her on the tip of her nose.

"She knows I love her. I'm just not responsive to some of her needs."

Soltec looked confounded at the unanticipated display of affection. But Sabrina came to his rescue. "He chose another, so I relinquished him to her." She tried to smile, but it turned into a sad smile.

Maria Callander looked so astonished that Sabrina started to chuckle. "Maria, I know this can be very confusing. It's the story of a young girl falling in love with her hero, only to find that he had chosen her friend instead. Tragic love stories still exist even in outer space."

"Ahem," Soltec coughed, turning to Maria. "Going back to my question, do you think Sabrina could stay with you?"

"Of course. We could make your love story into a ballad. I write the words and you think up the tune."

Sabrina gave Maria one of her long looks. "I think this company is rubbing off on you," she said in a low voice.

"I hope it has. I have never had such an entertaining afternoon. Please do stay. Sabrina?"

"I can go back to my accustomed name. Right, Sargon? Soltec?"

"I'm confused. This calling card says Jim Thalon," Maria called attention to the discrepancy. "I heard Sabrina calling you, Sargon?"

"Sargon is an acronym of my name, which is unpronounceable in English, so I chose the name Jim Thalon."

"And what am I to call you, then?' Maria asked.

"How about Jim."

"Well that would make it easier," Maria replied. "Right, Sabrina?"

"No, it won't. He hasn't been called Jim for ages. Right, Sir." Sabrina stood at attention, and saluted.

"I think I can dispense with this confusion. Call me Jim," he told Maria, "and you," giving Sabrina a pointed look, "can call me, Sir."

"Maria," Soltec said, "I think we best ignore these two. How is Sibyl? You're taking her to the United Nation's meeting?"

"Oh, you don't know? She fell down the stairs and broke several ribs. She's in the hospital."

"You're going by yourself?"

"No. I have a temporary secretary. She's very efficient," Maria said, hesitantly.

"But?" Soltec prompted.

"I hate to say it, but I don't especially care for her. She's very impersonal, almost cold."

"I think we have found Merden," Sargon said.

"An Altruscan?" Maria asked in disbelief.

"Yes. If this is Merden, we will have no problem locating Garth." Sabrina said. "Can you contact her?"

"No problem. My office is closed for the holidays, so she is right here in the house, updating files. I will call for her."

Maria's new secretary came in. "Signora?" she said, and abruptly stopped, recognizing Soltec standing beside Maria. Sargon moved behind her to block an escape. When she saw Sabrina, Merden knew the game was over and she let herself be led away. After all, as a realist, she knew any denial or resistance would have been futile. Through mind-scan, Sargon ascertained the whereabouts of Garth. Later, he called Maria's house and asked if Sabrina could remain with her until Garth was apprehended.

Chapter 19

Maria considered Sabrina's stay to be a god-sent because tomorrow afternoon she was to meet with a Papal Legate who had proven in past dealings to be a difficult man.

Also within this month Sabrina and she were slated to travel to New Atlantis, she in the capacity of Europe's delegate of the World Management Commission, and Sabrina, as a member of the Alliance Counsil. As soon as her travel destination became news, she was approached by the Papal Legate, inquiring is she would present the Vatican's proposal to the Alliance Counsil. According to the Legate, the Vatican wished to join the alliance as an independent member of the World Management Commission.

*   *   *

For a moment Maria contemplated Sabrina standing by a window, then walked quietly into the room. "Sabrina how would you like to join me in the library for breakfast. I finished your book last night. It must have been very interesting to have known Jonathan Wright."

Sabrina came toward her smiling and shaking her head. "I didn't think so at the time."

Maria linked her arm through Sabrina's and led her into the library. "Sit down and I'll call Shelton to bring breakfast."

After she rang for Shelton, she asked him to bring breakfast in here, instead of the dining room. Seated opposite Sabrina, she gazed at her for a several seconds. "Now, what about him didn't you like?" Maria wanted know. "He sounds fascinating."

"He brought too many changes into my life and they were not appreciated at the time. I was only thirteen years old when all of a sudden my parents became very secretive and distant. Being kept in the dark, I naturally blamed Jonathan for it."

"But Sabrina . . ." Maria stopped as Shelton came in with the breakfast tray. She remained silent until he finished with his ministrations. When the door closed behind him, Maria took up where she had left off. "But just think, had he not discovered the Altruscans and this Cartel's conspiracy, Earth history might have taken a very different course."

"Yes, I understand that now. Can you imagine this Henry Dixon thinking he was signing an interstellar trade agreement with the Altruscans?"

"You know more about the Altruscans than we do here on Earth."

Sabrina shifted slightly in her chair, remaining silent for a few moments while staring at the floor. "Yes," she said hesitantly and then her face turned cold. "I had several run-ins with them. They are a vicious, war-like people. They wield a tyranny no one should experience."

Maria, serving Sabrina a plate of crepe-suzette, asked, "Then it wasn't a trade agreement they were interested in?"

"No! They wanted Earth as an outpost. When they take over a world, they first eliminate the leaders, then, enslave the people."

"We should be very thankful to you for . . ."

Sabrina quickly interrupted her with a wave of her hand. "Maria, I was only doing my job."

"Well, the least I can say is it seems you're finishing what Jonathan Wright and your parents started."

"Yes, it's an irony isn't it?"

"What?"

"Coming back after all these years and I seem to be stepping into their foot-steps"

"What happened to your parents, Sabrina?"

"They were assassinated by someone from the Cartel. My parents had asked Jim Thalon to take care of me if something should happen to them, and that is how I came to live on the Antares."

"I think our morning is being crowded with too many sad reminiscences and what I'm about to suggest won't lighten your mood, either." To Sabrina's questioning look Maria continued, "This afternoon I have an invitation from a Papal Legate, and I would like for you to accompany me."

"Why?" Sabrina asked, with a glint of amusement in her voice. She already had an idea why Maria wanted her to come along.

"As a chaperon," Maria explained, smiling over the rim of her cup. "I have met him several times, but I have very little information about him," she hedged. Not to prejudice Sabrina, Maria wanted to say as little as possible about him. She had developed an active dislike for him. Finally, she added, "The Legate's name is Paul Bouchard."

Sabrina pursed her lips. "Tell me, how much of the Vatican is still in existence?"

"It is rumored that the Pope and a few members of the Curia survived, but nothing was ever heard from him. This is the first time there has been word about him, and then only through this Legate. I have been informed that the Pope would like to establish the Vatican as an autonomous state again."

*   *   *

It was late afternoon when Sabrina knocked softly on Maria's bedroom door.

"It's me, Sabrina. May I come in?'

"Yes, of course," Maria answered

Sabrina stood in the door smiling diffidently. "You think this comportment and outfit will do to meet this Nuncio?"

Maria, sitting in front of her mirror looked up. When she saw Sabrina, she broke into laughter. "You might just fool him," she told Sabrina.

Sabrina wore a dark blue dress, which did nothing for her complexion, also a small hat and gloves, and she carried an attaché case.

"You're sure you want to part with your preamble of the Alliance's Charter?" Sabrina asked, while checking her hat in the mirror. "I have never worn a hat in my entire life," she groused, shifting it around on her head.

"I can always get another preamble. Are you sure you want to be introduced as Sabrina ra Thalon and not as Mary Hennesee?"

"Introduce me as Sabrina ra Thalon, representative from the World Ship Antares. I'm going to leave the Hennesee part out," Sabrina stated. When Maria looked at her, Sabrina wrinkled her nose. "It sounds too Irish," she explained. "Now, how are we going to handle this Nuncio?"

"With kid gloves," Maria replied.

"That doesn't sound very encouraging."

"He is a very peculiar man. I wish Soltec would take care of this Nuncio, who I think responds better to men."

"How did you come to know Soltec, Maria?"

"Just before the Earth underwent the axis alignment, my father and mother were rescued and found themselves on the same spaceship as Soltec. My father became involved in organizing the people and their activities. When my father and I resettled on Earth, we stayed in touch with him."

"Your father and you?"

"My Mother died when I was ten. She never saw Earth again."

There was a tap and the butler opened the door. "Signora, your transportation has arrived," he intoned formally.

"Thank you, Shelton." She looked at Sabrina and said, "I guess we better go."

"No limousine, no courtesy car?"

"Sabrina, the Vatican is very poor. They have lost everything. The Pope is supposed to be taken care of by Benedictine Monks. They maintain a small monastery and hospice inside the Vatican's old enclave."

"No more palaces for the clergy?"

In answer, Maria only smiled.

"I remember coming back from Japan," Sabrina told her, "when my parents stopped in Rome, and also at the Vatican. I'm sorry to see St. Peter's Basilica destroyed. It was beautiful."

"Much that was beautiful is gone and much that was ugly," Maria said, entering the taxi. "Vatican Hill," she told the driver.

The taxi was an electric car which drove almost noiselessly through the streets that now was Rome. The rubble had been cleared away and only a few empty shells that once had been buildings were still standing. The stones and bricks were used as material for the new houses which now clustered around the government structures. The broad avenues were now only narrow streets.

174

Sabrina looked sadly at the ruins. However, there was nothing sad about the people. There was a spring to their steps as they were busy with shopping or going places. They noisily greeted each other, some stopped to gossip.

"How many people are now living in Rome?" Sabrina wanted to know.

"When we returned to Earth, there were two thousand who settled in and around Rome. But not all were Italians."

"And the other cities?"

"Sabrina, there are no other cities in Italy. There are outlying farms and some vineyards. Earth is a strange and empty world and the people like to stay close. In America, Virginia Beach is one of the big cities and so is the one on the bay at the West Coast . . ."

"I know. I flew from Virginia Beach to the West Coast and there was nothing but empty land. Now back to your Nuncio. I will stay in the background and you will have to do most of the talking." To Maria's questioning look Sabrina added, "I always like to observe to get a feel of an individual."

The taxi halted in front of a church with white-washed walls and steps leading up to its entrance. Toward the back were buildings that housed the cloister, dormitory and the chapter house. Adjacent to the church was the Abbot's lodging. There was also a graveyard with crosses already marking gravesites.

Maria looked at her watch. "Two minutes until four. Should we brave being a little early?"

"Well, let's ring the bell and see," Sabrina said.

They walked up to the Abbot's lodging and pushed the unlit button. The door was opened, but only partially, by an elderly monk.

"We are here to see his Excellency, Cardinal Bouchard," Maria said, handing him her card.

"Come in, please," he said, barely above a whisper, and opened the door the rest of the way. He led them to a small sitting room on the right. As soon as Sabrina and Maria were seated, he left silently, closing the door softly behind him.

The room was bleak with a single cross adorning the bare walls. There were several wooden chairs placed side by side, and a somewhat larger, upholstered one against the opposite wall.

Sabrina raised her eyebrows. As an answer, Maria lifted both shoulders.

They sat in silence for at least ten minutes before the door was opened again by the same elderly monk. Following closely behind, Cardinal Bouchard entered the room.

Maria and Sabrina respectfully rose to their feet.

The Cardinal was tall and gaunt with a pale face and a long sharp nose. He was dressed in black, except for the white collar designating him as a priest. His hands had long, slender fingers which were clasped in front of him.

"I wish you God's peace and blessing," he said in a cool, but courteous voice, making the sign of the cross.

Maria dutifully crossed herself.

Sabrina, whose aunt had been a Catholic nun, naturally was familiar with the proper etiquette.

"Signora Callander, Signorina . . ."

"ra Thalon," Sabrina pronounced for him.

What a curious name. He thought of her as insignificant with the dowdy dress and down-cast eyes. Maria Callander, petite, with auburn hair and light brown eyes, he remembered meeting before. He approved of small women, especially those who heeded their position in the world.

"Please be seated," he invited, after he had taken his seat and straightened the folds of his cassock.

He sat ramrod straight, and after folding his hands in his lap, he began without preamble. "I am here to convey greetings from the Holy Father. He has asked me to lay out a proposal that would maintain the Vatican's position as a Sovereign State. Also, if our proposal is accepted, we would like to send legates to countries with a Christian population. We would also like to conduct a census to ascertain which population is Christian, and then send bishops to form regional offices."

Sabrina was slightly taken aback, and pursing her lips, shot a glance at Maria.

"And you wish us to convey this to the Counsil of United Europe or the World Management Commission?" Maria asked him guilelessly, discreetly dropping her eyes.

The Cardinal compressed his lips and looked meditatively at Maria. His narrow aristocratic countenance became even more narrow and tighter. "As you know, Signora Callander, we have already presented this writ to the European Council, and also to the World Management Commission."

"And they have rejected it?"

"As you know, they have."

"What is it that you wish of me, then?"

"To arrange for us to present our request to the Planetary Alliance Counsil."

Maria shifted in her chair and was silent for a moment.

For the first time, his gaze shifted to Sabrina. He had forgotten her.

Sabrina had been sitting silent and motionless in her chair, observing the Cardinal's deportment. Maria was right, she thought, he is not an easy man to like. Something about him deeply disturbed her. There was an unnatural rigidity in the way he held himself, and an intensity to the glare of his eyes.

After a short but deliberate silence Sabrina said, "My first question is, what do you expect the Alliance Counsil to do for you?"

"I only wish for you to arrange an audience with the Council's coordinator," the Cardinal responded.

"The Alliance Counsil is a secular organization and does not deal in ecclesiastic matters."

The Cardinal clenched his hands, and an impatient expression flickered across his face. His nostrils flared as he responded. "My wish is to present to the Counsil the greetings of the Vicar of Christ and his request."

It was hard for Sabrina to maintain her demure demeanor. So, with a very subdued and reasonable voice she said, "I see. Your position is to continue as in the past. The world has changed, your Eminence, and maybe with it, the perception of religion. Of course God is God," she injected quickly, noting the expansion of his chest and cut short what might have been a diatribe. "As we grow, our understanding changes, as well as out realizations, or need for spiritual guidance."

Cardinal Bouchard rose and regarded her silently. He turned to Maria, and in a stinging voice said, "I have here a request for an audience with the Coordinator of the Alliance Counsil. I beg you to indulge me in presenting it at the Council's meeting."

Sabrina and Maria rose. Maria took the document from him and handed it to Sabrina who placed it into her attaché case.

He only nodded his head and departed. The monk, who had shown them in, appeared at the door. As he escorted them out of the house, his hand surreptitiously brushed Sabrina's. When she looked down, he slipped a piece of paper into her hand.

Maria and Sabrina stood for a moment in the street in silence.

"No car, no taxi? Are we expected to walk home?" Sabrina quipped, still irritated by the tone of the meeting.

"It's a nice day and only a forty minute walk. Do you mind very much?"

"Not at all; I enjoy walking," Sabrina replied. Puffing out both cheeks, she expelled a forceful breath. "What colossal arrogance," she told Maria.

Maria began to chuckle. "An understatement, my dear."

After a thoughtful moment, Sabrina turned to Maria, "Would you mind very much going home by yourself?"

"What do you have in mind?"

"A stroll and the solitude to collect my thoughts," Sabrina replied.

There was a curious look, but Maria acquiesced and slowly walked away. After Maria was out of sight, Sabrina looked at the piece of paper in her hand. It was folded very small. She unfolded it and with growing surprise read, please, come back and knock on the door. I will let you in.

Sabrina pursed her lips. Well, to find out what this means I guess I better go. She returned to the monastery and knocked on the door per instruction. Again the door eased open and the same brother peered out.

When Sabrina started to ask what it was all about, he put his fingers to his lips and whispered, "Please, come with me." He led her near the Chapel. Sabrina paused and listened spellbound to the sonorous voices of the monks singing a Gregorian chant.

"Wait for them to come out, then, follow the Abbot. He will probably go to a walled-in garden."

When Vesper was over, the monks came out in single file. There was a tall, gaunt monk with his cowl drawn over his head, and she recognized him as Bouchard. He was now dressed in the simple habit of a brother.

As she watched Bouchard moving toward the cloister, she had that eerie feeling of something not being quite right.

The click of a door made Sabrina turn around. A tall, sparse monk came slowly down the steps and walked along the path that led behind the chapel. Sabrina followed him at a distance. He entered through a wooden gate into a small enclosure. It was the beginning of a rose garden. A statue of Jesus stood in an alcove with a stone bench beside it.

He sat down and brushed back his cowl. The thick black hair circling his tonsure was barely touched with grey. The profile was sharp and the face intelligent. At Sabrina's approach, he slowly looked up, then, rose in bewilderment. There weren't supposed to be any women within these walls.

"Good evening," Sabrina said in Italian, with a small bow. "I surmise you are the Abbot of this monastery?"

"Yes. What can I do for you?" he asked as he resumed his seat and refolded his hands.

To the Abbot's surprise, Sabrina sat unceremoniously down beside him.

"I have come to inquire about a Nuncio name Bouchard."

There was a startled movement and he looked vaguely astonished as he half turned toward her. "I do not know a Nuncio Bouchard," he said, shaking his head, "only a brother named Paul Bouchard."

Why doesn't this come as a surprise? Sabrina thought as she turned her gaze upon the Abbot. "Maria Callander and I were asked to come to the Abbey today to meet with Cardinal

Bouchard, a Papal Nuncio. We believed him to be sent by the Holy Father to ask us to intercede for a hearing with the Counsil of the Planetary Alliance. He proposed a concordance for the Vatican to remain an autonomous state as it had been in the past."

It was quite apparent that the Abbot was taken aback by what she said. He sat silent for a long time. Finally he turned and scrutinized her with his deep-set eyes, which lingered thoughtfully on her face.

"Then he has given you a document?"

"Yes." Sabrina picked up her attaché case and placed it on her lap. She opened it, took out the document, and handed it to the Abbot.

He read it carefully, especially the signature. "A good forgery," he said, enjoying the perplexed look on Sabrina's face.

"Would you clarify this for me?"

"Paul Bouchard is a very troubled soul, and he is only a lay brother . . ."

"But he wore a priest's collar."

"He has never been ordained. He was an aide to the late Pope . . ."

"Late Pope?" Sabrina's eyebrows went up as she rose from the seat. When she stood, the Abbot was compelled to rise. Sabrina was as tall as he and they locked eyes. "The late Pope?" Sabrina asked again, this time her voice firm, going into command mode.

"The Holy Father died a long time ago. He barely survived the upheavals. In the last year of his office, he had been very frail."

"Paul Bouchard? What of him?"

"He had been very attached to the Holy Father, or maybe his office." There was a wry quirk to his mouth as he looked at Sabrina. "We know that he would like to see the past resurrected and can't accept that the world has moved on. We didn't know how far he had initiated his plan."

"He approached the Counsil of United Europe and the World Management Commission."

"And as I suspect, he had been turned down?"

"He was."

"My apology. We had no idea."

"His mind is unbalanced?"

"Paul is chasing a dream he can't relinquish. We know he did some furious writing and was sending out questionnaires."

"Then you have no intentions of contacting the Counsil of the Planetary Alliance?"

He gave her a whimsical smile. "Yes, I do." To Sabrina's questioning look he said, "You see, I inherited a Legacy. I'm the custodian of more than two thousand years of history. I would like to have Vatican Hill maintained as a historical site. And I would like to have help in restoring what is left of the Vatican's extensive library. Also, we have managed to save some precious art works. Neither the World Management Commission nor United Europe have the funds to undertake such an endeavor."

"If you would formulate a request and give it to Maria Callander," Sabrina said, "I will see that it is passed on to the proper authority."

"Thank you . . ." Somewhat shocked, he said, "How remiss of me. I have never asked your name.'

"I'm Sabrina ra Thalon. Will you appear before the Counsil?"

"No, I'm not much of a diplomat. I will send a real Nuncio with all the right credentials. After all, we have to maintain the dignity of the Papacy," he said, his lips curling into a touch of a smile.

"Will the Papacy be revived?"

"No." The corners of his mouth turned down slightly as he contemplated Sabrina for a moment. "There was a prophecy, the Malachi Prophesy that the name of the last Pope is supposed to be Peter of Rome. Before the Pope died, he conferred this Abbacy on me. With it, his mantle so to speak, passed on to me. Sabrina ra Thalon, I am Pedro de Romano.

*   *   *

Three days later, Sargon returned to Maria Callander's house and told Sabrina that Garth had been found and that he and his daughter been shipped back to the Altruscan home world. He also brought a tape Miri had made and gave it to her. "Now you don't have to travel. Miri has done it for you."

"That's very sweet of her, but what am I going to do in the meantime? The United Nations' meeting is more than a month away."

"You could go back to the Space Station. Ian isn't very proficient in the Altruscan language. He ran into a lot of trouble trying to translate a manual he needs in order to put the navigational system of the Constitution together."

Sabrina's face puckered. She knew he expected her to instantly alter her plans. There were sights she wanted to see, and she had hoped to have some time off. "Is that an order, or a request?" she asked testily.

Sargon was prevented from replying in kind by the untimely arrival of Maria Callander.

"Well, hello Jim," she said, delighted at seeing him again. "Can you stay for lunch?"

Sargon gave Sabrina an icy stare, then, beamed at Maria. "Yes, I would be delighted, but only if you can get rid of that irritant," pointing to Sabrina, "it could be a very enjoyable lunch."

Sabrina immediately turned on her heels and slammed out of the house.

Chapter 20

Sabrina landed on the Space Station and searched unsuccessfully for Soltec. At Command Central, she asked the man at the operations desk where she might find Ian McPherson. Without looking at her, he handed her a computer printout of Ian's status and berth number. According to the sheet, Ian was assigned to the Constitution as a civilian engineer.

"Where's the Constitution?" she asked him.

"She's docked . . ." and for the first time, he looked up. His Adam's apple bobbed up and down as his eyes roved appreciatively over her figure, "But to get there, you'll need clearance."

"How do I get clearance?"

"I don't think you could get it. It's kind of hush, hush. You know, secret."

"I see. Who's in command of the Constitution?"

"I think a Captain Daniels. An alien named Soltec is in command of the Station, if that means anything to you."

"It might," Sabrina told him evenly, trying very hard not to show her annoyance with this incompetent and unresponsive yeoman. "How do I get to his office?"

"Just follow the green marking on the wall. It should lead you there."

"Thanks, you have been very helpful," Sabrina said and gave him one of her sparsest of smiles.

She found Soltec's office, but his secretary informed her he would not be back at the station until the next day.

Sabrina requested a layout of the station, then, walked out of the office, studying it as she went. There was a large undesignated grey area on the map, and she surmised it was where the dry dock was located. As she walked along, she noticed Altruscan ideographic writing on the walls. At some time in the past, with the help of the Altruscans, the Cartel had built the station as a safe haven in the event of a war on Earth. It was then that Sargon, with the help of Brook and Noel, and a young man named Roger, had moved the station beyond the Cartel's reach. The station had been brought back later with the assistance of Soltec. Since she knew Altruscan, it was easy to locate the spaceship, and she found Ian in the Engine Room. Work on the Constitution had been halted since the disappearance of the Altruscan engineers.

"Hey Ian," she said, walking up behind him.

Ian jumped, then, whirled around. "Should'na do that lass; you could get a black eye, sneakin' up on me like that."

Sabrina only laughed at him. "What's going on?"

"Since you made all the Altruscans disappear, there's no one who knows how to work these contraptions."

"What you are saying is, that you could use some help?"

"Aye lass, that's the gist of it."

"Well, let's see what you have here."

The two worked in silence. Ian knew he had only to think at Sabrina in his mind, and she would know what he wanted. Suddenly, their work was interrupted by an individual in uniform standing over them as they came out from under a console.

Sabrina squinted one eye as she looked up at him. "Ian," she said, waving her finger, "that stuff on his shoulders, does it mean he is a Captain?"

Ian rose. His pockets were bulging with tools and his face was smudged.

"Sir," Ian said, dusting his pants off, "may I introduce . . . Damn girl, I never know as what or whom do I introduce you," Ian said exasperated.

"Mary Hennesee, Sir," Sabrina said.

"Miss Hennesee, you are in a restricted zone. If you don't have clearance, I will have to escort you off the premises."

"Don't do that," Ian exclaimed, almost in panic. "I need her, or I'll never get this thing installed."

"Explain yourself!"

"The lady here is an engineer, and she knows more about this Altruscan stuff than I do," Ian said, moving a step toward the Captain of the Constitution.

"Captain . . . ?" Sabrina queried, before Ian could say more.

"Captain Daniels."

"Thank you." Sabrina inclined her head. "Who is in command of this base in the absence of Soltec?" she asked Daniels.

"Admiral Denver."

"I see. Ian, would he know who I am?"

Ian considered it for a moment before replying. "Don't think so lass. I thought you were coming back with Soltec."

"So did I, but I got delayed by a side trip to Rome. I thought Soltec came ahead of me."

"Then what are you doing here?"

"There is a meeting two days hence, and I was invited to attend," Sabrina informed Ian.

Captain Daniels had been listening to this conversation with incredulity and he finally cleared his throat, "Miss Hennesee, you still will have to leave here and you both will have to answer for these irregularities."

"Now you've done it agin," Ian complained to Sabrina.

"What has she done?" Daniels asked.

"Trouble," Ian muttered darkly. "Trouble follows her wherever she goes," Ian grumbled, shaking his head.

"I get the impression that neither of you consider this situation serious," Daniels said, harshly. He was becoming annoyed by their complete disregard.

"Captain," Sabrina said, "if Soltec were here, there would be no problem." Then, turning to Ian, "Don't you think you could call it quits until I have a chance to talk to Soltec?"

"I guess I could since Captain Daniels is not going to allow you to help me, I'm stuck, and you know it. I can't read this damned Altruscan manual as you can. Sir," he turned to Daniels, "she would be a help, because she can read those manuals."

"Where did you learn Altruscan?" Daniels asked, suspiciously.

"My teacher told me to always learn my enemy's language," Sabrina intoned, her voice taking on a mocking tone of formality, which gave Ian a sudden coughing fit. As he turned his face away, he saw Daniels staring at them in disbelief.

Suddenly Sabrina felt a presence, "Basra?" she mind-sent, and asked him for assistance. When he acknowledged her, she greeted him with gentle laughter.

"Sabrina, are you having difficulties?" he sent back, amused.

"You may be able to help Ian out of a spot of trouble I got him in."

When Basra appeared in the Engine Room, Daniels bowed respectfully to him. "Sir," he said, "this lady is in here without clearance."

"Also, she won't take this situation serious," Basra commiserated with Daniels, suddenly using speech.

"You can talk!" Sabrina exclaimed, taken aback.

"Dealing with humans, I had to avail myself of this mode of communication," Basra replied with a smile.

"Can you vouch for this lady, then?" Daniels asked.

Basra looked sharply at Daniels. His smile widened, then, his face creased into a comic mixture of humor and indecision. "To tell you the truth," he said slowly, "where she's concerned I don't know where I stand."

Sabrina held up her hand when Daniels was about to talk. She sensed Basra contacting someone because his shield went up as a precaution against her rifling through his mind.

The intercom came to life with Soltec's voice, "Captain Daniels, Miss Hennesee has clearance to all areas of the station, including the ship."

"Aye, Sir," Daniels answered.

"Well, Laddie, now we can go back to work. You see this symbol there?" she said to Ian. Both immersed themselves in the manual, totally ignoring everyone else.

Ian turned to Daniels before going back underneath the console, "I never behave as badly as that. It only happens when she's around," he added as an apology.

"Making me into the heavy again. I tell you Ian, I'm going to get you for that," then falling into his Scottish brogue, "an me only wanten to help oot."

*   *   *

189

Admiral Denver contacted Sabrina and gave her the itinerary for the next day. After being assigned guest quarters on the Space Station, she asked for a wake up call, then, promptly went to sleep.

Next morning she awoke before the call came. When she answered it, she was told she would be escorted to the conference room on the third level.

Half-an-hour later, there was a knock on her door. A young boy with fair hair and a narrow, anxious face said, "Ma'am, are you ready to go?"

"In just a second." Sabrina picked up the folder lying on top of her bed, then, followed her guide to the third level of the Space Station.

When the door to the conference room opened, the first individual she saw was Commodore Doers. "The proverbial bad penny you can't get rid of," she mumbled under her breath. Then her eyes moved to the others sitting at the table. She nodded to Serenity the Arachnid sitting in her human form next to Elkatma, the Chiron Ambassador. She winked at Basra. There was only one stranger in the room. Elkatma introduced him as Ambassador Najoth of Ramath, from the Altair System. Sabrina's eyebrow rose in astonishment as Elkatma still adhered to calling her Miss Mary Hennesee.

Sabrina inclined her head, "Mister Ambassador," she said formally.

"Please sit next to me," Serenity said. As soon as Sabrina was seated, Serenity continued, "We have been discussing your qualifications. Captain Thalon described you as amply qualified and I agree with him up to a point. You are the best expert to know if Earth is ready to join the Alliance, but still, I suspect there would be a trace of bias in your assessment."

Without a moment's hesitation, Sabrina agreed. "I concede there might be," she said even voiced.

"Have you read my folder?" Doeros somewhat pompously inserted himself into the conversation.

Sabrina gave him a long, deliberate look. "No Sir," she said. "I plan to have an open mind and any conclusions I reach will be without undue influences by outside opinions," she said.

"Really?" His voice rose in surprise and he looked at her to see if she had made some obscure joke. "What makes you believe Earth is now ready to join the Alliance?" Doeros said, coldly.

Sabrina grimaced, trying to contain the annoyance she felt at his pontifical attitude which never failed to irk her. "Since the last vestige of detrimental influence has been removed, Earth is now able to chart her own course, unhindered. I think she'll make a trustworthy and dependable member for the Alliance," Sabrina said, slightly strained. There was an impish part of her that refused to listen to anything Doeros said, but she did try to be civil to him, at least this time. Sabrina looked at Ambassador Najoth. "Is there anything you would like to ask?"

"I am quite aware that, until recently, the Earth was under the influence of the Altruscans. You have met with the people of this planet? Do you think their warlike propensity is a thing of the past?"

"Most patriarchal societies have the unfortunate predisposition to settle their differences with a show of force. Earth has an unfortunate record of aggression and conquests. But they also have been an enterprising and determined people. Since I have been there, I have seen a more racially integrated society. Also, the form of government has changed from an individualized style of governing to a cooperative management for the good of their whole world. There is also a more egalitarian interaction where the sexes are concerned." Sabrina all of a sudden faltered, her attention drawn toward the door. There was the sensation of a presence invading her awareness. The small hairs on the back on her neck began to prickle; her whole posture became more alert.

When the door slid open, Sabrina shook herself a fraction. An overwhelming power radiated from the man who strode into the room. Sargon and Sabot had just as strong a presence, but on a different scale.

The newcomer had light skin, black hair and eyes, and was as large and powerfully built as Sargon. His eyes took in all who sat at the table, lingering on Sabrina.

She had slammed her shields down the moment he had entered the room, and now she met his eyes with guardedness.

"Miss Hennesee, I am Heiko, the Coordinator of the Alliance Counsil" he said, his great, dark brooding eyes resting on her. "Have you come to a definitive conclusion?"

Sabrina straightened her shoulders; there was a long moment of silence.

Weighing her thoughts and her feelings she looked gravely at him. "Yes, I think this is the time," she answered.

*   *   *

Sabrina had just exited the airlock which connected the Constitution to the Space Station's dock, when she sensed a familiar presence. "Sargon!" she sent out her mind-call. At a distance she could see him standing beside Heiko, both deep in conversation.

"You two know each other?" she asked astonished, as she approached.

Sargon fixed her with a level and penetrating gaze. "Just because you don't know everybody, doesn't mean I don't," he informed her.

She let out a snort and refrained from commenting. Then another presence inserted itself into her awareness, no, not one, but two. She whirled around and saw her two boys coming toward her. At the sight of their mother, Jason let out a whoop and started to run with Logan at his heels. Sabrina spread her arms wide and embraced her two offsprings.

"Bet you didn't expect to see us so soon," Jason said, his green eyes twinkling as he looked up at his mother.

"No, not quiet this soon," she acknowledged, kissing him.

"Dad said you're going to make a speech at the United Nations. Got it all worked out?" Logan asked. He was now almost as tall as she, and when she looked closer at him, she began to laugh. Teasing, she asked, "What happened to your tiger eyes?"

"Well, Dad said Earth people weren't ready yet for tiger eyes, so he made me wear contacts."

"Since Sargon has to hide his too, Logan didn't make too much of a fuss about it," Jason commented, his arm around Sargon's waist.

Turning to Sargon, Sabrina smiled up at him, her face radiant with joy. "Thanks for bringing the boys along."

Sargon smiled. "They would have never forgiven me if I hadn't," he told her.

Heiko watched the reunion and it intrigued him that Jason called him Sargon, and Logan, Dad, but both boys being as familiar with him like sons.

Sargon and Sabrina both discerned his curiosity, and Sabrina grinned at Heiko. "House rights," she said dead-pan.

Sargon chuckled. "Heiko, I wouldn't touch that with a ten-foot-pole."

"To understand your aphorism, you mean it's not quite appropriate to investigate deeper?" he asked.

"Precisely. Sabrina has a very peculiar sense of humor. Both boys are her sons. I'm Logan's father, but parent to both."

"Very nicely put," Serenity remarked, joining them. "There is a use for a male after all."

Sabrina looked at her in disbelief. Trying to sound scandalized, Sabrina said, "It would be devastating if you'd developed a sense of humor."

Sargon's expression had gone blank, shielding his thoughts. But Heiko's mind was reeling with incredulity at Sabrina's levity, which was very easy for her to read. His mind ran through what he knew of spiders. He recalled that some spiders devoured their mates. He didn't know if Serenity ever had a mate or what she did with him. He decided that he was never going to ask.

Serenity, totally oblivious to the imagery her pronouncement created, watched the different reactions she received from Sabrina's boys.

Logan stepped back, almost shielding himself behind his mother, while Jason's eyes nearly bulged from their sockets as he looked closely at her. "Mom," he said breathlessly, "she came through the wall. She can do the same thing I do."

"Almost, but not quite," Serenity told him.

Jason, unlike Logan, had no PSI ability, so he did not sense the non-humanness and absence of feelings emanating from Serenity. He was only full of bubbling curiosity. Logan sensed what Serenity was, pulled Jason back.

"I'm not interested in younglings," Serenity assured him, her obsidian eyes disregarding them, as she turned back to the adults. "We will be sitting in the gallery tomorrow," she told Sabrina.

Jason was still bubbling, but this time with excitement, "Mom, Sargon said after all that hubbub is over, we can go planet-side and have fun."

"Oh, did he now," Sabrina said acidly.

"What's she mad at you about?" Jason asked Sargon.

"He rerouted her itinerary . . ." Logan interjected.

"You quit rifling though my files," Sabrina chided Logan.

"Well, what do you want me to do, shut down like a clam?" he defended himself.

"No, I guess not. I'm just a little cagy about going to the United Nations and having to make a speech," Sabrina admitted. "Sorry I bit at you."

"Now that this reunion is over, are you ready to go to Atlantis?" Sargon asked.

Atlantis, named after the mystical continent of the same name, was a landmass that had risen to the southeast of the Americas as a balance for the land that had disappeared during the upheavals. It was now being terra-formed to make it inhabitable.

"You mean now?" Sabrina asked.

"I'll give you enough time to pack your things," Sargon conceded. "The ship will leave in twenty minutes."

Sabrina gave him a sour look, "Very generous of you," she told him sarcastically, then turned and sped toward her quarters. Since she always kept her belongings semi-packed anyway, she arrived at the departure area within fifteen minutes.

As she was getting settled, and in the process of strapping in, the shuttle departed. Sargon was seated next to Serenity, and Heiko sat with Doeros. Her boys were in front of her, busily peering out of the window and commenting on the planet that was seemingly rushing toward them.

After landing on Earth and disembarking the shuttle, they were met by the hotel's courtesy car. When Sabrina, carrying her duffle bag, walked into the hotel lobby ahead of the others, there was an audible sniff from the desk clerk as he looked down his nose at her.

Since Sargon hadn't given her much time to change, she still wore her baggy pants and baggy top. They had been woven from an unbleached material, and it looked rather grey. Her duffle bag was travel-worn, and as she plopped it on top of the desk, the clerk turned toward the others coming in, ignoring her.

"Wrong boyo," she muttered, just audible enough for him to hear," I'm the VIP here, those others are incidentals."

He gave her a scalding look. "Sirs," he said to Heiko and Sargon, "may I help you?" He totally ignored Sabrina.

"We have reservations, I'm Commodore Heiko."

After Heiko gave everyone the keys, Sargon turned to Sabrina. "I assume you want to be with your boys," and before the clerks startled eyes, he handed Sabrina the keys to the most expensive suite.

Logan, having gleaned what was happening with his PSI awareness was relating it gleefully to his younger brother. Both were giggling and somewhat boisterous as they went up the stairs. A short cough from Sargon ended it abruptly. Falling back, they walked the rest of the steps sedately beside their mother. Sabrina didn't say a word, only gave them an amused look.

Sabrina's suite consisted of a sitting-room and one bedroom for the boys, and another one for herself. She had just deposited the duffle bag on the bed when someone knocked on the door.

"Come," she said. It was only the maid. She came in with an armload of towels.

"My name is Amy. Can I help you unpack, Ma'am?" she asked, staring at Sabrina. She was supposed to be an alien, but didn't look like one.

"No thank you, but you can put the towels in the bathroom."

Amy was heading toward the bathroom just as the boys came in, Logan without his contact lenses. The girl let out a loud gasp, and the towels went tumbling to the floor.

Sabrina gently touched the girl's arm. "Just think of them as cat eyes," she told her.

"What do you mean . . . cat eyes?" Logan protested. Turning toward Amy, "Don't you think they look more like tiger eyes?" he asked with an ingratiating smile and batted his eyelashes at her.

Amy giggled. "I agree, they look more like tiger eyes," she conceded, looking up at him. He's handsome she thought, he is exotic. Both Sabrina and Logan perceived her arousal.

Sabrina noticed his reacted to it with an imperceptible body posture and cockiness. No, Sabrina thought, it was more, like some-kind of condescension, no, it was something else. She became uneasy. The first time she noticed it was after Logan had been enthralled by the kaleidoscopic display of colors of the Nursery cell walls. Something in him had changed.

"A girl with exquisite taste," he commented to his mother, which made Amy blush and giggle even more.

Sabrina laughed. "Okay, Logan, that's enough," she told him. "Sorry, Amy, we didn't mean to startle you. Would you put the towels in the bathroom now, please?"

"Yes of course; I'm sorry ma'am."

Sabrina gave Logan a stern look.

Well," he said," I hate those things. They bother my eyes. I'll wear sunglasses," he conceded, then stalked from the room.

"Wonder where he gets that bad temper from . . ." Jason quipped.

"Because you're always such a sweet tempered and obedient child," Sabrina finished for him.

Jason looked at her a little piqued, and commenced stalking out of the room too.

Chapter 21

The structure that housed the United Nations had been built on the new land as the symbol of a new world. It stood on a hill, facing the sea. It's long sweeping horizontal design in a smooth curved exterior of brick and glass was built in three tiers into the hill and blended nicely with its natural surrounding. The approach was an open plaza. In the center stood a flagstaff flying only one flag, the old symbol of the United Nations, but with the sub continent of Atlantis placed at its center.

The artist in Sabrina was impressed by the building's clear lines and functional design, and as she entered, with the airiness of the wide lobby.

A woman detached herself from one of the windows and came toward her. "Miss Hennesee, I'm Selma Strindberg," she introduced herself; "I'm Secretary General. Miss Callander has asked if you would be so kind to join her. Please come this way."

Maria Callander met Sabrina outside the door of a conference room. "I'm sorry to change your itinerary. The Vatican has sent the Nuncio promised by Pedro de Romano. His name is Sebastiano Roncalli and he is here to petition the Alliance for assistance."

Sabrina showed only a flicker of surprise at the name Roncalli. It had been her fraternal grandfather's name. Juliano Roncalli had been disowned by his family because he wouldn't marry the woman they had chosen for him. Instead, he had married Kathleen Anna Mary Hennesee, the Irish lass who had stolen his heart. After their marriage, he adopted her family name, Hennesee.

"Miss Strindberg," Sabrina turned to the other woman," Would you be so kind and inform the Russian delegation that I will be delayed and explain why?"

"It has already been rescheduled. They decided to have breakfast and then meet with you.

Sabrina chuckled. "Not a bad idea. That will give us time to meet with this Nuncio. Thank you, Miss Strindberg." Turning to Maria she couldn't help commenting, "Well this time it is supposed to be the real article."

At her previous stay in Rome with Maria, they had both gone to a Benedictine Abbey to meet someone representing himself as an envoy of the Pope. He turned out to be only a discontented monk who yearned for a return to the Vatican's former glory. Later Sabrina did meet with Pedro de Romano, the Abbot, who promised to send a legitimate Nuncio to the United Nations to meet with her there.

Sabrina and Maria entered the room, and as soon as the Nuncio's eyes came to rest on Sabrina, they widened. She suddenly felt a violent explosion of anger rushing toward her. His thoughts were loud and clear. This misogynic, brainless fool described her as inconsequential.

Ah, Sabrina thought, that must be about the so-called Nuncio. As he rose to greet her, a turn of his head made her hold her breath. His profile reminded her of her Gramps; her Grandfather Juliano. It had the same contour.

He gave her a studied look as he walked toward her. "Miss Hennesee?" He greeted her with a minute bow of his head. "I am Sebastiano Roncalli. I'm here to extend Abbot Romano's greeting to you. I am indebted to you for taking time out of your busy schedule. As you know, we are not interested in reviving the past, but need help in preserving a more than two-thousand year history. We are asking for assistance in saving Vatican Hill as a national monument.

Sabrina had already scanned his surface memory. Hmm, she thought, we have a Cardinal Roncalli. "Your Eminence," she addressed him to his surprise, "I have already presented Commodore Heiko, the Coordinator of the Alliance Counsil, with your request."

Logan's presence suddenly invaded her mind. He was coming down the hallway, dressed in the Antarean uniform. When he opened the door, without looking back, she said, "Cadet, step forward," and she held her hand out for the slip of paper he carried. Before she looked down to read, her eyes fell on Roncalli. He was staring in disbelief at Logan. She turned quickly to look at her son, then, chuckled. Logan had again dispensed with his contact lenses.

"Interesting, wouldn't you say?" Maria Callander said.

Maria had already seen both Logan's and Sargon's eyes and the Nuncio's undisguised surprise amused her.

"That would be an understatement," he answered, his gaze still locked on Logan.

The memo informed Sabrina that Heiko and Sargon requested the presence of the Nuncio and Maria Callander in the conference room across the hall.

"We are asked to join the Coordinator of the Alliance and Captain Thalon next door," she informed Roncalli.

After crossing the hall and entering the room, Roncalli suddenly stopped. He looked at Sargon and then back at Logan.

Sargon's mien showed no reaction.

"Your Eminence," Heiko greeted him with a slight bow of his upper torso.

Sargon only nodded his head. Then, to Sabrina and Logan," You are dismissed," he commanded. "Miss Callander," Sargon said, "I believe you have met Commodore Heiko."

Sabrina turned and walked out, but Logan gave his father an angry look before following his mother.

Outside the door, "Mom, you let him do that to you all the time?" he upbraided her.

"Logan, he's the Captain."

"But Mom, you have the same rank as he."

"Nevertheless . . ." she stopped and regarded him for a second, "Son," she told him," there is only one Sargon."

"And that's suppose to settle the issue?" was his rebellious reply.

*   *   *

The United Nation's auditorium was filled to capacity. Many of the delegates from Earth had already met with beings from different worlds and established a dialogue. When Sabrina entered the theater, she walked into the hum of many voices and an aura of energy and expectancy permeating the room. All eyes followed her as she walked down the aisle toward the podium. She was dressed in her Antarean uniform.

"Ladies and Gentlemen," she began, after stepping up to the podium. Her voice rang clear, her diction precise. "I have been granted the honor of giving this speech. You may wonder why an alien was thus singled out. I am an Antarean from the Worldship Antares, but before that, I was born on Earth. My name is Sabrina Mary Hennesee. I have had the privilege of working with people who sponsored the admission of Earth into the Planetary Alliance. Belonging to the Alliance entails privileges, but also responsibilities, responsibilities toward other members of the Alliance. The Alliance is made up of a large variety of sentient beings. Not all are in human form."

"One thing I will like to make clear . . . there must be respect toward other beings, even if they don't look like you, sound like you, or even smell like you. There must be tolerance for the diversity of all forms of life. When you go out among the stars, you will find civilizations which differ from your cultures, philosophies and religions. Many may be antagonistic toward what you believe or feel is right."

"Ladies and Gentlemen, let me advise you; leave your beliefs, your philosophies, and your religions at home. When you go among the stars, your view of your world must stay with your world. When you join the Alliance, you pledge to protect and cherish all other forms of life and their right to live as they choose. The purpose for which the Alliance was founded was for mutual protection against aggression, but its main directive is non-interference. That means for each world to be able to develop in its own way, without undue interference from outside sources. The laws enacted through the Charter give you that protection. Ladies and Gentlemen, when you go among the stars, bring your energy, your curiosity, and love of life and you will find it returned many fold. I wish you well and joy in what ever your discoveries will be."

When Sabrina stepped down from the podium, Heiko rose and restrained her from leaving by touching her arm. Then he mounted the podium.

"Ladies and Gentlemen, we have just heard a beautiful speech which says much about the woman whose name is Sabrina. What she did not tell you is her valor beyond the call of duty. Many times, because of her actions, the integrity of the

Alliance had been preserved. The honor to address the United Nations was not given because she was born on Earth. The honor is ours. She is honoring us by being here today. It was Sabrina who discovered the recent Altruscan conspiracy, and she finished the work begun by Jonathan Wright. Jonathan Wright was among the first to discover the Altruscan plot. With the help of Brook and Noel Hennesee and others, they were able, if not to stop, but to hinder their machinations. Thanks to them and to Sabrina, Earth is now free to chart her own course." There was a deep silence in the auditorium, then, everyone rose and bowed in deep reverence.

When Heiko came off the podium, Sabrina smiled at him. "Thank you for your kind words, but if you don't mind, I would like to disappear." Doing just that, she left through a small door behind the speaker's platform.

Chapter 22

Just before the break of dawn, Sabrina was jogging along the beach when she detected a disturbance ahead. Extending her PSI awareness, she sensed the blurring of a form, then, perceived Serenity in her primary form, a spider. But, also running nearby, was a human. She picked up his fear, and his intense abhorrence. The sudden report of a gun rang out from the vicinity of an outcrop of rock and she sped toward it.

The first thing she saw was an enormous spider. Then, she noticed a man lying on the ground. He seemed to be unconscious. She remembered that spiders sting their prey. Keeping her distance, Sabrina slowly squatted down, knowing not to interfere with whatever Serenity was doing.

There was a hand-held radio lying on the ground and the dubious voice of a man asking, "What you mean a gigantic spider? Man, answer me. Larry, answer me!"

Sabrina picked up the radio. "This is Sabrina Hennesee, who are you?"

"I'm Ed. What's happened to Larry?"

"I'll take care of him," Sabrina answered.

"There's a bunch a guys coming out in a jeep."

"Call them back; do you hear me. Call them back immediately."

But it was too late. The jeep careened around the corner, spewing sand in all directions.

"Sargon, priority one, priority one, "Sabrina sent mind to mind. "Come to the beach at the rock outcrop."

Sargon picked up her call, and so did Logan and related it to his brother. Logan piled into a jeep behind his father, but Jason, changing into a cat, raced ahead.

In the meantime, on the beach, three men piled out as soon as their jeep skidded to a halt, and squatting down, aimed their rifles at Serenity's bulk.

"Don't!" Sabrina yelled and ran toward them. "Don't shoot!" She swooped down and with both hands picked up sand and threw it at them. "Damit, are you deaf?" she shouted at them. "I said, don't shoot!"

They finally heard her. She was about to explain that she would take care of Serenity, when she was knocked down by a rather large cat. She sprawled in the sand, face down. Jason had arrived at top speed, and thinking his mother in danger, had jumped on her back to knock her out of harm's way.

Sabrina groaned, spitting sand. "Aw, for the love of beans, Jason, get off of me. Will you?"

There was a blurring of form and Jason sat astride his mothers back, "Is that the thanks I get trying to save your hide," he complained

Sabrina was saved from replying to her offspring's accusation by Sargon and

Logan's arrival. Sargon drove the jeep up beside her, and sticking his head out the window, asked, "What's your emergency?"

"Serenity," she said, pointing toward the rock.

Sargon went to see about Serenity. He found her burrowed into the sand with only her head showing. She was sated and sublimely oblivious to the crisis she had provoked. Since Serenity seemed to be all right, he bent down to examine the man lying on the ground. He had a small bite mark at the back of his neck. Sargon turned him over and lifted his eye lids, then laid his hand on his heart. "He's all right," Sargon called toward the men who still crouched in the sand.

"What happened to him?" the one named Ed wanted to know.

Sargon held up his hand. He was in communication with Serenity.

Serenity had been severely put out. The man named Larry had interrupted her feeding. She had been out early to hunt, snaring a deer in her web when the man happen to come along and freed it. In her fury she had stalked him. After immobilizing him with her venom, she had used him as prey instead. Serenity's kind only fed on body fluid without killing. On the planet Coronis, they keep herds and took only enough fluid to assuage their hunger. In their hunting mode, they used a different strain of venom which only immobilized their prey. In the killing mode, they were deadly. Serenity's information to Sargon flowed to Sabrina through the mind-link, and from her to Logan. Jason was left out. He went over to the men, curious about their rifles. Sabrina sensed their uneasiness and watched as they backed away from Jason. They had witnessed his transformation from cat to a boy.

"He's harmless," she called to them. "He's only a fourteen-year-old pest."

"I wonder where I heard that before," Sargon commented, then chuckled. A long time ago Jonathan had tried to explain Sabrina the same way.

A commotion to the right drew everyone's attention. A group of people were coming toward them.

Suddenly Sargon chuckled. "Chiara, over here," he called out and waved his arm.

Logan and Jason raced to meet them. Sabrina walked toward Sargon, and recognizing Benjie, began to run too. Benjie had been a little boy from South Africa she had raised since his was eight years old.

"Benjie," she said, hugging him, "let me look at you. You're gorgeous, you know. Oh, I'm so glad to see you." He had grown, her scrawny little boy. Benjie was not as tall as she, but he was lean, and as the kids on the Antares said, 'mean.' He was Antares' science officer and often served as instructor at the Academy on Acheron.

After kissing her on the lips, he asked, "Are you staying out of trouble, sister?"

"Sabrina? Are you kidding," Sargon said, coming up behind her. He caught Sirtis just as she flung herself into his arms. Sirtis, the same age as Jason, was Sargon's daughter by his wife, Chantar.

"Big Sister," Benjie said, wagging his finger at her, "I think we need to have a talk. I need a good example for my daughter. I don't know if you make the grade," he teased her, and finally released her from his embrace.

"Your daughter?" Sabrina asked, and looked at Chiara. Benjie, after seeing Chiara only a very short time on Antares, had fallen hopelessly in love with her.

"Hi Sabrina," Chiara, in turn, embraced Sabrina. "Yes, we have a daughter. Sizzy, come let Sabrina see Noel."

Sizzy was Serenity's youngest daughter, and she was in human form. Sizzy's paternal parentage was much speculated about, because Sizzy, unlike Serenity, exhibited feelings. She also knew how to relate to people. In her human form, she appeared to be a bubbly ten-year-old. Serenity had wanted her to learn about humans, so she attended school on the Antares.

Sizzy stepped forward carrying a three-year-old girl. "Hi Sabrina," Sizzy said, "You want to hold Noel?"

"Hello Noel, would you like for me to hold you?" Sabrina asked. But Noel turned her head and hugged Sizzy tighter.

"I guess after she knows you better, she will come to you," Sizzy assured her. "Little kids are like that . . . shy."

"Thank you, Sizzy. I think you're right."

"Where's my mother?" Sizzy asked. "She wanted me to come to her, but I can't see her."

"Let's go and see about Serenity," Sabrina invited everyone. She reached for Sirtis, "Let go of you father for a second, and come and give me a hug, Sweetie." After Sirtis had been born, Sargon had asked Sabrina to bond with Sirtis since Chantar did not have the necessary PSI abilities to tune into her. Sabrina was bonded to Sirtis as Sargon was to her two boys.

"Hi Sabrina," Sirtis said. "You know I don't get to see him often enough, so when I have him, I like to hold onto him as long as I can."

Logan lined up on the other side of Sargon, "That's a fact," he said, joining in his sister's complaint.

With his arms around Sirtis and Logan's shoulders, Sargon walked toward the beach. "Let's see about your mother, Sizzy."

The three men stood a little aside in a group, and Larry, still recovering from Serenity's attack, joined them, standing on somewhat wobbly legs.

Ed approached Sabrina." Miss," he said hesitantly, "I heard your speech yesterday in the Auditorium. When you talked about different forms of life, were you talking about that spider, too?"

"Yes, and other forms. Serenity is only one of them."

Sabrina looked down at Sizzy who was leaning against her. She had wriggled her hand into Sabrina's.

209

Ed smiled at her. Such a pretty little girl, he thought. "Are you afraid of Spiders?" he asked, and patted her on the head.

"No," she answered him matter of fact, "I think they're nice."

Before Ed could asked another question, Serenity had decided to emerge and her form erupted from the sand.

Suddenly, Sizzy's form blurred and she scuttled in her spider form toward her mother.

Ed nearly fainted.

Sabrina caught him by the arm and had him sit down in the sand. "Ed, out there are many surprises," she told him, and pointed toward the sky.

"No wonder she wasn't afraid of spiders," he remarked dryly.

Sabrina chuckled, "Neither are my kids."

"Well, you got one that turns into a cat," Ed remarked, looking at Jason. "Turning into a spider probably doesn't look strange to you."

"By the way," Sargon remarked as he approached, "Why didn't you tell me about Jason's talent?"

"I didn't know, until he jumped on top of me," Sabrina said. "I was going to ask you the same question."

"You didn't?"

"No. Honestly."

"Logan!" his father bellowed. When Logan came running, Sargon nailed him with a stare. "How long did you know that Jason could change shape?" he asked.

"Oh . . . well," Logan said, scratching the top of his head. "You see, there was this kitty in my chair, and I tried to give it back to Meghan, but she said it didn't belong to her. Then, suddenly it turned into Jason. I was never so surprised in my whole life," Logan concluded.

"I guess you were," Sargon replied dryly.

"How old was he?" Sabrina asked.

"Oh, about three, I think."

"And you two thought to have fun?"

"Well, Mom, what's a brother to do, you know?" He threw up both hands and shrugged his shoulders.

"So there are even surprises for you." Ed chuckled.

Sargon turned to him, but before he could say anything, a hum was coming from the sky. A craft, looking like a giant blob with spidery legs, settled down on the beach.

"God, alive!" Ed exclaimed, "What's next?"

It was Serenity's ship. As soon as it landed, she and Sizzy boarded and it took off again.

"I see they are on their way home." Sabrina said. "I wondered why Serenity stayed so long."

"She was waiting for Sizzy," Heiko said, as he stopped next to Sargon.

"You know about those spiders too?" Ed asked him.

"Spiders and other not so pleasant-looking beings," Heiko replied.

"I don't know if I want to go out there," Ed said, shaking his head. "I think I will go back to human civilization," and pointed toward the hotel. "I think I need a stiff drink."

Sargon laughed. "I guess you could use one. But before you do anything, get your friend, Larry, here to eat a big meal. He might not feel hungry, but it's important he eats, okay."

"What happened?" Heiko asked.

"Larry interrupted Serenity's hunt, so she got him instead, "Sargon informed him.

Heiko let out a long, drawn-out whistle. "Does Larry remember?"

211

"No, I don't think so. His subconscious probably blocked out what happened. He may remember later. I would have him looked at by a psychiatrist."

"I will inform the medical staff."

"Ed, would you mind taking Larry and the others back to the hotel."

"I don't mind at all," Ed said, shaking his head, "I had enough surprises for one day."

Sargon and Heiko laughed as they watched Ed and company drive off.

In the meantime, Jason was chasing Sirtis, edging her toward the water when Sirtis suddenly grabbed him and dragged him in.

She came up sputtering. "Of all the dirty tricks!" Sirtis said outraged, hitting the water with her flat hand

"What happened?" Sargon asked, amused.

"That bum turned into a fish," she said, affronted. She naturally knew all about Jason's talent, and like Logan, had kept mum about it.

Sargon glanced at Sabrina who stood wordless, like she was thunderstruck.

Her eyes darted to Sirtis, "Of all the bombshells, that tops it. And no one ever let me in on it." Sabrina told her, aggrieved. Stalking toward the water, she began shucking her sweat suit and tossed it out of the water's reach.

Heiko, moving toward Sargon, paused. Then Sargon heard him suck in his breath. He quickly looked at Heiko and couldn't help grinning, Heiko stood transfixed. Sabrina was tall, sleek, with long and slender legs. Her small breasts were round and firm. She was tan all over.

Before she jumped in, Sargon quipped, "Don't let that fish bite you."

Sabrina only gave him a baleful look and swam with clean flashing arm-strokes out to a platform anchored off shore, while Logan, Jason and Sirtis played along the water's edge, dodging the waves.

There was a light breeze and the morning clouds were beginning to dissipate. The water was still cold, but the sun was now midway in the sky, making the air comfortably warm. A little off to one side, Benjie, Heiko and Sargon stripped. Sabrina watched from the platform as they swam out to join her.

After the three men were contentedly stretched out, Sabrina propped her foot on Sargon's rump so she could examine where a splinter had been jammed into her toe when she pulled herself on to the wooden platform.

"I don't think I can pull it out," she commented, running her finger gently over the injured digit

"Let me see," Sargon said, and Sabrina proffered her foot for him to inspect. "No, I don't think so, either," he told her.

Heiko was amused by the intimacy Sabrina showed toward Sargon. But his amusement turned to astonishment when the splinter came out, seemingly all by itself.

Concentrating on the splinter, Sabrina used body control to eject it. She then contently moved her head on Sargon's back until it was in a more comfortable position.

Gazing up into the sky and feeling the gentle sway of the platform, Sabrina began to relax and spin a daydream. When her eyes fell on Benjie and Heiko, she began to weave them into her fantasy. As her thoughts wandered lazily over Heiko's body, she invaded his drowsy mind and initiated sexual images.

Sargon, suddenly aware of her activity, gave her a resounding slap on the thigh.

Sabrina catapulted into a sitting position and grinned sheepishly at him.

"Not fair," Sargon said, shaking an admonitory finger at her. "Go cool off."

Sabrina rose, and diving into the water, swam toward the shore.

"She did that to me?" Heiko asked. He had finally connected Sargon's reaction to his daydream about Sabrina.

"Sorry about that, Heiko."

"Heiko grinned, "Oh, I didn't mind."

*   *   *

After taking a shower, Sabrina dressed and came down for breakfast. She met her sons coming from the breakfast bar with loaded plates. When she raised an eyebrow, "We're growing boys," Logan reminded her.

Sabrina sat down across from Sargon, but he ignored her as he talked to Chiara. When Heiko joined them, his chair touched Sabrina's, so she moved a fraction.

Reaching idly for a strand of her hair, Heiko began to finger it, then tugged her head toward him, "One only needs to ask," he told her. "It would be a pleasure to oblige."

Sabrina stiffened. His breath was in her face. She closed her eyes and felt the horror rising inside. Instead of it being exciting, his nearness brought on fear and the dreadful memories of the rape so long ago. Before Sargon could move, Logan inserted himself between Heiko and his mother.

"Move over," he told his mother curtly, then looked at Heiko," If you don't mind, Sir," and sat down between them. He had clearly read his mother's panic relating to Heiko's attention.

Later that day, Heiko asked Sargon if he had misread Sabrina's message.

"I'm sorry Sabrina chose you to engage in her first attempt at reaching out." When Heiko gave him an uncomprehending look, Sargon explained further. "Sabrina was once severely beaten and gang-raped. I think this is the first time she had engaged in any fantasy of that sort."

"Why did Logan feel he had to intercede?"

"Heiko, Logan is very aware of his mother's feelings, and immediately felt her panic, as I did."

"You mean he knew what was going on?" Heiko asked with incredulity.

"No. He knows when she's sad, or happy, or in danger. Logan responded to her emotional reaction."

"I see. I'm deeply sorry. Had I known, I would not have teased her. It must be a terrible nightmare when that happens to a woman. Will she be all right?" Heiko asked, sincerely concerned. He loved women. To him they were companions to share one's life with. What he didn't tell Sargon that he was married to three women.

"Would it be all appropriate to apologize to Sabrina?"

Later, Heiko did just that. As they walked along the beach, talking, Sabrina told him about the rape and how difficult it had been just surviving day by day. Heiko talked to her about his wives and what they meant to him. When he mentioned that he had three wives, Sabrina stopped in mid-stride and looked at him. "You don't say! And they all live peacefully together?"

Heiko flung his head back and laughed. "That would be a miracle I think. All three are quite different. My first wife owns an estate and does not tolerate any interference in its management. It is the reason she married me. I have no idea

215

about running such an enterprise. My second wife is a trial judge. She is very busy and does not desire a full-time husband. So I fill that description. I'm not home very much. My third wife is a diplomat, the same as I."

"Do they know about each other?"

Again Heiko laughed. "Yes of course. They each have a child and naturally want the children to know one another."

"But how do you arrange meeting them?"

"They get in contact with me and we arrange an assignation." As he said it, a broad grin split his face.

Sabrina paused thoughtfully, "I see. This is very interesting," she conceded.

Heiko took her hand and kissed her fingertips. "It would also have been interesting knowing you. You are a very beautiful and desirable woman."

Sabrina gave him a long look, then, smiled.

When they parted, they parted as friends.

Chapter 23

Next morning, her boys, her friends, everyone was gone. Sabrina didn't have the heart to stay on New Atlantis. As soon as a flight became available, she boarded a plane to return to the Dehners.

When Martha pulled the door opened, she stood holding the handle, pointing an accusing finger, "Mary, indeed!" She exhaled gustily, her mouth twitched. "Now you're finally found out, Sabrina." Giving her a critical once-over, "You know Sabrina really fits you much better. Mary was a much too tame a name."

Sabrina leaned against the door post, laughing. "I see you're keeping up with the news."

"Yes, so we no longer will be calling you Mary. Did you have a good time?"

"Yes. My two sons were there, so I got to be with them for a couple of days."

"Where are they now?"

"They had to go back to school, Martha."

"How old are they, then?"

"Logan is fifteen and Jason is fourteen. Jason will be joining the Cadets this year, so all my kids will have flown the nest," Sabrina said somewhat sadly.

"Come in off the stoop. We can't have you blubbering in front of the whole neighborhood."

She led Sabrina into her sunny kitchen.

"A cup of tea, I think, would be in order," Martha said briskly, and went about putting on the kettle. "After it came out in the news about you and the United Nation, Robert told me what you have been up to. You must be about the bravest person in the whole world." After she said it, she gave Sabrina a funny look, "I guess I shouldn't have mentioned it."

Sabrina smiled. "Martha my love, I had a lot of help. I didn't accomplish any of it alone."

"But still."

"It's my job, Martha."

"I heard that, too. You're a Captain."

"Among other things. Most of all, I'm a mother."

"What's your husband doing?"

"I don't have one."

"You mean your boys don't have a father?"

"Oh, one has, and his father looks after both."

"Oh, I see," she said slowly and poured the tea.

"I think I better tell you, or you'll have a lot of erroneous impressions."

As they sat drinking tea, Sabrina told Martha about her life on the Antares, about Sargon and her sons. The afternoon went by and Martha was just getting up to turn on the lights, when Robert walked in.

"Ah, there you are," he said to Sabrina, "I was told to expect you."

"Hi Robert, I'm glad to see you too," Sabrina said. "I didn't know Earth people disregarded the niceties of greeting friends."

"I'm sorry. I'm just angry. I thought to have you around for a while, but I have orders for you to join the Constitution."

"Whose orders?" Sabrina asked curtly, her irritation clearly showing in her face.

"Doeros."

"Who requested my presence on the Constitution?"

"A Commander McPherson."

"Ian? I'm going to make him a head shorter," Sabrina stormed. "Could I call the Station?" and immediately added, "I'll pay."

"No, no, it's all right," Robert said quickly, but was relieved because the cost was stiff for a call from Earth to the Space Station.

Sabrina dialed and had Ian paged. When he came on screen, "Ian, how would you like to acquire a shiner?" she asked, her anger clearly visible to him.

"Sabrina I would na have doon it, but I need ya. It's her maiden voyage, and with those Altruscan contraptions, I'm not too easy about em. Sabrina, if you come, I would na mind two black eyes."

"But why Doeros?"

"Weel, otherwise you would na have come."

"I still need to find Elisheba. The more time passes, the harder it will be to locate her."

"Only this one time," Ian begged.

"You owe me."

"Until me dying days," he said, placing his hand to his heart.

"I'll be there," she said, and hung up.

She dialed the operator and asked for the charge. "Sorry Martha, duty calls, as the asinine cliché goes."

"Well, so it won't be a complete loss, why don't we go and eat out?" Robert suggested.

*   *   *

Two days later, Sabrina arrived in the Shuttle-bay of the Constitution. There was no courtesy reception, only Ian waiting for her. She wore her Antarean uniform and when she looked at Ian's jeans, and polo shirt, she gave him a cold glare. "Are you assigned to the Constitution?" she asked him curtly. When he shook his head, "You are out of uniform, Mister," she told him icily.

Ian knew she wasn't going to let him forget, and she was also going to make a point to the Captain for failing to show her the courtesy of receiving her. She was going to make him wear the Antarean uniform. Ian came to attention and said, "Yes, Sir."

"The Captain knows that I'm here?"

"Yes, I told him that I requested you through Doeros."

"Okay, let's go to Engineering."

"Don't you want to deposit yer duffle-bag first? We share cabins," Ian informed her with a broad grin.

Sabrina wasn't going to pick up on this banter. She only looked at him. "Lead on," she said.

His cabin was small and contained only one bunk. When she looked at him with one raised eyebrow, he assured her quickly, saying, "I requisitioned a cot for me to sleep on."

"All right," she said, and dropped her duffle bag. "What now?"

"Have you had anything to eat yet?"

"Nope. I came as soon as I could arrange transport."

"Let's go to the cafeteria first," Ian suggested.

"After you get into uniform, Mister."

Ian gave her a long, suffering look, but did as she ordered. While he dressed, she put her things away.

220

When they entered the cafeteria, they received curious stares from everyone. Before they had time to sit, Captain Daniels walked up to the table.

"Ian, what's up?" he asked, looking at his uniform.

"Sir, I was ordered by my commanding officer to get into uniform."

Captain Daniels looked questioningly at Sabrina. "Ma'am, would you please explain?" he asked, civil enough, but underneath, Sabrina could sense his affront.

"Very simply," she told him evenly. "First, if I am in uniform, I am addressed as Sir. Secondly, Ian is not assigned to the Constitution. As an Antarean officer, he was out of uniform."

Daniels scanned her uniform for indication of rank and said, "You and he are not wearing any insignias."

"On the Antares, it isn't needed. To non-Antareans, if you look it up, the color orange along my collar marks me as an officer. The insert says that I have the highest rank attainable on the Antares. Also, because of my other qualifications in the Alliance, I outrank any captain on any Alliance ship. If you wish to launch a complaint, do so to Admiral Okada. McPherson's orange marking on the tip of his collar also marks him as an officer. His rank is Commander. Now if you please, I would like to sit. I think we attracted enough attention."

To Sabrina's satisfaction, Daniels looked discomfited and now understood that he had been greatly remiss.

Once Daniels was seated, he asked, "Are you taking command of my ship?"

"No Captain. I'm here to help McPherson with the engines since I can read the Altruscan ideographs better than he."

"We are to be underway in three hours," Daniels said, checking his watch. "If you will excuse me?" He rose and quickly left.

"Did you have to pin his ears back like that?" Ian griped.

"Yes, he's been remiss in checking his personnel. Did you notice his surprise when I told him you were a commander?"

"I noticed. But you see, I never made it a point to tell him either."

"Still, he should have known."

*   *   *

"Shut her down, Ian, shut her down," came Sabrina's frantic shout.

The scaffolding had been removed and the lifeline to the Station reeled in. The engines just started and as the ship slowly accelerated, Sabrina gave her muffled shout.

Ian obeyed instantly.

"McPherson! What's going on?" the Captain called from the Bridge.

"I think we have a problem," Ian informed him.

There had been a small flicker on the analog dial. A gut feeling told Sabrina to take it seriously. Her first thought was sabotage. Knowing the Altruscans hunger for revenge, it could not be ruled out. She swung under the console, going though wiring and running her fingers over the modular units to feel for any irregularities. After going from console to console she pulled herself up into the service crawl-ways and inspected all the wiring bundles. Nothing. She was getting frantic, because the Constitution was beginning to float out of the station, and soon was going to hit something or drift. She even inspected the air shaft. Puzzled she came back down, and nearly landed on top of Captain Daniels.

"Why did you belay engine start?" Daniels asked.

"Because I saw a flicker on the analog dial that should not have been there. Now leave me alone, so I can think."

"Lady, you might outrank me, but you will have this ship on its way." Before he could finish, Sabrina, gave him a distracted look and vanished before his eyes. He stared at Ian, who only shrugged like it was an everyday occurrence.

Sabrina had raised her vibration as Sabot shown her and reappeared in the station observatory. She quickly scanned the people who were waiting to see the Spaceship float out into space.

Got you, she thought. She had spotted the Altruscan. He was eager to see the Earthling's ship blow. He was also getting a bit edgy because the Constitution was still not all the way out of the hangar.

Sabrina rifled through his thoughts and found the information she needed: two devises, their identity, and their location. Also, he had a detonator-switch implanted in his chest, just underneath the muscle. One of the devices was in the Engine Room, and on the ship was a very uncomfortable young girl tied up in a lavatory wired with an explosive.

Shouts of surprise erupted from many of the people standing around the windows as Sabrina grabbed the Altruscan from behind and yanked him backwards. To prevent him from contracting his chest muscles, she broke both of his shoulder blades. Turning him over, she slammed him to the floor with her knee pressed against his Adam's apple. Then she took the knife from her boot and cut into the muscle. He fainted from the pain when she dug with her hand into his chest and carefully lifted the device out.

Her actions had been so swift she was done before anyone could react. Once the people saw the gadget in her hand, no one tried to interfere with her. She removed her knee from his throat and finally took a look at him. She remembered him. She moved off slightly to one side and everyone watched as she squatted on her haunches and began to carefully disable the contraption.

In the meantime the Altruscan regained consciousness and when she looked at him, she saw that he remembered her. His eyes were ablaze with fury. He spit at her. Dodging the spittle, she rose and kicked him in his groin. Groaning with pain, he arched his back to kick at her, but she hit him with her foot so hard his head bounced off the floor. Then she bent down, grabbed him from behind and broke his neck. She quickly walked away, ignoring the horrified exclamations.

On one of her previous mission with Miri and Lara he had been one of her tormentors.

Sabrina went into the ladies' room to wash her hands and to disappear. She materialized back on the Constitution.

Entering engineering she demanded, "Ian, give me your satchel. There is a small ampoule with a helium molecule in the antimatter injection chamber. I think you can get to it without my help. Captain, please follow me," she said to the flabbergasted Daniels. To a young ensign she said, "Tell the doctor to come to the head on the far end of deck four, and to bring his bag and a gurney"

To her surprise, Daniels followed her without commenting.

Entering the head, she went to the stall on the far end and when she opened the door, she was still shocked by what she found. A young female ensign, with the bottom part of her uniform missing, was gagged and her back was tied to the water pipe. She was barely alive. She looked up at Sabrina, her eyes nearly insane with fear.

"I'm Sabrina. Don't be afraid. I know about the device. I can disarm it. So be patient just a little longer." Sabrina gently removed the tape from her mouth.

The doctor coming up at the door, blanched, "Oh my god," he exclaimed.

"Doc, I need some gel for my hand. Come on. Don't gape, do it," she told him impatiently as he hesitated. Somewhat confused, he did as he was asked. Sabrina looked at the girl, "Since we are going to get very familiar, I would like to know your name?

A ghost of a smile came and was quickly gone. "Jenny," she said, barely audible through her dried lips.

"Jenny, this is going to be very uncomfortable. I will try not to hurt you more than I have to. You will need to hold very still. You think you can do this for me?"

When Jenny nodded, Sabrina inserted her fingers into Jenny's the vagina, and feeling along the device, found the two prongs. Jenny held still, but her rapid breathing and the sweat running down her face told Sabrina that she was in extreme pain. Bending the prongs inward, she slowly pulled the devise out.

"Captain, hold this very carefully. Don't even move it an inch. "Now Jenny," she said to the girl, "sit still for me just a little longer. Doc, pull a rubber glove over my hand." Sabrina reached down into the messy bowl. Fear had loosened Jenny's bowels, so Sabrina had to feel her way around for the detonator. She found the wire and using a laser cutter separated the detonator from the explosive that had been jammed up inside the girl.

"Now you can dispose of it," she told Daniels, as he moved aside to let Sabrina get out. "Doc, you can remove Jenny." Then smiling she added, "Take good care of her, she has been a very brave girl. And Captain, if you get a query from the space station, tell them to contact Commodore Doeros. Tell him the name is Sabrina Hennesee."

When Daniels gave her a confused look, she told him, "That's all Doeros needs to know."

Before going up in the elevator, she hit the intercom, "Ian, did you get that contraption."

"Aye lass, I got it oot," he replied.

"Good, let's get this ship underway."

*　　*　　*

The elevator door hissed open and Sabrina walked onto the Bridge, ignoring the stares and whispers.

"Now, how would you like to put this baby through its paces?" she asked Captain Daniels.

"I've been waiting for you to give the word," he replied.

She activated the intra-ship communications. "Now hear this. We will be going through training maneuvers. They will hold surprises even for your captain. So look sharp." Then switching to the Engine Room, "Ian, give Mister Brandon his engines," she said, "It's time he's coming into his own."

"Aye, Sir," Ian replied.

"Mister Brandon, give me warp three," Sabrina said.

"Aye . . ." there was a small hesitation in Brandon's voice before he said, "Sir."

Sabrina's mouth twitched, as she leaned over the navigational console. "Lieutenant," she told the navigator, "for now, the computer will take over, so only react to compensate where necessary." Turning to Daniels, "I programmed several maneuvers in to test the ship, and also the crew's reaction."

The ship accelerated smoothly. Sabrina had programmed three programs into the computer, all surprises. Since this was her maiden voyage, the Constitution only carried essential crew.

Sabrina had just gone to check a reading on the engineering console when the ship's surgeon and Ian walked in.

Daniels swiveled his chair around. "I know you have met. But still, let me introduce Don Shaw, our ship's surgeon. Don, this is Captain Sabrina Hennesee."

Doc Shaw looked at Sabrina and shook his head. "Woman," he said, "you look like death warmed over. Let me do something for you, if it's only to prescribe a little sack time."

"He has nice bedside manners," Sabrina remarked to Daniels. "But thanks. I'll stay until the maneuvers are over and know the engine's performance comes off all right. We can't have any more glitches."

"Lady, I don't think you heard me. I can order you off this Bridge when I decide it's in your best interest."

"I know that, Doctor, but I'll stay until I'm finished."

When Shaw tried to persist, Ian laid a hand on his arm, "Don," he said, "the Captain knows her capacities and limits; best leave her be."

When Shaw ran his med-scanner over her, he received the shock of his life. He rechecked the reading twice.

Sabrina, noticing his shocked reaction, gave him a fraction of a smile. "Nothing wrong with your scanner," she assured him. She knew her reading wouldn't check quite human. "See, there isn't much you can do for me anyhow."

But he was right . . . she felt like death warmed over. The altercation had drained her. Taking a life, even an Altruscan's,

227

was never easy on her. Meeting him again had reawakened memories and old fears. To turn in right now wouldn't guarantee sleep. She was afraid of nightmares. Working in familiar surroundings and being busy gave her time to readjust.

She put the ship and crew through its paces. Her commands were terse, to the point, and given in a soft but clear, audible voice.

After the Captain gave the stand down for the crew, Sabrina stretched and left the engineering station on the Bridge and went to the Mess Hall. She sat in the farthest corner, just wanting to be alone. After she finished eating, she went to Ian's cabin. He was already asleep on his cot. Exhausted, she threw herself down on the bed, staring wide-eyed at the ceiling. When sleep finally came, so did the nightmares. She tossed and turned and cried out in a loud, piercing scream. Someone passed the door and called Doc Shaw.

Ian awoke immediately and jumped from his cot. He squatted beside Sabrina. Her face was contorted with an odd mixture of fear and hatred and he wondered what nightmare she was reliving. Suddenly there was a knock at the door.

"Ian, it's me," Doc Shaw called out.

Ian opened the door, but blocked his entry. "Don, don't interfere. She's not quite human, and she could hurt you.

"But man, I can't just stand here and do nothing."

"I know the feeling, but that's precisely what you must do."

As they spoke, Sabrina's tossing and moaning subsided, and her face smoothed out. During the nightmare, her mind had called for Sargon and Karsten. Their never-failing presence enveloped Sabrina with feelings of love and peace.

"I am here," Sargon sent. "You are not alone."

"I love you, Sabrina child," Karsten sent. He knew it always elicited a smile from her, and he didn't fail this time. Dreaming, she smiled. They remained with her until her dreaming became peaceful.

Ian received a mental message from Sargon, telling him that Sabrina would be all right now. Ian smiled at the Doc, "I told you so. See, she's all right."

Don Shaw gave him an inscrutable look, and harrumphed. "I better get acquainted with alien physiology, or I'm going to feel as useless as a fifth wheel on a wagon. Know anyone who could give me the help I need?"

"Maybe. I could talk Sarah into berthing on the Constitution," Ian mused. She's an expert on alien physiology."

"She's anything like Captain Hennesee?"

"No, she's all human."

Later, Don reported to Captain Daniels that Captain Hennesee was staying in Ian's cabin. But when he wanted to help, he was prevented by Ian.

Next morning, Daniels went to see Ian in his cabin. He heard a commotion inside. When the door opened, Ian was wearing only a towel wrapped around his middle. From the bathroom came the sound of running water and a set of ladies' underwear was lying on the bed.

Daniels looked shocked.

Ian chuckled. "It's not what you think, Sir." he assured the blushing Captain. "Like you can see, I slept on the cot."

"Ian, who's in here?" came Sabrina's voice from the bathroom.

"Captain Daniels just walked in," he informed her. Then, turning to Daniels asked, "Which one of us do you want to see?"

"Well, I wanted to see you. But I guess it can wait."

Just as Daniels turned to leave, Sabrina's acrimonious voice demanded, "Ian, stop chattering and start handing me my clothes, before I come out minus this towel."

"Okay lass, keep your towel on."

"Since when are you concerned about that anyway?" was Sabrina's retort.

Ian's eyes danced as he looked at Daniels. "She's a devil of a tease, but don't ever overstep your bounds. The lady is dressed, even if she's stark naked. Get my drift? She's staying in my cabin because no one was provided for her."

"You mean . . ." Daniels began.

"Yes. There were no accommodations ready for the lady."

"Damn," Daniels muttered.

"Yea, an oversight, and she won't forget it either."

Sabrina came out of the shower, fully dressed. "Captain Daniels, how nice to see you," she said sweetly. "Is there anything we can help you with?"

Ian winced, but to his surprise, Sabrina behaved herself.

Daniels replied, "In three hours we will arrive back at the Space Station and you are invited to a party.

*   *   *

After the party, Daniels invited Sabrina to visit a night club on the station. Ian had found companionship elsewhere.

When the waiter came, Daniels asked," What would you like to drink?"

"A glass of red wine would do nicely."

They talked for a while. Neither wanted to touch on the Altruscan incident.

The band played old rock and roll music. Daniels looked at Sabrina. "Do you dance?" he asked.

"Of course," she said, and let him lead her out on the dance floor. Daniels discovered that Sabrina danced well. When the band took up a slower rhythm, they stayed on the floor. Suddenly they kissed. Sabrina never remembered if she kissed him or he kissed her. But it didn't matter. She rested her head on his shoulder and they moved with the rhythm. It was morning before he took her to her hotel room. He followed her inside. As she stood by the mirror to remove her earrings, he put his arms around her, reaching upwards to cup her breasts.

Instantly, she stiffened, and arched her back to push herself away from him. She spun around, assuming a defensive position. She was shaking all over.

He looked at her, startled. "What have I done?" he asked, incredulous.

Sabrina stood silent with her head bowed, and still in the ward-off position, sent out a mind-call for Ian.

Only a moment passed before the door burst open and Ian came in at a run. Shooting a glance at Daniels, then at Sabrina, he quickly came to her side. Putting his arms around her, "Lass," he said gently, lifting her face, "Everything's okay. I'm here." Then to Daniels, "Sir, you better leave."

"Tell me first . . . what did I do?" he asked her again.

"Nothing, Sir. It's not you. She's the one having difficulties."

Ian guided Sabrina to her bed and had her lie down.

Before Daniels was through the door, Sabrina looked at him from the bed. "Peter, not your fault," she told him. "Bad memories."

After the door closed, Sabrina breathed out slowly. "Ian thanks for coming," she told him. "I'm all right. You can go now."

"Not so fast. Did he try to get fresh with you?" Ian asked as he sat down beside her on the bed and brushed back her hair.

"No, of course not."

"Did you lead him on?"

Sabrina said nothing.

Ian, of course, knew of the rape and guessed that Sabrina had tried to reach out. There was still that lingering aversion.

Her face was white and drawn. Anxious, he tried to read her emotions. Not having Sargon's talents, the only thing he could do was scold her with, "Lass, don't you scare me like that again."

Sabrina gave him a wane smile.

"I'm not Sargon, but from your reaction I sense you have never put the rape behind you."

"Ian!" she warned.

"Don't Ian me. You're still caught up emotionally. You haven't dealt with it."

There was an angry glare as she raised herself on her elbow. "When do you think I had time? I had to deal with one disaster after another. You remember that slip of a girl who turned out to be a shape-shifter? Had it not been for Sabot, I would not have had Jason. Maybe I would not have been alive either. Then I had to raise two children by myself, plus I had the Antares. Then there was Sarah's problem. Then I've been assigned to check out Earth. And do you know what happened here? There was a nest of shape-shifters that had to be cleaned out. And then I had to kill that damned Altruscan!"

Her voice had risen and the iron control on her emotions nearly broke. But seeing Ian's woebegone face she softened and relented. "I know. You're right. I haven't taken the time."

"Lass, I only said it because I care about you."

"I know."

"You think you can sleep?"

"I'll try."

Before he left the room, he turned back for one more look, but Sabrina dismissed him with, "Good night, Ian, and thanks."

Next morning, she saw Daniels walk into the breakfast room and watched him curiously as he approached.

He felt awkward and hesitated for a moment before asking, "Can I sit with you?"

She smiled, hoping it would put him at ease. "I would love your company," she told him.

Reaching out with his hand, "Friends?"

"Yes Peter, friends," she said and taking his hand, pulled him down for a kiss

Chapter 24

After leaving the Constitution, Sabrina reported to Doeros on the matter of the Altruscan, and for once, she was civil to him. Then she left for Israel to begin her search for Elisheba.

Sabrina vividly remembered her first command. They had been mining for ores and minerals, and cut timber on a sparsely populated continent. Toward the end of their stay, Elisheba had been abducted by natives. They had come suddenly upon her, and as she fled, rode her down on their horses. She had been captured as a present to their chief. When he tried to play with his new toy, using what little martial art she knew, she viciously kicked him. Incensed and in pain, he had her beaten and then raped. Later, the chief had her staked out on a hill infested with insects that reminded Sabrina of ants, but looked more like scorpions.

She, Yoshi, Benjie and Kara had arrived just in time. Disregarding Sargon's order not to use advanced weapons, or the space-crafts, she had called Charlie the Android and commanded him to come in with the Shuttle's engines roaring. On their way back to the Antares, Elisheba's life hung on a thread, her body almost succumbing to the scorpion-ants poison.

Irrationally, Elisheba had turned her anger on Sargon. To give Elisheba space, he sent her to stay with Sarah who interned on Madras. One night, she fled Sarah's home and took a berth on the Doran, a cargo-ship. Sargon tried to find her, but she kept changing ships. Mendes, a friend of Sargon, finally traced her to Haifa.

Using Mendes' the information, Sabrina procured a ride on a windowless cargo plane to Tel Aviv. Sitting next to two people on a long hard bench, the noise of the engines made any conversation impossible. For most of the time Sabrina dozed. She was startled awake by hail and rain pinging on the hull. Worst of all, the turbulence jerked the plane up and down. When the plane dropped several feet, she hoped it meant they were landing. Sabrina felt more than heard the breaks screeching as the wheels slid on the wet tarmac.

The landing had been a controlled crash on the rain sleek airstrip that once was a part of the Tel Aviv Airport. Because of the rain, she stayed over. The facilities were scanty. It only contained a hangar, a small cafeteria and sleeping quarters for the crew. There were no guest facilities, but she was furnished with a cot. When one of the young mechanics apologized, she waved him off, telling him that she had slept on worse.

* * *

The next day dawned sunny and bright. The rain had cleansed the air and it smelled fresh and sweet-scented. Driving toward Haifa in a rented vintage car, Sabrina wondered what it must have smelled like before with all the dirty air.

Haifa turned out to be a small fishing village with few houses and a synagogue. But every house had a garden with a white picket fence and flower-boxes full of geraniums on the windows. On the unpaved streets, children played an old hoop game as she drove through the village.

Her first stop was the police station and then the synagogue. But there were no records of an Elisheba Thalon. Lastly she walked through the market-place and then all the small shops lining the main street. Everywhere she went, she showed a picture of Elisheba, but nobody recognized her.

Fairly discouraged, Sabrina began to walk the streets again and in desperation used her extra-sensory awareness. But it was no use. Maybe the Elisheba she knew did not exist anymore. People changed with time.

On her second day, late in the afternoon, on a hunch, she went down to the waterfront. The fishing boats had just come in and a crowd gathered to watch and later haggle over the fishermen's catch. Out of the corner of her eye she noticed something familiar about a heavy set woman with a basket. As the woman bent down to talk to two little girls about five years old, she noticed the peculiar tilting of the head,

Sabrina moved rapidly to get closer.

"Elisheba?" she questioned, looking into a freckled, heavy cheeked face.

Dropping her basket, "Oh my God!" came the startled exclamation. Sabrina hadn't changed at all. She was instantly recognized.

"Oh, Elisheba Love," Sabrina said, embracing her. "Sargon has been looking for you all these years."

"Sargon?" she asked unbelieving. "Why would he look for me? I brought him nothing but disappointment." Her eyes teared up, and sniffling, she searched for a handkerchief.

"Silly woman," Sabrina said, shaking her by the shoulders. Then looking down at the two girls, they were twins, "Your Mom is okay," she reassured them.

Uncomprehending, they stared back at her.

"Don't they speak English?" she asked Elisheba.

"No, they only speak Hebrew. Sabrina, go away, please go away." Her voice was flat, heavy, and hopeless. Ponderously, she picked up her basked and started to shuffle away. Her daughters, their inquisitive eyes glued on Sabrina, slowly followed.

"No, Elisheba," Sabrina said determined. "No, I will not just go away." She caught Elisheba by the arm and made her turn to face her. "Can't we go somewhere to talk?"

Elisheba looked at her, knowing Sabrina would not relent. "My place. My husband won't be home for a while."

Her voice was full of anxiety. Sabrina sensed the unhappiness and suppressed a shudder. There was a feeling of utter hopelessness she knew Elisheba desperately tried to hide.

The house was small, sparsely furnished, but immaculately clean. Elisheba put the basket down on the kitchen table and pointed to a wooden chair. "Do sit down. I don't have anything to offer you," she told Sabrina. "We are poor."

"I came to talk, not to have tea with you. I came to find out how you are faring. I will tell you right from the start, like Sargon, you can't lie to me, or hide your feelings. I already know that your marriage is a very unhappy one. Am I right?"

"You are right, Sabrina, as always," she said tight lipped.

"Yes, I am right, as always. Now tell me what happened after you left the Doran?"

"Sargon traced me to the Doran?" she asked, incredulous.

"No, Sarah traced you to the Doran. But Sargon followed your trail from there to the other ships you boarded, and lastly to a liner, then from Jerusalem to Haifa."

Laying her head on the table, Elisheba wept.

Sabrina waited patiently until she was composed enough to talk.

Elisheba looked at Sabrina with a dark hollowness to her eyes. "I feel like such a fool," she began. "I thought that coming back to Israel, I would be coming home, and everything would be all right. I thought becoming Jewish would make it right with God, and the world would smile on me, and the pain of failure would go away. Then I married a man who belongs to a strict orthodox sect. I tried to live his way. I tried to be an obedient wife. I try to be a good mother. I try so hard, Sabrina. Our life is austere, but that's not it. He is so harsh, so cold. There's no warmth in him. He treats me and the girls correctly, but I can feel that he is disappointed; I didn't give him a son. My life is so lonely . . ." She drifted off.

"And so unhappy," Sabrina finished for her.

"Yes. But I made my bed and I guess I have to lump it," Elisheba said with a crooked smile.

"No, that is where you are dead wrong. I was sent to ask you a question. Sargon asks if you want to stay here, or to come home."

"How can I go home and face him? I have caused him nothing but trouble. I was such a feather-headed fool. I only wanted to have fun. I never learned anything he tried to teach me."

"And that made you feel like a failure?" Sabrina asked harshly. "You were just a young girl at that time. You expect a lot of yourself. What was it that really made you feel you were a failure?"

"I jeopardized your first command."

"That was my problem," Sabrina told her firmly.

"I got myself raped, and I didn't defend myself. I just let them do it to me," Elisheba wailed.

"Elisheba, look at me," Sabrina commanded. She cupped Elisheba's chin in her hand; she made her look up. "I was raped, twice," Sabrina told her. "I couldn't prevent it no more than you did. I carry an enormous pain inside of me that hasn't gone away. I was violated."

Elisheba's look changed from surprise to incredulity. "You?" she asked slowly.

"Yes. Me. The invincible Sabrina, master of the martial arts. Now tell me, what could you have done?"

"Nothing."

"That's the first honest truth you have told yourself," Sabrina said to her. "Now to my next question. Do you want to stay here, or go home?"

Elisheba looked at her wistfully. "Oh, if I just could," she said and then again broke down crying. Her daughters looked confused and frightened as they huddled together on a wooden bench under the window.

Sabrina pointed to the girls, "Do you want them to grow up like the children on the Antares, or you want them to grow up here? They're frightened. Why are your daughters frightened, Elisheba?"

"Their father . . . he is harsh. He demands absolute obedience from them. Most of the time, they are not even allowed to be little girls. This religion . . . I've began to feel is a scourge. Oh Sabrina . . . I don't know."

Suddenly, the door opened and a thin man with a beard and long locks of hair curling down each side of his face entered the room.

Sabrina noticed the girls cower even closer together.

His face darkened as he looked with distaste at his wife's tear-streaked face. "Elisheba," he said harshly, "what is this unseemly display of emotion?" When he looked at the stove, he said astonished, "You have not even prepared dinner. If you want to have company, do it when it is not interfering with our

239

family schedule." he scolded her in Hebrew. "We are to be at the Synagogue in an hour."

Sabrina had followed the conversation with her PSI awareness and she looked him over with an unreadable expression. Then her lips curled and her nostrils flared. She became angry at his surliness. "Well, Elisheba, your choice," she told her as evenly as she could.

Elisheba took a long look at her husband who was feeling self-conscious at Sabrina's harsh, scrutinizing stare.

"Woman, you are to leave. We have no time for idle chatter," he told Sabrina.

After translating for Sabrina, Elisheba suddenly began to giggle uncontrollably. "We have no time to chatter, Sabrina," she repeated inanely. Then it was as if for the first time she focused and a ray of hope crept into her eyes. "Possible?" she asked Sabrina.

"Would I be here otherwise?"

Elisheba rose, and getting her daughters, she told Sabrina, "Let's go. They have a right to a happier way of growing up."

"That's the stuff, kiddo," Sabrina answered back.

When they tried to leave, her husband barred the door.

To his utter astonishment Elisheba told him in Hebrew, "Yussuf, get your butt out of my way!" He winced at the warning in her voice, and stood there in disbelief.

"Where are you going?" he demanded. "What is going on?"

"I'm going home," she told him. "The girls and I are leaving."

He spread his arms across the door, "But you can't. You and I belong together."

Sabrina took his arms and pinned them to his side. "Elisheba, say it in Hebrew, so your girls will understand too, okay." Sabrina then used the Acheron formula of disengagement. "Tell him, Yussuf you are divorced. You are free. Find someone else to share your life. I'm going home with Sabrina." And to Elisheba, "You need to pack. Do you want to take any toys," pointing her chin toward the girls.

"They don't have any toys," Elisheba told her sadly. "It's frivolous. God has forbidden it."

When they left, he followed them into the street, berating her, exhorting her not to forgo her religious beliefs, or blaspheme God by leaving him. One of the girls broke loose from her mother's grip, and putting both hands to her ears, fled.

Sabrina sprinted after her and picked her up. She hugged her, stroking her hair. "It's going to be all right," she told her mind to mind, and when the girl looked at her in astonishment, Sabrina laughed. Lifting her into the air, she repeated orally, "It's going to be all right."

They drove back to the air strip at Tel Aviv in the old, but good vintage car. From the office she called Dehner to see if there were any messages.

"Several, Sabrina," he told her. "One says Scout I is orbiting Earth, and Benjie wants you to call him when you've found Elisheba. The other is from the Space Station. You are to report to the Constitution. It's about an Ambassador named, Elkatma?"

There was an unmistakable noise on his end, but Dehner still asked, "What was that?"

"Nothing, just letting off steam. I want to go home. I have two boys I want to see. I hate when he does this to me. I don't . . . aw . . . never mind. Robert, I'll see you when I get there. Thanks. Bye."

To Sabrina's and the twin's astonishment, Elisheba broke into laughter.

"What's so funny?" Sabrina asked, irritated.

"Sabrina Love, you just made me feel like I'm home already. It was just like old times."

"Well, if it made you feel good, it was worthwhile. I still need to blow off steam once in a while."

Sabrina activated her communicator bracelet and contacted the Scout. A female voice responded. She told her to inform Lieutenant Hennesee, that Captain Hennessey needs a shuttle to pick her and party up at the Tel Aviv air strip."

An hour later, the shuttle, piloted by Benjie, landed and the little girls eyes grew like saucers.

"Are we going on that?" Leah asked. "Oh Mommy, are we going out into space?"

The other twin, Ruth, said, "This going to be so exiting. Are we going to see the stars?"

When Elisheba came on board, Benjie looked startled for a moment. "Boy, there's a lot of you there," he said not too delicately.

Elisheba looked ruefully down at her body, "Will the extra pounds make a difference to lift off?"

"Oh girl, it's good to have you back." Benjie hugged her and landed a kiss smack on her mouth. Her daughters looked scandalized. Their mother was doing the unimaginable; kissing. Not just kissing, but kissing a strange man!

Sabrina gleaned their reaction from their minds and began to laugh. Then she told Elisheba what her daughters had been thinking.

"They're going to have a lot to unlearn," Elisheba said. "I earnestly pray that there wasn't too much damage done with all that religion. I hope it's not too late for them."

"It's never too late," Benjie told her. "Now let's go, so I can fill you in on what's happened on the Antares since you left. Come girls, climb in."

When Elisheba started to translate, Benjie gave her a resounding slap on the backside. "You didn't teach them English?" he said, pretending to be outraged.

"I didn't think I would ever get back home."

"Ye of so little faith. Did you think we would forget about you?"

When they arrived above the Air Academy and Benjie was about to beam Sabrina down, she told him, "Have Spitfire readied for me, Lieutenant."

"Little Lady gives big orders," Benjie's grumbled before he engaged the transporter.

Chapter 25

This time, when Sabrina walked onto the Constitution, she received the attention accorded her rank. Captain Daniels and his second in command were there to greet her.

"Captain Hennesee, welcome on board."

"Hello Peter. Nice seeing you again."

"Ambassador Elkatma would like to see you in his quarters at your convenience." Daniels told her. Walking toward the lift he added, "How do you interact with a Chiron?"

"Very carefully," Sabrina quipped, and then laughed at him. "Already having trouble dealing with diplomats?"

"Sabrina, you're full of it. I'm serious. I don't know how to talk to that . . . individual."

"No one clued you in?"

"No. I was only told that I was to take a Chiron Ambassador named Elkatma to Khitan."

"Well, whoever gave you that assignment was very remiss. The Chirons are a telepathic race. It is very painful for them to be among people whose emotions are unchecked and allow their thoughts to run rampant. It takes a lot of effort for them to screen out all of the mental noise you're generating."

"Damn, no wonder he's keeping to his cabin."

"What else were you told I was supposed to do?"

"Ambassador Elkatma probably has the answer to that."

"Thanks, Peter. Now, where do I sleep this time?"

Daniels blushed. "I'm sorry about that. Let me escort you to your cabin first."

Her room turned out to be officers' quarters, nicer and roomier than the one assigned to Ian last time. Sabrina bit her lip. Apparently Ian had been given crew quarters. But then he wore civilian duds. Blue jeans and polo shirts were still in style, even in this century, she mused.

After stowing her meager possessions, Sabrina went in search of Elkatma's cabin. When she arrived at the door, and before she could knock, she heard him say, "Come,"

When she entered, he rose from his desk. "Welcome, Sabrina. I have requested your presence because we need to work out a protocol for dealing with humans."

"Thank you, Elkatma, for your kind consideration and your confidence in me."

"Ah, you had other plans?"

"Yes, my desire was to go home."

"I see. Are humans always so noisy?"

"If you mean their mental activities, yes." When he looked pointedly at her, she gave him a twitch of a smile. "Elkatma, I always had PSI awareness. Captain Thalon developed it and trained me to use it. Also, there was some meddling by Serenity, as you know. I'm the exception to the rule. You will not find many humans with my abilities."

"Then it will be difficult for humans to work with Chirons."

"That needs to be seen. Humans are very adaptable."

"I perceive your attempt at humor," he said, looking benignly at her. He had great respect for her abilities and had learned to tolerate her idiosyncrasies. In his way, he enjoyed her company because she never tried to be other than herself.

He expected her to work right then and there.

She began by explaining common human behavior to him, mannerisms of talking, beliefs, general mode of thinking and emotions. Now the Chirons have deep feelings, but never express them in emotional terms. She also discussed with him her plans to start a handbook for the humans that would help them in dealing with Chirons and other races they would meet in Space.

"Elkatma," she suddenly said, "I will stop now. We can continue tomorrow.

"But we have only started." he said.

"I will be back tomorrow." She left knowing explanations were not welcome, so she gave none. She was tired, and needed to stretch. Also, her stomach was rebellious; she had not eaten since breakfast.

In the Mess Hall, several old acquaintances greeted her. She filled a plate and sat down just as Peter Daniels walked in.

"Sabrina," he said, without preamble, "I received this packet," and tossed it at her.

After she read it, she laughed. "It means you're going to be on display on Khitan. I guess we better get a script together."

*   *   *

Members of the Alliance Security Council were meeting on Khitan to inspect the crew members of the Constitution. They especially wanted to meet the captain to pose a few more questions. Sabrina knew the ones requesting this session had not been overly eager for Earth to join the Alliance. She saw that the Chirons were represented, also Serenity; Acheron was on the side of Earth. It was pure harassment that Helva and Madras still wanted to ask questions even though the treaty with Earth had been ratified. Sargon was conspicuously absent, and Sabrina suspected that it was because of the two vacillating planets. They probably considered him too biased since he was in the forefront in sponsoring Earth.

A week before their approach to Khitan, Sabrina presented Daniels to Elkatma.

"I have tried to coach him on his strategy for dealing with the members of the Security Council. If there is anything you find amiss, I would consider it a kindness if you would counsel me," she said to Elkatma.

"Knowing you, I suspect you were thorough. But should I find something inappropriate, I will inform you."

*   *   *

"Boy, was that unfair!" Daniels complained at the end of the interview.

"I agree; they really grilled you. They were prepared for you to cave in," Sabrina told him. "Let's get something cold to drink."

"Is it always this hot here?"

"For most of the year. Khitan is an arid planet with very little rainfall. Population centers exist only close to underground water sources. Recently, the Chirons contracted the Antares for the water makers; machines that extract moisture from the air. Captain Estel had seen them on the Antares and asked Captain Thalon if they could be manufactured. Individual households now used them for their drinking water.

Later that evening, Capt. Daniels met Sabrina at the Space Port. Unbeknownst to him, this afternoon she had disappeared, and just now landed Spitfire. She took him to see her ship. "Are you impressed?"

"Green with envy," he replied, playfully jostling her.

"You are on Khitan, you must preserve decorum."

"Damn their decorum," he said, and pulled her into his arms. He kissed her passionately. "That's how I feel about you. What do you say to that?"

"My dear, you only have the hots for me. You're just trying to get me to go to bed with you."

"What's wrong with that?"

"I'm not interested in what's wrong with it." When he continued to grip her waist, she slapped him, and ran away.

He ran after Sabrina and catching up with her, both tumbled down a small hill. She laughed and playfully wrestled with him, but suddenly realized that he was getting serious.

"My dear Peter, I thought we were friends?" She warned him.

"Friends be damned. Don't you know I want you?"

"I think we have company," Sabrina told him, pointing toward Estel and Serenity.

Peter knew he was overreacting. But he did not want any interference. He had enough of aliens for one day. He jumped up and spun around, going into a crouch with his fists doubled up.

A sharp, "Captain Daniels," from Serenity made him suck in his breath. "I would like for you to accompany me." She said it in such a way that didn't brook any refusal, and he left, walking beside her.

Sabrina rose slowly, dusting off her slacks. She gave Estel a questioning look.

Unexpectedly, the Chiron's composure broke and his anger suddenly erupted. "You have no self-control," he ground out between clenched teeth. "Your amorous tumbles could be felt by every Chiron."

Sabrina gave him a cold look and turned to walk off. Estel grabbed her by the arm, and spun her around. His breath hissed through his teeth. "You will answer me. You will not walk away."

"I go as I please, Estel n'el Halim," she said, controlling herself as she tried to leave again.

"I will say what you will do."

Sabrina stood silent for a moment, and for the first time felt the anger emanating from him. She was stunned. Her fist impacted against his jaw, and he went down. When Sabrina stood over him, he rolled, and with a scissor chop of his legs, upset Sabrina's balance. She fell hard, but caught herself like a cat, and came up rolling into a crouch. He dived at her, using his weight to pin her underneath. With his hand clenching her hair, he pulled her head up. Using his PSI abilities, he began to reach deep into her mind. She panicked when she realized what he was doing. He was trying to gain control over her. He had a strong mind, full of vitality. Furious, she fought back. As her last resort, Sabrina focused on his bonding centers knowing instinctively that this would be the only way to force him to release her mind. In an instant he realized it, and tried to break free. But now it was she who controlled. In her anger, she wanted to punish him. It was gratifying to feel his fear. She pushed deeper.

Again, he tried to break free, but now her mind was gaining in power and she held him. If he did not break free now, she would forever overshadow him.

At first, Sabrina was exhilarated by the power she gained over him. But then, she suddenly felt the resonance of a matched mind. She saw him as he truly was. One does not tame a tiger she thought, and pulled back a fraction. When she pulled back again, he realized what she was doing. Both disengaged slowly until they felt free of each other.

Estel's whole body bespoke of the fear he felt. He had underestimated Sabrina's strength. She could have superimposed her personality over his. He would never have been free of her. For a moment he had experienced feelings so intense, they had been painful. Now he understood. He had desired her from the start. Even on the Trefayne. Watching the easy and almost familiar way she interacted with Daniels had enraged him.

With his head resting on his knees, he fought to regain his composure. He took a deep breath and staring straight ahead, said, "Thank you, Sabrina."

Sabrina rose and left, not looking back.

She boarded Spitfire, and minutes later, roared off toward Space

Chapter 26

Sabrina's face was pale and the emotional encounter had drained her. She leaned heavily on the console, staring at the monitor. Her immediate need was to be alone with no interference from anyone. She needed to sort things out.

Daniels was forgotten.

The incident had been frightening and at the same time exhilarating. She glimpsed a part of Estel's personality she never envisioned. When she served on the Trefayne, he appeared reserved; even cold toward her. During the struggle she had gained impressions of his feelings for her she never suspected.

Now she understood why most Chirons opt to remain single. It took enormous trust between partners to form the kind of intimacy required in a marriage.

She was just beyond Khitan's planetary pull, about to engage Spitfire's special effect, when she had a foreboding, a feeling of alarm. She sent her mind searching outward, questioning. What she encountered was a familiar feel, someone she knew. Her attention was momentarily diverted when she switched from manual to computer. Spitfire gained speed from sub-light to warp. Suddenly the mind reaching for hers was back stronger and she recognized it as Logan's. He was calling for help from her, or Sargon.

"Logan," she sent. "What's going on?"

"Mother, we are under attack," he sent back, and gave her the coordinates.

"Who's in command?"

"Yoshi."

"Tell him I'm coming."

"Come soon."

"Hold onto your hat; I'll be there in no time."

Sabrina programmed the coordinates into the computer, before she engaged Spitfire's special effect. As the ship reappeared in real space, dropping into sub-light, Sabrina was a parsec from the battle scene. Her sensors picked up a huge ship. Putting it on screen, she recognized it by its configuration. It was from Voltar, a planet at the far horn of Taurus. That meant slavers from Anshar.

Using the huge bulk of the Voltar ship for cover, she slowly advanced. There was a sharp intake of breath. Six ships, identical to her Spitfire, engaged an Alliance ship, the Minoan, in battle. She watched as the raiders dived toward the Minoan, their weapons exploding off the hull. The Minoan fired back, but a split second before impact, the ships arched away, and the Minoan's fire passed by harmlessly.

Sabrina keyed into the Minoan communications. She heard Yoshi's voice, "Status on the raiders." A young voice replying, "They're coming around again."

"Bring us around! Engineering, all shields to starboard!"

She listened to the damage reports coming in from all stations.

"Logan, tell Yoshi I'm here," she mentally sent. "Get ready to bug out at my command."

The enemy ship's sensors and shields were all aimed toward the Minoan. No one dreamt of someone being audacious enough to sneak in the back door. Then Spitfire looked like one of their own. Slowly she crept up on the mother ship. She knew its design well, and she knew its weak points. And she found them.

Using her tractor beam, she placed explosives under three pylons, then, backed away. Opening her communicator, "Yoshi, count three, then, bug out."

She watched the Minoan angle away and going into warp. Before Spitfire's special effect took place, she saw the mother ship explode.

*   *   *

When Sabrina reentered real space, the Antares loomed up ahead. As she approached, Chandi was at the com.

This is the Antares; identify yourself."

"Chandi, this is Sabrina. Let me in."

"Hi Sis, we have been expecting you. The Minoan called in and said you saved their hide. Where have you been?"

"Chandi, stow it. Open antechamber one and let me in?"

"Okay, will do."

Once the antechamber was pressurized, the door opened into the hanger deck. When she exited Spitfire, she saw Sargon striding toward her.

Her first question was, "How are the boys?"

"As you know, Logan is on the Minoan and Jason is on a three month training mission on the Explorer.

"And Elisheba?"

"She's doing well, working with Sarah."

"I'm glad."

Sargon studied her. She appeared to be weary. "What's wrong?"

She glared at him, and her expression tightened. "Sargon, buzz off. I don't want to talk or see anyone right now."

"Sabrina!" he said sternly and reached for her forehead.

Her mouth opened as if to protest then closed without a sound. She allowed his touch.

Sargon gleaned details about her encounter with Daniels and how it had left her with feelings of frustrations and impotence. It had ignited the smoldering fear and mistrust. Then Estel. He experienced her initial exhilaration by the power to conquer, then the guilt of taking enjoyment in subduing another individual. Also, there was still a lingering aftereffect of horror being near the shapeshifters.

"Girl, what you need is a vacation," he told her, then pulled her into his arms. "You had a hell of a time. Miri and Lara are here. They have plans to visit Lara's planet. You should go with them."

He contacted Miri through their mind-link.

"What's up?" came Miri's query.

"Sabrina is here, and she needs a break, maybe someone to talk to."

"Big problem?"

"Very big."

"I'll see what Lara is doing, then, I will get back to you."

In a matter of moments, Miri appeared in front of them. "You look lousy," she told Sabrina bluntly, but soften her tone after a searching look, but without invading her mind. "What happened?"

"Miri, stow it," Sabrina said tiredly.

Miri let out a long whistle. "That bad? Too much happened at once, huh? I understand. You need to go somewhere, a place where no one can reach you for a while." Checking her watch,

"What's keeping Lara?" she mumbled just as her communicator came on.

"This is Lara. You both want to beam up?"

"Yes, we're ready."

"My things?" Sabrina asked.

"They're already here," Lara told her.

Sabrina looked for Sargon, but he was gone.

Chapter 27

The trio landed the Peregrine on Lara's planet. It was called Lara's planet because she discovered it and never shared the knowledge about its existence with anyone, except Miri and special friends. The planet was similar to Earth, but smaller.

Miri set her craft down on a long stretch of beach, on a large island way out in the ocean. On a peninsula, under large shade trees, stood Lara's bungalow with an all-around screened-in porch.

After shutting the Peregrine down, Miri and Lara grabbed their belongings and walked off. Sabrina was left to follow them as best she could. When she came close to the house, the first thing she heard was the screen-door slam. "Well, hello Sabrina, welcome to my domicile," Sabrina muttered very audibly after she entered the house.

Miri came back for her, and hearing the muttered jibe began to laugh. "You don't expect Lara to play hostess?" she asked.

"Apparently not. Where do I bunk?"

"We have a small problem."

"What? Cassandra isn't here, is she?"

"No. But the house is full."

"I thought this was Lara's secret hiding place?"

"Martel!" Miri called.

Sabrina stared at the individual coming around the corner. He was bare except for a kilt around his middle. There was something about him. It wasn't that he looked familiar. But she could feel a faint stirring at the back of her mind. Suddenly it came together. "Mendes?" she asked. Then looking at Miri, "Well, which is it," she asked, tartly.

"My friends call me Martel," he told her.

"Then, well hello, Mendes. Surprised seeing you here."

Miri laughed, eyeing Sabrina, "You better learn to get along with him, because you two will be sharing a room."

"He could sleep outside on the porch," Sabrina suggested.

"Well, so could you," Mendes/Martel retorted.

"Okay, you two can work this out all by your lonesome," Miri said and walked off.

Sabrina watched Miri disappeared, and then . . . "Well, what's your full name?" came out a bit uncivil. She wanted to be alone, still feeling raw inside. She didn't care to have company.

"My name is Martel Alemain. I only use Mendes and a few other names when I'm working undercover. And yours is still Sabrina?"

She gave him a chilly look and ignored his question. "You work in the Alliances' special branch?"

"Yes," he said, barely masking his grin. She had not forgiven him yet for the Sarpedion incident.

"Well, okay," she finally conceded. "Show me where to put my things."

Martel walked ahead and back around the corner to the door at the far end of the hallway. When he opened it, the room was large, sunny and very neat. Nothing was out of place.

"I hope you're not a mess." She couldn't help needling him.

For the first time Martel scowled at her. The room contained only one very large bed.

"My bed, your floor," Sabrina told him.

"No my dear, there's another room."

He opened the door and let her walk in ahead. It was quite a bit smaller and so was the bed.

"Your room," she said, and pointing to the bigger one, "my room."

"No. You sleep in here and I sleep in there."

"You're no gentleman."

"Am I supposed to be one?"

"Aw . . . stow it Mendes, and get lost."

"My goodness," Martel said in his old nasal and fussy Mendes voice, "Charm just oozes from you," and loudly slammed the door behind him.

*   *   *

When a gong sounded through the house, Sabrina ignored it and went back to sleep. Shortly the door opened, and Miri stuck her head in.

"Sabrina, dinner time."

Sabrina sat up in bed and looked at her. "You know, I don't have a thing to wear," she said testily. "All I have are two uniforms and my coveralls."

"I figured that, so I brought you a piece of cloth. You can wrap it around you which ever way you want."

Miri tossed it to Sabrina and closed the door.

Sabrina gingerly picked at it with her forefinger and thumb, spreading it out over her blanket. Not bad, she thought. It was silk with a floral print of deep red, green and yellow, and it was long enough to wrap it several times around herself.

"Well, that will take care of the bottom, now what for the top?" she muttered. Then she remembered the chemise among her undergarments.

Dressed and ready she followed the voices. When she walked in, she wore a sari.

Lara gave her an approving look and Miri smiled.

"Not bad," Miri said.

As Sabrina looked around the room, her eyes fell on Teva. She had last seen him on Karsten's ship.

"Hello, Teva," she said surprised.

"Sabrina," he answered pleasantly, and offering his arm, escorted her to the table. "Come sit with me," he invited, and pulled out a chair.

"With pleasure." She smiled at him and throughout the meal she deliberately ignored Martel.

When dinner was over, Lara and Teva rearranged the table and chairs.

"What are you doing?" Sabrina asked.

"We're going to play cards. Want to join?" Miri asked.

Lara was already seated and shuffling a deck.

"You ever play poker?" Teva asked her.

"Well, you could teach me," Sabrina told Teva sweetly, trying not to grin. Of course, she knew how to play poker.

Martel and Miri took their chairs and picked up the cards.

"Are you going to play or just be in the way?" Martel asked Sabrina rather curtly. Her total disregard of him, even if he didn't like to admit it, had nettled him.

Sabrina sat down. "Deal me in," she told Lara.

While Lara dealt Sabrina's hand, Teva explained the rules. When everyone paid for chips, Sabrina, acting scandalized, asked, "Are you playing for money? This is gambling!"

"Where did this kid grow up?" Martel asked. "Put your ante in the pot or get out."

"How much are you playing for?"

"How much you got?"

"Martel, you're not being very nice to me," Sabrina complained.

"I have no reason to. Now, how much are you going to wager?"

"Will a hundred be enough?"

"For a starter," Lara told her. "And Sabrina, dear, no file rifling."

"Well, I never . . . !"

"Yes, you have and we know you can," Miri told her.

They played for a while and Sabrina was neither winning nor losing. She was observing their wagering and mannerism. Also her eidetic memory helped her remember which cards had been played, and which were still in the deck. After a while, Sabrina's play became more aggressive, and she won several hands.

"Sabrina," Teva said aggrieved, "I thought you didn't know how to play this game."

"Whoever gave you an idea like that?"

"Oh forget it," he said and folded, raking in his remaining chips.

"Let's go out on the porch and have a drink. Anybody like some wine?" Lara asked as she went toward the kitchen.

Sabrina hesitated briefly, then, followed to see if she could help.

When she entered the kitchen, she didn't find Lara, but another woman.

"Who are you?" Sabrina asked, surprised.

"I'm Nina."

"Hello, Nina. Where did Lara go?"

Nina only shrugged, but gave Sabrina a glass of wine. Sabrina almost had it to her lips when she smelled something odd.

"What did you put into this wine?" she asked suspiciously, and began rifling through Nina's mind, and gulped. She had never been so astonished in her life. Nina had put a laxative into her wine . . . out of jealousy? Even more shocking was Nina's strong feeling of love for Lara, but for Lara as a male. Nina was Teva's mother and Teva considered Lara his father. Sabrina got really confused. All the time she had known Lara, she thought of her as female.

Suddenly the door opened and Lara came in.

"Sabrina!" she said angrily.

As an answer, Sabrina held out the wine to her. When Lara sniffed it, she looked astonished, first at Sabrina then at Nina.

"What gives?"

"Ask her," Sabrina said.

"Nina?"

Nina began to cry and went to Lara, putting her arms around her neck. "I'm sorry," she sobbed.

"How much did you glean from her mind?" Lara asked more composed than Sabrina had expected while she emptied the glass into the sink.

Sabrina sat down at the kitchen table and seriously regarded her. She knew she was treading on dangerous grounds. Lara might not respond rationally. Sabrina heaved a sigh of relief when the door opened and Miri came in.

"I sensed trouble on the ether," she joked. "What's up?"

"Nina put laxative into my wine," Sabrina told her.

"Very unpleasant, unless you need it. Nina, Sabrina works with Lara, that's all."

Nina renewed her sobbing until Lara lifted her face and kissed her fully on the mouth. Miri gave Sabrina a quizzical look. "Have we let the cat out of the bag?" she asked.

"Only partly," Sabrina told her, scratching her head. "Is she Teva's mother?" she asked Lara.

"His birth-mother."

"And you?"

At this point Lara switched to Galactic. "I'm Teva's biological mother."

"But why does she consider you male?"

Miri coughed gently. "You remember the mad scientist?"

"Frankenstein," Sabrina couldn't help wisecracking.

"Drop it, Sabrina," Miri said harshly.

"Okay, I know it's serious. I'm not taking it lightly."

"Most of the time, Lara is gender-neutral, meaning she has no gender. But at times she undergoes hormonal changes and then she becomes either female or quasi male."

When Sabrina raised a questioning eyebrow, Miri turned to Lara, "I think we need to go the whole nine yards with her."

"Might as well. Sabrina, I'm part Altairian and part Orion . . ."

"Yafo?" Sabrina injected, and smirked. "But he has no hair,"

Lara looked at Miri. "She's just like you, you know," she said, irritated.

"Now come on. I'm not as bad as Sabrina," Miri defended herself.

"Okay Lara, continue. I'll try to contain myself." Sabrina told her.

Lara gave her a doubtful look. "Like I said, I have a mixed parentage to begin with. You met Yafo. Right now, he is gender-neutral. He's allowed to leave the planet until he goes into puberty. After that, he will be either male or female and so can become a parent. From then on he will be planet-bound. I have some similar physical aspects, but I am a female, and I ovulate. When I'm a female, naturally I seek out males, as many as I can to get a variety of genetic material. When all my eggs are fertilized, the development of the zygotes is arrested. After a while there is a second hormonal change where I implant the zygotes into a female's womb much the same way a male injects his sperm."

"You don't say," Sabrina said ingeniously. Pointing to Nina, "This is why she's Teva's birth-mother. But . . . doesn't she guess . . . no, let's put it this way," Sabrina said after a pause. "Do all the women get as attached to you as Nina?"

"No. Nina has been with me the longest and for some reason she loves me."

"But surely she must know that you're a female? Do you think she's a lesbian?"

Lara looked at her with a raised eyebrow, so Miri said, "Karsten thinks so."

"That would explain her attachment to you." Then she asked, having sensed from Nina that their relationship was anything but platonic between hormone changes, "But having sex is not contingent to your hormone changes?"

"Nope," Lara said, dryly.

Nina had endured silently during the whole conversation, sensing that some of it was about her. Now she looked at Lara with an aggrieved expression.

"Sorry, Nina," Sabrina said, changing back to English, "but there were some questions I had to ask, and I hate to talk about you like you weren't present. I understand things better now, and let me assure you, I only work with Lara and Miri, sometimes." When she rose, she walked by Lara and said,

"Thanks for trusting me." Before she was through the door she stopped and looked thoughtfully back at Lara. Stroking her chin she said, "That's a hell of a deal," and quickly shut the door.

As she walked away, she could hear Miri's laughter.

*   *   *

When Sabrina awoke next morning it was late and the house was curiously quiet. She showered and when she walked into the kitchen, it was empty. Searching through the whole house, she found no one there. Even the beach was deserted.

Going back into the house, she fixed herself breakfast and later went down to the beach. For three days she wandered the hills and swam and snorkeled in the ocean. She windsurfed and fished for her dinner.

On the fourth day it started to rain. Sabrina stood by the window and looked at the churning sea. In order to keep herself busy she went into the kitchen and started to empty the cabinets. She cleaned the oven and then the floor. She even waxed the table and chair legs. On the fifth day, it still rained and she began cleaning the rest of the house. On the sixth day, she was still deep asleep when she was startled out of a dream by Miri bouncing on her bed.

"Hi Sabrina, the house looks nice."

"If I were you, I'd fire the housekeeper," Sabrina grumbled.

"Are you volunteering?"

"It's still too early in the morning, so don't be funny."

"How would you like to go rafting?"

Sabrina lifted her head off the pillow and looked toward the window. "No kidding, the sun is shining. Rafting? Sounds great!"

"Then get ready."

"What do I wear, Sari or birthday suit?"

"Your coveralls will do fine."

When she joined the others in the kitchen, Martel was at the stove fixing breakfast.

"Where's Teva and Nina?" she asked Martel.

"They are both on the Antares. Teva needs some additional training in science. He wants to become a science officer," Miri answered.

Turning to Miri, Sabrina asked, "You talked to Benjie?"

"Yes. Benjie said he'll watch over him."

"Benjie is the best, next to Sargon."

"You're biased."

"Just because he's my little brother?" Sabrina asked with her eyebrow going up. "No, it's because I taught him, that's why he is the best."

"Sabrina, set the table," Lara ordered.

"Yes Sir. Table-setting coming up."

* * *

They used a small craft to fly to one of the continents and decided to follow one of the rivers to see where it began.

As they followed the fast-flowing waters, Lara warned them that it was icy cold. Its source was a glacier-lake.

The lake, high up in the mountains, lay motionless and dark, mirroring the ice-covered peaks. A clear rivulet issued from the glacier-lake, and farther down, it tumbled lustily over rocks and squeezed through gorges with many rapids and waterfalls along its course. Smaller tributaries joined and it grew. At the place Lara decided to camp and build the raft, the river was already broad and running deep.

After the camp was set up, Miri took the small craft back to the island and then popped back in again.

The next morning after breakfast, Martel handed Sabrina an axe and she looked at him like he had lost his mind.

"What do you mean handing me an axe? What happened to lasers?"

"The trees still need to be notched so they fall right."

"Why all that primitive tree cutting and raft building? Whatever happened to inflatable rafts?"

"This is part of the script. You wanna play or gripe?"

Sabrina made a face at him."

"And only notch the ones marked," he told her as she began to walk away.

Sabrina turned back and playfully swung the axe at him.

*   *   *

Two days later they had the raft built and at the water's edge. On the third day, very early in the morning they loaded the supplies and set out.

Their first stop was late in afternoon after shooting rapids and going over waterfalls. During one of the more hairy situations, Martel, standing close by Sabrina, grabbed the pole and augmented her in pulling the raft around a pile of rocks as they shot through a narrow gorge.

Miri wondered at the ease Martel exhibited standing so close to Sabrina. Usually he was very cagey about someone touching him.

Farther down where the river ran calmer, Sabrina grounded the raft on a narrow, pebbled beach with a meadow stretching above them.

There had been little conversation that day, or even later. While Sabrina and Miri gathered firewood, Lara and Martel unpacked the provisions and set up a small tent.

The meal consisted of rations everyone just opened and ate. Dessert was hot tea. No one complained about going early to bed.

Again, Miri wondered. Martel, sleeping at the far end of the tent had made sure Sabrina slept next to him. Usually, he put Lara between himself and the others.

On the second day, they drifted with the currents and took it easier.

"How long are we going to stay on this river?" Sabrina said to no one in particular.

"Tired already?" Martel asked.

"Can't go swimming unless you want to turn into a Popsicle," Sabrina complained.

"What's a popsicle?" Martel wanted to know.

"Frozen dessert," Miri told him.

Both sides of the river were forested and tree branches hung over the water. They drifted into a bay the river had gouged out of the bank. Lara suddenly let out a yell. Jumping for an overhanging branch, she scrambled up the tree.

A massive wall of water was rushing toward them.

Miri disappeared.

Sabrina had drifted off to sleep, and when the warning sounded, rose up and a tree-branch hit her on the back of the head. She tumbled into the water.

Martel, crouching down, was hanging onto the raft for dear life as he rode the swell and at the same time frantically searched the churning debris laden waters for Sabrina.

A tree shot by him and he could see Sabrina hanging onto its roots, her head barely out of the water. He jumped from the raft to the tree, and straddling it, inched his way toward Sabrina.

The only saving circumstance was that they had entered the bay before the wall of water had come down on them.

Martel, careful not to roll the tree-bole, worked his way through the root system and toward the bottom Sabrina was clinging to. Just as he reached for her, her fingers let go and she slipped into the water.

Miri suddenly appeared, clinging with one hand to the extended taproot and reached with her other hand for Sabrina.

"Martel, I got her," she called out. She seized a handful of Sabrina's hair and held her face clear of the water.

A sudden jar shook the tree as it plowed into the bank, nearly dislodging Martel. Before the tree could get torn loose, Martel and Miri grabbed Sabrina and hoisted her on land. Carrying Sabrina, both began to run for higher ground before being swamped by another swell.

"Is she still alive?" Miri asked, as she helped to put Sabrina down on the ground.

Martel bent over Sabrina and touched the artery on her neck. "Yes, but barely. We need to get her warm before she dies of hypothermia."

"Hold on and I'll get the Peregrine." She disappeared instantly.

Martel laid himself atop Sabrina trying to keep her warm.

It seemed like an eternity to Martel, but it took only moments for Miri to disappear and reappear with the ship. She located Martel's life-reading and hovered above to beam up Sabrina and him.

When Martel and Sabrina materialized on the pads, Miri helped him strip her clothes.

"Get her to the infirmary. I'll look for Lara," Miri told him. She found Lara still clinging to the top of a tree.

When everyone was on board, Miri told her, "Use the Zirbelnuts-meal and make a hot drink. I'm going to the infirmary to heat blankets. Come to the infirmary as soon as you can."

Lara only arched her eyebrow at the abrupt orders before she raced off to the Galley.

When Miri entered the tiny room, Martel already had dried Sabrina off and wrapped in a blanket. Again, Martel was trying to augment her body's warmth by lying on top of her.

"I will heat a blanket," Miri said.

Martel only looked up at her. Using his empathic ability, he contacted Sabrina. He felt an overwhelming sadness, even past pain, and almost a willingness to let go.

Martel took the sadness and pain and enveloped all with a warm feeling. He barely noticed as Miri and Lara came in to wrap Sabrina in the heated blanket. He held Sabrina in his arms, pressed tight to his body until she gave a small sign of life, a long sigh.

Her whole body started to shiver. "I'm so cold," she finally whispered.

"Sabrina, you're on the Peregrine," Lara told her. When she didn't respond, Lara took her chin and turned her face toward her. "Sabrina, can you hear me?" There was still no response, "Miri," Lara said tersely.

Miri's mind reached out until she touched Sabrina's. "You're safe," she told her. "It's time to come around. Come on girl, we have something hot for you to drink." Looking into the cup, she saw that Lara had made it chicken soup, the universal cure-all Karsten once called it.

Martel, who was still in contact with Sabrina, put his arm around her waist and pulled her into a sitting position, drawing her against his body. Miri, lifting her chin, put the rim of the cup against her lip, "Come, drink, Sabrina," she urged.

Suddenly there was a shimmering and Karsten materialized.

"What's going on?" he asked.

"How did you get here?" Lara asked surprised.

"I was rerouted by a very troubled and insistent Logan. He told me where to find his mother and that she is in distress."

Logan, bonded to his mother, was always subliminally aware of her presence. Ever since she once withdrew her awareness to shield him, he panicked whenever he couldn't feel her.

Karsten bent over Sabrina and ran his hand-held diagnostic instrument over her body. "She's still hypothermic," he said. "Sabrina, can you hear me? Martel, tell me what's going on?"

But Martel was again deeply in contact with Sabrina, unaware of Karsten's presence.

"We can't beam them over to the Borealis this way," Miri said. "We may lose Sabrina."

"What do you mean?"

Miri gave Karsten a depreciating look. "She's acquired another talent. She can disappear like me. But not quite like me. I don't know what she does."

"You mean she might not materialize?"

"That's what I'm afraid off. Try and see if you can reach Martel. We had him a while ago. But he went back into contact with Sabrina."

Karsten carefully inserted his consciousness into Martel's awareness and telepathically told him, "Martel, we need to beam Sabrina over to the Borealis. Can you hold her?"

When Karsten received a very detached affirmative, he activated his com-bracelet and said, "Marcus, scan and energize."

Lara's eye widened when she heard the name and asked, "Who's minding the store?" meaning her own home-world, Starburst, a conglomeration of spheres connected by tubes.

Before the beam took them, Karsten quickly told Lara, "Marcus wanted to come and I left Livia in charge."

When they all materialized on the Borealis, Miri said, "That's going to be another surprise for Sabrina," and giggled.

Marcus and Livia were Lara's children by Sargon. During her need to mate she had enticed Sargon into an amorous situation. Although she gave Sargon, whom she considered a friend, a way out. During her mating cycle, if the male she had chosen proved reluctant, she generally used persuasion, but was not above using force.

In the infirmary, Karsten took Sabrina from Martel and placed her into a life-support unit. He was adjusting the gauges when Marcus walked in. To Karsten's questioning look, he said, "Minerva just called. Miri, Lara you are to report to Daugave. There was a query about a Captain Hennesee."

"Okay, Marcus, we'll take care of it," Lara told him. "Karsten, what about Sabrina?"

"I'll take her to the Antares." Then turning to Martel, he asked, "What's on your agenda?"

"I'll come with you."

271

"And the message to Minerva?" Marcus asked.

"Tell Minerva that Sabrina has not been located yet and that I'm delayed, but should be there shortly. I'll let Sargon handle Sabrina's affairs," Karsten finished.

"Okay, we'll see you on Daugave then," Lara said before she beamed over to the Peregrine. Miri went over in her own way.

* * *

On the Antares, Logan stiffened and looked past his instructor. "Sir, I need to leave."

"You're not finished with your demonstration."

"Sorry," he said and pushed past him while mentally contacting Jason, "Mom's here. She's in the hospital. Go to her, now."

Jason left the schoolroom before his teacher could object. After going through the door he became invisible. Materializing in the hospital's corridor, he startled Zaida into almost dropping a chart.

"Jason! Someday you're going to give someone a heart attack," she told him while grabbing a shock of his hair.

"Zaida, cut it out. Where's my mom?" he asked, slapping at her hand.

"Sargon's with her."

"Okay, where?"

"In there," pointing to the room she had just left.

Logan, not needing to be told where his mother was, just rounded the corner and opened the door.

"Dad?"

"She's all right."

"Then why is she in a life-support unit?"

"To keep her warm."

"Hypothermia?" Jason asked, coming up behind his brother.

"Yes."

"How long will she be in there?"

"Until she wakes up. You two better get back to your classes."

Logan grinned. "I think you will be hearing from Mister Bates."

"You two didn't just walk out of your classes?" Sargon asked both.

The answers were two grinning faces.

"You didn't disappear?" Sargon asked Jason.

"Of course not, Sargon. I waited until I was out of the room. But you're sure she'll be okay?"

"Yes, she'll be okay. Zaida is going to release her as soon as she wakes up. Now, you two better get going," and he shooed them out of the room.

Martel, entering the room just as the two left, asked Sargon, "Who are those two?"

"Those are her sons."

"I see."

In the meantime, Sabrina began to stir and hit the side of the unit. Shocked, she opened her eyes, but Sargon was already opening the top.

"Where am I?"

"On the Antares, Sabrina."

She looked at him searchingly and then remembered. "Oh! Okay. You know that damned water was as cold as hell." When her eyes fell on Martel, she smiled. "Sorry, I gave you a hell of a time."

"It's all right."

After disconnecting the IV and letting the sides down, Sargon tried to help Sabrina stand.

"I'm all right. I can do it by myself," she groused. But when she stood up, her knees buckled. "I guess I'm not," she said and grabbed at Martel for support.

Sargon watched in surprise when Martel's arms went around Sabrina's waist and he helped her into a bed. Usually Martel flinched when someone touched him.

Martel looked at Sargon. "Can you give us some privacy?"

"Sure, you only need to close the door and put this sign out."

"What are you up too?" Sabrina asked Martel.

"I'm going to finish what I started," he told her.

"Finish what?"

Sargon watched astonished as Martel told Sabrina to go down into meditation. Sargon turned and quietly left the room.

Sabrina balked. Martel curtly ordered, "Do it."

When both reached the same level of depth, Martel touched on all of Sabrina's feelings. Soon he realized she had only worked with her pain and feelings until they didn't pinched anymore, then, filed it away to be looked at a later date. Which in Sabrina's case never came.

He began with the death of her parents. Along with her, he felt the shock and terror and then the feeling of abandonment. In his mind he told her, "Give it to me."

Reluctantly she relinquished the pain.

Martel saw Sargon becoming the sole source of her security, and possessively, she still clung to him. In her need, she never dared to think that he could ever leave her. When he didn't respond to her needs, especially the needs of a developing adolescent, again she felt rejected and became despondent.

She liked Joran until he intruded too much of himself into her life and slowly she began to resent him.

The shapeshifters had left her with an indescribable horror.

Machir Aram she hated and despised him for what he did to her. She still felt violated and lumped him and Prince Sarum al Mashad together, thinking of them as scum. They had left her with a distrust of men, albeit mitigated by her feelings for Sargon.

Martel took all her pain, hatred and despondency upon himself.

Still in her meditative state, Sabrina became aware of Martel's distress. She realized he was in shock after dealing with her pain.

She took his hands and gently infused a feeling of warmth and let it grow. Then she shared with him her memories of Logan and Jason as babies. When she thought of the joy of life, she thought of Logan and Jason, and their total abandonment to experiences. She let him feel her happiness when she thought of one beautiful spring day spend with her parents on a mountain meadow.

He emerged from his trance and smiled at her. His face relaxed and he squeezed her hands, then, released them. He rose, and without saying a word, left the room.

Sabrina, leaning back into her pillow, tentatively touched her emotional centers and to her surprise realized that her pain was gone.

Zaida, entering the room, looked annoyed at the bed. It was empty. Sabrina was gone. She called for Sargon, and he assured her that Sabrina had only gone home and was now sleeping in her own bed.

Chapter 28

Logan, tuned into his mother's life-signs, knew precisely when she awoke. Even before she had her eyes opened, the two came bouncing in, and behind them came Medea.

"Back from the dead?" Logan asked solicitously,

"Aw, Logan, you're not supposed to ask a question like that," Jason teased his brother.

"Okay, you two, what gives?" Sabrina asked.

"How would you like to have us back for a week?" Jason asked, batting his eyelashes at her.

"Off and on, I think I could stand it."

"You two, out of here," Medea commanded. "Let your Mom get a breathing spell before you pounce on her." Grabbing Logan and Jason by their collars, she turned them around and still scolding, headed them toward the door.

When the door closed behind them, Medea turned on Sabrina. "And now to you. Can't you let a body know when you're coming home? The house is still shrouded in dustsheets. Nothing is ready for you and here you're popping in."

"Medea, your concern is touching as always. Stop nagging me," Sabrina demanded, and then grinned. "It's nice to be home."

The door opened again and Tomar entered, pushing a tea cart.

"Look who is back to give us trouble again?" she said to Tomar, indicating Sabrina. "Now come, bring breakfast over here," she chided Tomar and pointed to a spot next to Sabrina's bed.

"That's just what I need, something hot. I'm still so cold." Sabrina shivered.

"What do you mean cold? Its seventy-three degrees in here," Medea remarked.

"When you nearly turn into a Popsicle, you'll stay cold for a long time."

Everyone looked toward the door when it opened again. This time it was Sargon.

"What'd she mean by turning into a Popsicle?" Medea asked him.

"It means that she nearly died of hypothermia."

Medea rolled her eyes to the ceiling and groaned. "Why do you ever let her off this ship? You know she needs constant supervision. With all the trouble she gets in, it's no wonder I'm getting old and grey."

Sabrina pulled Medea down on her bed and hugged her. "Medea Love, if you hadn't me to worry about, what else would you do?"

"Get off that bed," Tomar told Medea. Then he fluffed Sabrina's pillows and made sure she was sitting comfortably before he took the tray off the tea cart to put across her knees. "Now you eat," he ordered. Turning to Sargon, Tomar asked, "Do you think that's enough for now?"

Sargon had watched, both amused and also touched by the solicitude shown to Sabrina, There was a teapot full of steaming tea, and when he lifted the lid off the covered dish, he saw eggs, toast, and an extra bowl of cream of wheat.

"That should do it. Medea, she mostly listens to you." Sargon chuckled when she answered with a humph. "See that she rests. No work."

"You mean I have to stay here and be bossed around by those two! How about a little substituting or something like that?"

"No. Enjoy being with your sons. Enjoy your home." With this he strode to the door.

Before he was out of the room she threatened him, "I could get used to this kind of life."

Holding the door, he looked back at her. "That will be the day."

Books to be published are:

The Antarean Odyssey

Matched

Book Seven

The Antarean Odyssey

I, Sargon

Book Eight